Praise for Keri Arthur

Nominated for *Romantic Times* 2007 Reviewers' Choice
Awards for Career Achievement in Urban Fantasy

Winner of the *Romantic Times* 2008 Reviewers' Choice
Awards for Career Achievement in Urban Fantasy

"Keri Arthur's imagination and energy infuse everything she writes with zest."
—CHARLAINE HARRIS

Praise for *Full Moon Rising*

"Keri Arthur skillfully mixes her suspenseful plot with
heady romance in her thoroughly enjoyable alternate
reality Melbourne. Sexy vampires, randy werewolves,
and unabashed, unapologetic, joyful sex—you've gotta
love it. Smart, sexy, and well-conceived."
—KIM HARRISON

"*Full Moon Rising* is unabashedly and joyfully sexual
in its portrayal of werewolves in heat . . . Arthur never
fails to deliver, keeping the fires stoked, the cliffs high,
and the emotions dancing on a razor's edge in this edgy,
hormone-filled mystery . . . A shocking and sensual
read, so keep the ice handy."
—TheCelebrityCafe.com

"Keri Arthur is one of the best supernatural romance
writers in the world."
—HARRIET KLAUSNER

"Strong, smart and capable, Riley will remind many of Anita Blake, Laurell K. Hamilton's kick-ass vampire hunter . . . Fans of Anita Blake and Charlaine Harris' Sookie Stackhouse vampire series will be rewarded."
—*Publishers Weekly*

"Unbridled lust and kick-ass action are the hallmarks of this first novel in a brand-new paranormal series . . . 'Sizzling' is the only word to describe this heated, action-filled, suspenseful romantic drama."
—Curled Up with a Good Book

"Desert island keeper . . . Grade: A . . . I wanted to read this book in one sitting, and was terribly offended that the real world intruded on my reading time! . . . Inevitable comparisons can be made to Anita Blake, Kim Harrison, and Kelley Armstrong's books, but I think Ms. Arthur has a clear voice of her own and her characters speak for themselves. . . . I am hooked!"
—All About Romance

Praise for *Kissing Sin*

"The second book in this paranormal guardian series is just as phenomenal as the first . . . I am addicted!!"
—Fresh Fiction

"Arthur's world building skills are absolutely superb and I recommend this story to any reader who enjoys tales of the paranormal."
—Coffee Time Romance and More

"Fast paced and filled with deliciously sexy characters, readers will find *Kissing Sin* a fantastic urban fantasy with a hot serving of romance that continues to sizzle long after the last page is read."

—Darque Reviews

"Keri Arthur's unique characters and the imaginative world she's created will make this series one that readers won't want to miss."

—A Romance Review

Praise for *Tempting Evil*

"Riley Jenson is kick-ass . . . genuinely tough and strong, but still vulnerable enough to make her interesting. . . . Arthur is not derivative of early [Laurell K.] Hamilton—far from it—but the intensity of her writing and the complexity of her heroine and her stories is reminiscent."

—All About Romance

"This paranormal romance series gets better and better with each new book. . . . An exciting adventure that delivers all you need for a fabulous read—sexy shapeshifters, hot vampires, wild uncontrollable sex and the slightest hint of a love that's meant to be forever."

—Fresh Fiction

"Pure sexy action adventure . . . I found the world vividly realized and fascinating. . . . So, if you like your erotic scenes hot, fast, and frequent, your heroine sassy, sexy, and tough, and your stories packed with hard-hitting action in a vividly realized fantasy world, then *Tempting Evil* and its companion novels could be just what you're looking for."

—SFRevu

Praise for *Embraced by Darkness*

"Arthur is positively one of the best urban fantasy authors in print today. The characters have been well-drawn from the start and the mysteries just keep getting better. A creative, sexy and adventure filled world that readers will just love escaping to."
—Darque Reviews

"Arthur's storytelling is getting better and better with each book. *Embraced by Darkness* has suspense, interesting concepts, terrific main and secondary characters, well developed story arcs, and the world-building is highly entertaining. . . . I think this series is worth the time and emotional investment to read."
—Reuters.com

"Once again, Keri Arthur has created a perfect, exciting and thrilling read with intensity that kept me vigilantly turning each page, hoping it would never end."
—Fresh Fiction

"Reminiscent of Laurell K. Hamilton back when her books had mysteries to solve, Arthur's characters inhabit a dark sexy world of the paranormal."
—*The Parkersburg News and Sentinel*

"I love this series."
—All About Romance

Praise for *The Darkest Kiss*

"The paranormal Australia that Arthur concocts works perfectly, and the plot speeds along at a breakneck pace. Riley fans won't be disappointed."
—*Publishers Weekly*

Praise for *Bound to Shadows*

"The Riley Jenson Guardian series ROCKS! Riley is one bad-ass heroine with a heart of gold. Keri Arthur never disappoints and always leaves me eagerly anticipating the next book. A classic, fabulous read!"
—Fresh Fiction

Praise for *Moon Sworn*

"Huge kudos to Arthur for giving readers an impressive series they won't soon forget! 4½ stars, Top pick!"
—*RT Book Reviews*

"The superb final Guardian urban fantasy saga ends with quite a bang that will please the fans of the series. Riley is terrific as she goes through a myriad of emotions with no time to mourn her losses. . . . Readers will enjoy Riley's rousing last stand."
—Midwest Book Review

Praise for *Darkness Unbound*

"A thrilling ride."
—*Publishers Weekly*

Praise for *Darkness Rising*

"Arthur ratchets up the intrigue . . . in this powerful sequel."
—*Publishers Weekly*

By Keri Arthur

KISS THE
NIGHT
GOODBYE

Keri Arthur

DELL
NEW YORK

Kiss the Night Goodbye is a work of fiction. Names, characters, places, and incidents either are the product of the author's imagination or are used fictitiously. Any resemblance to actual persons, living or dead, events, or locales is entirely coincidental.

2013 Dell Mass Market Edition

Copyright © 2004 by Keri Arthur
Excerpt from *Circle of Fire* by Keri Arthur copyright © 2001 by Keri Arthur

Published in the United States by Dell, an imprint of The Random House Publishing Group, a division of Random House, Inc., New York.

Originally published in different form in paperback in the United States by ImaJinn Books, Hickory Corners, MI, in 2004.

DELL and the HOUSE colophon are registered trademarks of Random House, Inc.

This book contains an excerpt from the forthcoming novel *Circle of Fire* by Keri Arthur. This excerpt has been set for this edition only and may not reflect the final content of the forthcoming edition.

ISBN 978-0-440-24654-1
eBook ISBN 978-0-345-53873-4

Cover design: Lynn Andreozzi
Cover illustration: Juliana Kolesova

Printed in the United States of America

www.bantamdell.com

9 8 7 6 5 4 3 2 1

Dell mass market edition: November 2013

One

MOTES OF DUST danced in the beams of light filtering through the grubby windowpanes. The room was narrow but long, and the dusky sunlight did little to lift the shadows. The silence crawled across Nikki's skin like a live thing, yet she knew she was not alone.

She flexed her fingers, trying to ease the tension that had sweat running down her forehead, and swept her gaze from left to right.

They were here, somewhere. Four of them, hidden among the dust and the shadows and the wooden boxes. Two vampires and two shapeshifters. All she had to do was reach the far end of the room unscathed. Easy—except for the fact that the others were allowed weapons and she was not.

She glanced quickly at the ceiling. The monitors were on, and undoubtedly those watching in the next room were growing impatient. She'd been standing in the doorway for a good five minutes. But Michael had told her not to rush, and it was a suggestion she was following to the letter. If she didn't pass this test, she'd have to undergo yet another month of physical training, and that was something she definitely didn't want. She and Michael were supposed to get married in thirty-five days, and she hadn't even gone shopping for a wedding dress yet.

She wiped the sweat from her eyes and scanned the shadows again. After three months of intensive training—training that was both physical and psychic—she was fitter than she'd ever been in her life. However, in some ways, she was no closer to understanding or controlling her most recent gifts than she had been three months ago.

But she wasn't about to admit it. And how much the trainers suspected about her lack of control was anyone's guess, though she had a feeling Michael might have told them. They'd been concentrating more on her psychic talents of late.

Worry about one thing at a time, she told herself sternly. Jake, her best friend and former boss, had passed this same test four days ago. Surely she could do the same.

Only she didn't like the feeling in the room. Someone in the shadows was not what he or she pretended to be.

She flexed her fingers again and wondered if all the knocks she'd taken over the last few months had finally made her crazy. How could anyone in this room *not* be what they pretended to be? Here in the heart of the Damask Circle's Washington training center, there were no secrets. Except, perhaps, where Seline was hiding. And why she was in hiding.

If Michael knew the answers to those questions, he certainly wasn't telling her.

Which wasn't really a surprise. He couldn't be expected to break three centuries of habit in a matter of months—even though that's *exactly* what she'd expected of him for a while.

She glanced at the monitors again. Was he in the control room, watching her? He'd said he wouldn't be, because he couldn't watch someone beating her up without wanting to intervene. And even if he *was* watching, she couldn't reach out to him with her mind, because this room was a psychic "dead-zone." She couldn't even use her gifts to protect herself if something went wrong.

She bit her lip, trying to ignore the cold sensation creeping across her skin. It was nothing more than nerves. Nothing more than the knowledge that she'd failed this test once already and couldn't afford to do so again. Not with all the wedding deadlines looming.

She took a deep breath and released it slowly. There was no delaying the inevitable. If she didn't move soon, they'd fail her anyway.

She stepped to the right, keeping her back to the wall as she inched along. In the wasteland of boxes and shadows ahead, something stirred. Air brushed past her cheek, rich with the scent of the sea.

Delphine, the dolphin shifter. The one who had caused her to fail the last time, simply because she'd never expected a shifter in human form to be as slippery and strong as her animal counterpart.

A mistake she would *not* be making a second time.

She reached the corner and stepped into the shadow of a large box. The scent of the sea grew closer, though she could hear nothing in the thick silence. Nothing other than the rapid pounding of her own heart, anyway.

She peeped around the corner of the box and felt, rather than saw, the strike of air. She twisted out of the way, barely avoiding the hand that punched only inches from her nose. Air stirred a second time, heralding the approach of another blow. She dropped, sweeping her foot forward, hooking Delphine's leg and knocking her off her feet. Before Del could rise, Nikki lunged at her, smacking her hand against the other woman's chest.

"Bang, you're dead."

The smoky blonde's green eyes twinkled in the hazy light. "Good. Now I can sneak out the door before they lock it and get that cup of coffee I've been craving."

"I wish I could join you," Nikki muttered, stepping back so the other woman could rise.

Del slapped a hand on Nikki's shoulder. "You'll do fine. Stop worrying."

"Thanks," Nikki said, wishing she could believe the shifter. But that sense of wrongness was increasing, and with it the certainty that the person behind it had an agenda that had nothing to do with today's test.

She went back to the wall and inched along until she came to another box. This one was short enough to peer over, so she did. The darkness beyond leapt at her.

She yelped and jumped back. The shadows dissolved, becoming a vampire. She clenched her fist and struck at him. He caught the blow in his hand, crushing her fingers just enough to hurt. She pivoted, twisting her arm painfully as she lashed out with a foot. He ducked the blow easily, so she dropped to her knees, using his grip on her fist against him, and pulled him off the box. He landed on his back at her feet, and she pressed her free hand against his chest.

"Dead, dead, dead," she muttered.

He raised her fist to his mouth and kissed her fingers. "Very well done."

"Thank you."

She rose and scanned the hazy room. Two more to go, and she was a third of the way down the room. It had been almost too easy so far. Maybe Michael had threatened the participants.

Yeah, right. As if he really wanted her to pass this test so she could start going on missions with him. They might have reached a compromise when it came to the Circle and his missions, but that didn't mean he was all that happy about it. Still, he was keeping his end of the bargain, so she should do the same. And if she didn't pass this damn test, it was back to training and goodbye wedding until she did pass.

Her gaze rose to the ceiling again. The second shifter was up there somewhere. She couldn't say why she was so sure—her psychic gifts were not supposed to be working in this room at all. Frowning, she glanced at the box to her right and tried to shift it with kinetic power. Nothing at all. Not even a tingle.

Strange.

She took a deep breath and crept forward again. The room seemed to be getting hotter, and sweat trickled down her spine. Had the air-conditioning gone off, or was it simply fear that warmed her?

Dust stirred the air, and a sneeze tickled her nose. She swiped at it, sniffing, and in that moment sensed movement.

Sweeping down fast.

She dropped to her stomach and felt claws rake along her back, tearing her sweater but not her flesh. She twisted, kicking upward at the rising hawk. She clipped a wing, and the bird squawked—a cry that was almost indignant.

It swooped around and arrowed in again. She scrambled to her feet and dove over the box, feeling the scrape of claws down her jeans. She hit the floor, rolled to her feet, and tore off her sweater. Twisting it quickly, she flicked one end at the hawk as it turned for another strike. It hit the bird in the chest, knocking it into the side of a tall box.

A golden haze crackled across the hawk's body, and by the time it hit the floor, it was a man with golden hair and rich blue eyes. A man she knew—Jon Barnett. And he held two halves of a quarterstaff.

Things were about to get tough.

She glanced around, but there was nothing in this room that could be used as a weapon. Which was entirely the point.

He leapt at her, his wooden staffs little more than a blur. She backed away, dodging and weaving, but there was no way she could avoid every blow. Yet for all his speed, the blows were little more than taps. Had it been anyone other than Jon, she would have killer bruises tomorrow.

Her back hit a box. She cursed and dropped, sweeping with a foot. He jumped her leg, then smacked it with one of the staffs. She cursed again and dove at him, tackling him at knee height and knocking him to the ground. Before he could move, she scrambled up his body and punched his chest.

"Trust a shorty to tackle someone at knee height," he muttered, blue eyes diamond bright in the dusky light.

"Blame Maddie. She's the one who told me that if all else fails, tackle them." Nikki grinned. "You're just lucky I didn't grab you where she told me to."

"My wife told you to grab me?"

"Yep. Said she didn't mind, as long as I didn't bruise you too much."

"Charming." He smacked her leg. "You'd better get going."

She nodded and rose. But her smile faded as her gaze swept the remainder of the room.

One vampire stood between her and the end of the room—and the end of this test.

And that was the one who felt so wrong.

"Why the hell is she just standing there?" Jake's voice echoed loudly in the control room.

Michael glanced at the screen. Nikki was a small, slender shadow, surrounded by the dusky confines of the testing room. Her breathing was rapid—a fact confirmed not only by the fast rise and fall of her chest, but by the beeping of the monitors on the main panel.

"She's afraid." He could feel it.

He didn't know what she was afraid of. She knew almost everyone in the room with her, and none of them would hurt her. Yet her fear crawled inside his mind and begged him to take action.

But she'd kill him if he did.

He flexed his fingers and resumed his pacing. He

knew this test was necessary, but he didn't like watching it. It was hard to stand back and let someone hit
her—even if he knew the attacker wasn't about to
hurt her. He should have stayed away, just as he'd
said he would.

But he couldn't. Passing this test was important to
her. When she came out of that room, he had to be here
to celebrate or commiserate—whichever she needed.

"The temperature's still rising in the room." Camille
pushed her blue-rimmed glasses back up her nose as
she glanced at him.

"It can't be Nikki," he said. "The room is a psi
dead-zone."

"Then explain how the temperature in an environ-
mentally controlled room suddenly shoots up ten degrees in a matter of minutes."

"You're the witch. You tell me."

"Doesn't that fire-gift of hers appear when she's
afraid?" Jake asked, brow furrowed as he stared at
the small screen. "Could it be that?"

"It could be," Michael agreed, "but it shouldn't.
That room is chock full of spells to prevent magic
and psychic gifts from being deployed."

Jake raised an eyebrow. "So how did Jon shape-
shift?"

"That's personal magic—magic from the soul,"
Camille said. "It's a totally different thing."

"So you can make a spell to target or confine one
type of magic and not the other?"

"You can make a spell to do anything you want, as
long as you've got the skill and the time." Camille
glanced at Michael. "So what's she afraid of?"

"I don't know."

"Yet you can sense her fear?"

"Yes."

Camille raised a silver eyebrow. "Another thing that should not be possible. Interesting."

It certainly was. If he could feel Nikki's emotions through all the barriers in that room, then their connection went far deeper than anyone had realized. Maybe Seline was right. She'd suggested that when he'd shared his life force with Nikki, more than a binding of minds had happened. Maybe it *was* a merging—one of hearts *and* souls. It would certainly explain why they were beginning to share some of their gifts—why his kinetic powers had gone off the scale, and why she now had night vision similar to his infrared vampire vision. And why she could now sense the nonhuman as well as he could. But it didn't explain why both of them were developing new psi gifts, such as clairvoyance and precognition.

"The temperature is still going up," Jake noted into the silence.

Camille glanced at Michael. "You want me to stop it?"

"Not yet." Not when there wasn't any certain reason to do so.

Besides, he very much wanted to see her in her wedding dress. Very much wanted to watch her expressive amber eyes as he said *I do*.

If he stopped the test, their wedding would be put on hold. Seline had insisted on that, saying it would be a waste of time and effort if they stopped Nikki's training halfway through just so the two of them could get hitched.

It was an insistence that worried him. He'd known

Seline a very long time, and there was something else behind her push to train Nikki—something the old witch *wasn't* telling him.

Actually, she wasn't telling him much at the moment—not even where she was currently hiding. Which suggested that whatever she had seen involved *him* in some way—and that he could be a threat to her safety.

He'd asked her about it, of course, but the old witch could be stubborn when she wanted to be.

The old witch also has very good hearing, so watch your thoughts.

Seline's sharp voice arrowed into his mind and he smiled. *If the old witch weren't so nosy, she wouldn't hear so many disparaging thoughts.*

What's the point of getting old if you can't be nosy? Amusement spun down the mental lines. *How's Nikki doing?*

He glanced at the monitor again. She hadn't yet moved, and the temperature had gone up another notch. *She has to get past Lenny and then she's done.*

If she got past Jon, Lenny shouldn't be a problem, Selene responded.

He shouldn't . . . but somehow he is.

Why? She's dealt with vampires a hell of a lot meaner than Lenny.

I know that—and she *knows that.* He stopped pacing as Nikki looked up at the camera closest to her. Sweat beaded her forehead, and fear sparkled in her eyes. But her expression was determined, and after a moment she took a deep breath and slid another step forward.

Then another.

Lenny didn't attack, and the temperature rose yet another degree.

"Another three degrees and I'm stopping it," Camille commented. "We'll be risking everyone's safety otherwise."

Maybe it's not so much Lenny as the wedding, Seline commented. *Maybe she's decided she doesn't want to marry such an old man after all.*

This old man will track you down and box your ears if you're not very careful.

Seline's sigh was a cool breeze through his mind. *You're annoyed because I won't tell you where I am.*

No, I'm annoyed because you won't tell me why you won't tell me where you are. He crossed his arms, watching Nikki duck around a box. Though Lenny had circled around behind her earlier, he now stood near the window, so she still had some breathing space before he attacked.

Remember that vision I had when you and Nikki were in San Francisco?

The one about someone coming after me in revenge for what I did to his brother?

Nikki took another step. Two boxes and some shadows were all that stood between her and Lenny now.

Yes. It appears the vision was slightly off. He had a go at me first.

What?

He almost shouted the word out loud, and Seline's wince echoed down the lines between them. *I'm fine, as evidenced by the fact I'm still here talking to you.*

Why didn't you tell anyone?

Because I fear the Circle has been infiltrated by our foe.

Nikki had passed the first box. One more box, a few more shadows, and Lenny were all that stood between her, the window and the end of the test. But she'd stopped again. Her fear swamped him, so strong it left a bitter taste at the back of his mouth. It was definitely Lenny she feared, though why was still unclear.

It wouldn't be the first time the Circle has been infiltrated.

No, but this time it was so cleverly done that it almost caught me. Remember Nadia?

He frowned. *She's a young vamp we recruited about five years ago, isn't she?*

Yes. I promoted her to my personal staff last year. Last week, she tried to kill me in my sleep.

Then she didn't know you as well as she thought. Or she'd have known Seline never slept without at least two protective spells active.

Few people know that. Most think I set only one spell, and I prefer to keep it that way. It was the second spell that caught her. She'd gotten past the first.

How? Nadia wasn't a witch, and few on your staff know anything about magic. Only Camille. And as acidic and annoying as the colorful crone could sometimes be, Michael trusted her—not only with Seline's safety, but Nikki's. Which was why Camille was here, supervising Nikki's training, rather than the usual trainers.

Someone obviously taught her enough to bypass common protection spells.

So did she say why she wanted to kill you?

No, and interrogation proved useless. Whoever sent her made sure they'd erased that section of her memory.

Then you still have no idea who is behind the attack?

No. Seline hesitated. *But I've had more visions, and I'm more than certain my suspicions are correct.*

And those suspicions are? In the room below, Nikki took another step. Michael found himself clenching his fists again and he flexed them, trying to relax. Which was hard to do when her fear was so all-encompassing.

He was so very tempted to stop the test, to run down there and ask what the hell was wrong. Only the knowledge that she'd be furious—that she'd think he was still trying to prevent her from joining him on his missions—stopped him.

Remember Hartwood? Seline asked.

Of course.

Then you remember Emmett Dunleavy?

He smiled grimly. How could he forget him? The bastard had killed Christine—one of the few people Michael had cared about in those dark years, a woman he'd spent ten years loving. Worse still, Emmett had turned her into one of his zombies.

He'd spent twenty years hunting Emmett down and when he caught him, he'd made him pay. *Of course. I destroyed all he held dear, then I took him apart, piece by tiny piece. At the very end, you consigned his soul back to the hell it came from.*

What neither of us knew at the time was that Emmett had a twin—Weylin.

Emmett died just over a hundred years ago. Surely

if Weylin Dunleavy was out for revenge, he would have done something before now.

I fear revenge is not his sole intention.

"The temperature has jumped again," Jake said, his voice edged with concern. "If Nikki's doing this, something is very wrong down there."

Camille glanced at Michael. "One more degree to go, and then I'm stopping it, whether you like it or not."

"Fine." Nikki wouldn't like it, but Jon and Marcus were still in the room, and the heat was reaching levels that suggested Nikki *didn't* have it under control. And if it wasn't under control, then anyone in that room could be a target of the flames.

To Seline, he said, *When we were in San Francisco, you had a vision that someone would be seeking revenge for what I did to his brother. You said he was a brother who had 'kissed the night goodbye.' I take it this is Weylin Dunleavy? And that he's a vampire who can walk in the sun?*

Yes. He's also a sorcerer, and he plans to make us pay for what we did—pay in pain, as that vision warned.

The shadows moved in on Nikki. She backed away, ducking Lenny's blows and throwing several of her own. The vampire might be little more than an indistinct blur, but she was just as fast.

He's had a hundred years to plan, Seline continued, *and now the time for action has come.*

The words seemed to echo through Michael's mind. On the monitors, Lenny backhanded Nikki. The force of the blow was enough to send her staggering.

But somehow she kept her feet, and she wiped a hand across her mouth. That was when he saw the blood.

And that was when her fear crystallized in his mind.

Lenny was another plant.

"Get that door open!" Then he turned and ran for the stairs.

Nikki hit the wooden box nose first. She grunted in pain but quickly pushed away, dropping to her knees as the whistle of air warned of another blow. As the vampire's fist stirred the hairs on the top of her head, she lashed out with a foot, trying to hook his leg and bring him down.

He jumped her leg, then pivoted, his heel smashing into her jaw. She flew backward, hitting another box before sliding to the floor in an ungainly heap. The room whirled around her and her face throbbed, the bitter taste of blood filling her mouth. She took a shuddering breath, but it did little to ease the sick churning in her stomach. Her heart raced so hard it hurt, and energy surged in response, the sheer force of it making every muscle shake. Or maybe *that* was fear. But fire flickered across her trembling fingertips, casting bright shadows through the dusky light.

It shouldn't be happening—not in this room.

She felt rather than saw movement, and she scrambled away on all fours. A hand twined through her hair, yanking her viciously back. She yelped—fighting fear, fighting the flames that seared through her veins.

"Hey," Jon said behind them. "I think that's enough."

"No, it's not," her assailant snarled. He twisted the fistful of hair so tight she yelped again, and he dug what looked like a small crossbow out of his pocket.

"Look out!" She lashed backward with a fist, hitting his arm just as he pulled the trigger. There was a hiss of air, then Jon's harsh curse and the smell of burning flesh.

White ash, she thought. It had to be, because it was the only thing that could stop a shapeshifter.

She knew then that this man didn't just intend to test her. He intended to kill her.

And he'd come prepared to kill anyone who got in his way.

She twisted again and swung her fist, this time sinking it deep into his groin. He grunted, his grip on her hair relaxing enough for her to pull free. She scrambled to her feet and turned to face him, but suddenly there was another body between her and the vampire.

It was the first vampire, the one she'd defeated after Delphine.

"Enough, Lenny. You've drawn blood." His voice was soft yet cold. "That isn't in the rules."

"Right now, I don't give a shit about you *or* the rules."

There was a soft twang, then a grunt, and the weight of her would-be protector hit her hard. She grabbed him reflexively and saw the wooden arrow sticking out of his chest, the fingers of flame beginning to spread from the wound. Dead for real this time. Tears stung her eyes, but she quickly blinked them away. Now was not the time to do anything more than survive. Surely those in the control room had to realize by now that something was wrong. All she had to do was hang on until they got here.

She dropped the vampire's body and retreated, then saw Lenny raise the crossbow a third time. She swore and dove sideways, rolling past the cover of a box. There was a thud against the side, then a rush of air, and suddenly he was on her again.

His weight pinned her, his fists smashing toward her face. She blocked the blows one-handed, then reached up, splaying her free hand against his chest.

"Burn, you bastard," she said, reaching for the power that surged through her veins, imagining him burning but not dying.

Fire exploded through her, around her. The force of it ripped the vampire free and flung him across the room. His screams filled the room, his body a blazing comet as it hit the far wall and disappeared behind several boxes.

Nikki took a deep, shuddering breath, then climbed to her feet and walked the rest of the way to the window.

She'd passed their damn test.

Now they could explain what the hell was going on.

Two

MICHAEL LEAPT OVER the banister and hit the floor with enough force to jar his spine. Grunting, he pushed upright and saw that the door was still closed. He swore viciously and punched the intercom button on the side of the doorway.

"Camille, get this door open!"

"It's not responding. He must have jammed it from the inside."

"Then I'll just have to break it."

"Be careful. The spell—"

He released the button, cutting off the rest of her warning, then clenched his fist and hit the door with everything he had—physically and kinetically.

For too many seconds, nothing happened. Then, with a screech that sounded like a live thing dying, the door exploded inward. Wood and metal fell around him as he ran inside.

The smell of burning flesh hit him immediately. Lenny's screams pierced the muggy air, the beat of his heart loud and erratic. Beyond that, farther down the room, two more heartbeats. Human heartbeats, suggesting Nikki and Jon. The slower beat of a second vampire's heart was nowhere to be heard. Obviously, Marcus was dead.

He swore under his breath and ran swiftly around the boxes, heading for those two heartbeats. Nikki knelt next to Jon, her hand on his shoulder, pressing a T-shirt into his wound.

She glanced up as he approached, a mix of anger, confusion and fear in her eyes.

"What took you so long?" She grabbed Jon's free hand and placed it against the makeshift bandage, then stood, facing Michael in fury.

Her anger burned through his mind, and he almost laughed out loud in sheer relief. There wasn't much wrong with her if her temper was this high.

"Surely you could see what was going on in here?" she continued tartly.

"We did." He grabbed her, pulling her into a hug that was as fierce as it was loving. "And I'm sorry, but Lenny barred the door. It took a while to force my way through. Are you all right?"

"Yes," she said, her words muffled against his chest and at odds with the trembling in her body. "It was Jon who got hurt, and . . ." She hesitated, her voice catching. "The other vampire was killed."

He held her away from him, his gaze sweeping the length of her, then coming back to her face. He gently brushed a tear away from her left cheek, which was swollen and beginning to bruise. "Any loose teeth?"

"A couple," she admitted.

He saw the blood on her teeth and knew she'd probably cut the inside of her mouth as well. He pulled her into his arms again, brushed a kiss across her lips and glanced down at Jon.

"Thank you."

Jon nodded. Pain still lingered in his blue eyes, but Nikki had pulled the white ash out of his shoulder, and the healing process would already have begun.

"Thank me by finding out how that bastard got a crossbow and white ash in here," he said. "I thought we had spells set in the foyer to detect such things."

"We did, but all spells can be countered if you know how." What they had to find out was how someone like Lenny, who had no apparent knowledge of magic, had managed it.

And what his connection to Nadia might be. Michael had no doubt that there *would* be a connection. Two attacks, both using magic to get around the spells in this building, and both performed by people with no talent for magic, was more than just a coincidence.

"You need a hand up?" he asked.

Jon's good hand clasped his, and Michael hauled him to his feet. "You'd better head to medical for a checkup, just in case those arrows were tipped with something."

Jon nodded and walked away, and Michael pulled back from Nikki and brushed the sweaty strands of dark chestnut hair from her forehead. Her skin still burned with the heat of the flames she'd directed at Lenny. "You'd better get to medical, too."

She raised an eyebrow. "You're not coming with me?"

His smile was grim. "I have a vampire to question."

Surprise and relief flitted through her eyes. "Then he's not dead?"

"No." And he was no longer screaming. Either he

was unconscious or the flames had stopped eating his flesh—though this second option suggested that Nikki had retained some control over her fire. It had not been so when the flames had first appeared in the sewers of San Francisco. Then, they'd incinerated all that they'd touched. "Did you mean to kill him?"

"No."

"Then that's surely a sign that the lessons have been of some use."

"Perhaps." Her expression was dubious as her gaze searched his. "But how did I raise the fire when this room is supposed to be a psychic dead-zone?"

"The fire must fall into the zone of personal magic rather than psychic abilities. Same as the connection between us must be personal magic."

Her frown deepened. "I thought personal magic was something you were born with. My pyrokinetic skills are a leftover from the time the flame imps inhabited my body."

"Suggesting, perhaps, that for the brief time they were in your body, they became a part of you."

"Meaning the flame imps are now part of whatever I am?"

He smiled. "Don't sound so horrified."

"Why shouldn't I be? I'm not human anymore. I'm not vampire. I'm not *any*thing, because no one seems to know exactly *what* I am."

He pulled her close again and brushed a kiss across her nose. "What you are is the warm and wonderful human being I intend to take home at the end of the day and ravish in the comfort of our bed." Home for the moment was the penthouse apartment he'd bought a few months ago. With Nikki and Jake both undergoing long-term training, it made more sense for him and Nikki to be close. Of course, they *could* have used the Circle's apartments, as Jake currently was, but he preferred the privacy of owning their own place.

Her sudden grin was both mischievous and saucy. "And what if she doesn't want to be ravished in bed?"

He briefly kissed her sweet lips, wishing he could kiss her more fully. But he didn't dare when there was blood in her mouth. The demon within him was under control, but he wasn't about to take a chance when it came to Nikki. "Then she may choose anywhere else she pleases."

Her amber eyes twinkled as she pressed herself closer. "Anywhere at all?"

He smiled, wondering for perhaps the millionth time how he'd ever survived without her light in his life. "Anywhere at all," he agreed softly.

"Cool." She glanced past him for a second, and in that moment he became aware of the others in the room, and of Jake approaching them.

"So tell me," she added, her expression becoming serious again as her gaze came back to his, "how is it possible for a creature like the flame imps to become part of *my* soul?"

"How is it possible for a human to transform into an animal?" He shrugged. "There is some magic in this world that just *is*."

"In other words," she grumbled, "neither you nor Seline can explain it, so I just have to accept it."

He laughed softly and squeezed her fingers again. "The day you accept something without question is the day I'll stop drinking blood."

"I don't question *everything*." Her tone was haughty, but a grin twitched her lips.

"You don't?" Jake said, appearing in front of them. His eyes still held a lingering sadness since losing his wife, Mary, several months ago, but he was slowly beginning to regain his life. "Since when?" His gaze raked her as he added, "Are you okay?"

"Besides some bruises and cuts, yeah, I'm fine."

Jake's gaze met Michael's. "So why in hell was Lenny trying to kill everyone?"

"I don't know yet."

"You want me to take Nik down to medical so that you can stay here and find out?"

"That would be good." Michael brushed another kiss across her lips, then released her and stepped away. "I'll be there as soon as I can."

"Make sure that you are. I want to find out what's going on every bit as badly as you do."

"Stop nagging the man," Jake said, as he slipped his hand under her elbow. "You're not even married yet."

"I'll start nagging *you* if you're not careful," she said, then glanced back and met Michael's gaze. "Be careful. I've a feeling Lenny is just the beginning of the problem."

So did he. He watched them leave before walking around the boxes to where Lenny lay. Camille was kneeling next to the young vampire, placing the last of five colored stones around his body. She made a sweeping motion with her hand, the vibrant pink of her sweater sleeve contrasting sharply against Lenny's blackened body. Energy stung the air, crawling across Michael's skin like fireflies.

"I thought magic couldn't be performed in this room," he said.

"It can't be unless you turn the spells off, which is what I've done."

He knelt down beside her. Lenny still writhed and moaned, his agony stinging the air. Michael felt no sympathy for him. Lenny had killed Marcus, and had attempted to do the same to both Nikki and Jon. He'd gotten exactly what he deserved.

"There was a spell on him," she continued, sitting back on her heels. "Buried so deep that we didn't sense it."

"It's deactivated?"

Camille nodded. "For the moment. But I've got a feeling that if I try and kill it completely, I'll kill Lenny."

Michael frowned at her. "Meaning that the magic is entwined in his life force?"

"It's the only way he could have gotten past all the spells." She raised the crossbow and ran her finger along the barrel. Symbols had been burned deep into the metal. "The weapons are spelled, too, which is why we didn't sense them."

"Someone has gone to a lot of trouble."

Camille's bright gaze met his. "Someone who wants you and Seline dead, as well as anyone you care about."

"You've no doubt Lenny and Nadia are connected?"

"None at all. The magic that binds them has the same feel."

"Is it safe to search his mind?"

"Yes. Whether you can trust whatever information you get out of him is another matter. Seline got very little from Nadia, and what she did extract has all been lies."

He nodded and pushed a hand through the barrier of the stones. Energy crawled up his arm, sharp and unpleasant. He spread his fingers over the other vampire's face, lightly touching his burned skin. Lenny made a gargling sound in the back of his throat, his body jerking in response.

Michael ignored it and psychically plunged deep into Lenny's mind, rifling quickly and none too gently through his thoughts and memories. There was little to be found. Once he'd left work, Lenny seemed to do nothing more than go home to sleep. His life beyond that seemed nonexistent.

Frowning, Michael reached deeper. Surely there had to be memories of friends, lovers, even the enjoyment of past victims, locked away somewhere. Something—or someone—that might provide a clue as to whom Lenny was working for.

But Camille was right. Lenny's mind was little more than a garbled, gray wasteland, suggesting Lenny himself was operating more on automatic pilot than on any real thought processes.

Michael withdrew and met Camille's grim look. "Nothing."

"As I expected."

And as *he'd* expected. A lot of planning had gone into the attack, and whoever was behind it wouldn't be careless enough to leave vital information hanging about in a mind as weak as Lenny's. "He's still living in that Massachusetts Street apartment?"

"Yes, but I wouldn't advise going there. It's you they want."

He smiled grimly. "They killed Marcus, and I'm not going to let anyone else die for me."

"That may be what they're waiting for."

"And it may be the last thing they expect." Either way, he had to take the chance. He'd learned a long time ago that the best way to reveal a hunter was by allowing yourself to be hunted. More often than not, the thought of easy prey led the hunter into making a mistake or revealing himself.

Camille raised an eyebrow. "And what will you tell Nikki?"

"The truth." Another thing he'd learned the hard way was that when it came to Nikki, anything *other* than the truth often had disastrous consequences— like her stepping into the middle of the very fight he was trying to keep her out of. When she'd set her mind on a particular course of action, "stubborn" didn't even *begin* to describe her. But as much as it annoyed him, it was also one of the many things he loved about her.

He rose, offering Camille a hand and helping her to her feet. "Are you going to brief Seline?"

"Yep, after I tend to this piece of shit." She sharply toed Lenny's thigh. "If you're going to search his place, I'd do it right away, before those behind this sense anything is amiss."

"My thinking exactly." He stepped around Camille and headed for the door.

"Watch for traps," Camille called after him. "This is far from over."

"I know."

"And tell that girl of yours she passed."

He smiled. At least some good had come out of this

whole mess. He took the stairs down to the fifth level and walked the length of the white corridor to the medical center. Jake was pacing the length of the small waiting room, and he looked around as Michael entered.

"She's being examined in Room Two," he said.

Michael nodded his thanks and continued on. Nikki's gaze met his as he pushed through the door, her relief a warm sigh through his mind.

"Anything?" she asked.

He shook his head and glanced at the doctor. "What's the verdict, Mike?"

The gray-haired doctor glanced at him over horn-rimmed spectacles. "She's fine. Several loose teeth she might want to see about, but other than that, just bruises and cuts."

"So there's no need to keep her in observation?"

"No."

"No," Nikki echoed, eyes flashing dangerously.

He smiled and twined his fingers through hers, then raised her hand to his lips and kissed it. "Then we have a job to do."

She hopped off the bed and grabbed her sweater with her free hand. "What job?"

"Lenny didn't give us anything. We'll have to check his apartment."

" 'We' meaning you, me and Jake?"

He nodded. Even if he didn't need their help, he doubted he could keep Jake away any more than he could Nikki. "I can't cross a threshold uninvited, remember?"

She grinned and stepped close to brush a kiss across his lips, then winced. "*Oww.* That hurts."

He slid an arm around her waist, pressing her lithe body against his, drinking in the heat of her, the smell of her—sweat intermingled with cinnamon, sunshine and honey. "Then I shall have to find other places to kiss." He brushed his mouth down her long neck. Her pulse raced against his lips, an intoxicating sensation that called to the man in him rather than the vampire.

Desire flooded the link between them. With her breasts pressed so snugly against his chest, he was profoundly aware of her arousal, just as she was no doubt aware of his. He wished they were home. Wished he could give in to passion's flame. Hoped he had an eternity to feel this way.

But right now, they had work to do.

He stepped back. Her gaze scooted down his body and a cheeky smile tugged her lips. "Keep that thought until later."

"I intend to." He tugged his shirt out of his jeans to hide his erection and led her toward the exit.

Jake fell into step beside them. "So, where are we off to?"

Michael smiled. "Lenny's place."

"Why?"

"To find clues."

"No luck with the mind-rifling, huh?"

"No. Is your car downstairs, or did you walk?" Jake's car had tinted windows, which would protect him from the effects of the sun. Though by the time they cut through the traffic, the sun shouldn't be a problem.

Jake's expression was horrified. "Me? Walk? I'm too old for that sort of foolishness."

Nikki snorted softly. "Old my ass. You did that test quicker and easier than I did. *And* you can out-sprint me."

"Only when I'm scared shitless. Fear does wonderful things to the feet." Jake's gaze found Michael's. "Is it safe for all of us to be going out?"

Meaning, was it safe for Nikki to go out? Michael pushed open the stairwell door and waved her through. "Yes," he said, following Jake into the stairwell. "Because we don't know who else might have infiltrated the Circle."

"So we stick together?" Jake asked.

"For the moment."

"There go my plans for tonight," Nikki murmured.

"Hey, old men can be deaf when they want to be."

Nikki's glance back at Jake was wry. "I wasn't planning to make bedsprings squeak. I had something more exotic in mind."

"Oh." Jake's expression was amused. "Well, you'll just have to be exotic some other time."

"I guess." But her thoughts slipped into Michael's, as heated as her skin had been moments ago. *How about we spend a little time in the Jacuzzi tonight? Not as exotic as I wanted, but at least the noise of the spa might cover . . . other noises.*

Heat flashed to his groin as he remembered the time they'd spent in the Jacuzzi last week. She might have a lot less experience than he, but she'd taught him a thing or two that night.

Sounds like a good idea to me.

Amusement and passion shimmered through the link, wrapping him in heat.

Say that a little more breathlessly, she said, *and I might think you were excited about the prospect.*

Just a little.

Cool. It's a date.

A smile tugged his lips. *We live together, so it can hardly be called a date.*

Don't use living together as an excuse for laziness. You will come appropriately dressed, won't you?

Oh, I intend to.

Her laughter ran through him. *Good. I can't wait.*

Neither could he. They reached the underground parking garage and walked across to Jake's silver Mercedes.

"Where to?" Jake asked as they climbed in.

"Massachusetts Avenue."

Once they got there, Jake parked the car up the street from the apartment building and they all climbed out. The apartment block Lenny lived in was not the run-down building Michael had expected—though why he'd actually expected that was beyond him. Chevy Chase was considered one of the more prestigious communities in the Washington area.

"You must have been paying Lenny a decent salary if he could afford an apartment in this place," Nikki commented, regarding the old but classy-looking apartment block dubiously.

"Apparently so." He walked through the old-fashioned concrete arch and approached the security doors. He directed a lance of kinetic energy at the locks, and the door opened with little protest.

"You would have made the best cat burglar," Jake commented.

"I was, once."

Nikki's gaze jerked to his. "You? On the wrong side of the law?"

His smile was wry. "Often."

Though his clashes with the law had more to do with the darkness within him gaining the upper hand than anything else. He'd walked the edge for more years than he cared to remember. If he hadn't met Seline, he might not have been around to find Nikki.

They took the stairs to the fourth floor. Michael checked the corridor and motioned everyone out of the staircase. Lenny's apartment was the third from the end. Though the echo of heartbeats came from the apartments on either side of Lenny's, no life beat in his.

Michael stopped and switched to the infrared of his vampire vision. No life at all inside, human or otherwise.

He stepped back and glanced at Nikki. "Your turn."

She pressed a hand against the door. Energy shimmered through the air, dancing lightly across his skin. The door opened without a creak or complaint.

There was little furniture in the living room—a chair, a TV and a ratty-looking coffee table dotted with dried coffee rings.

"What are we looking for?" she asked, stepping through the doorway.

"I don't know. Something unusual. Something out of place."

She nodded and began searching. Jake followed her in. Michael leaned against the door frame and watched them explore.

They were going through the drawers when he

heard the distant sound of footsteps in the stairwell, footsteps that were moving up toward them. He looked toward the stair door, his gaze narrowing as he listened. Two sets of steps. Two sets of heartbeats. One human. One not.

He pushed away from the door frame. *Nikki, someone's coming.*

She looked over her shoulder, expression pensive. *Shall we leave?*

No. *Warn Jake, then close the door. I'll go check it out.*

Be careful.

Definitely. We have a date I have no intention of missing.

The warmth of her smile ran through him, fueling his desire. *Good.*

He turned and walked toward the stairwell. The footsteps stopped, and for several seconds all he could hear was the drumming of hearts in the apartments around him. Then the footsteps echoed on the stairs again, this time heading down in a hurry.

They've sensed me, Nikki. Stay in the apartment until I get back.

Be careful.

Always.

He slammed through the stairwell door and took the stairs two at a time. The two men were several floors below him, their footsteps as rapid as their hearts. The second man had the feel of a shifter rather than a vampire. Had they been intending to visit Lenny? If so, why run when they sensed *his* presence? The fact that they did might mean they knew who he was.

Might know something about Lenny's attack on Nikki.

He heard a door open and close, and he swore. He couldn't afford to lose them now. Leaping over the banister, he dropped to the floor, jarring his spine for the second time that day. He pushed through the door and saw the men running down the street.

He ran after them. The sun caressed his skin, warming without burning. It was well after two now, and the sky was clear. Once upon a time, it would have proven his death to be out in the sun like this. But sharing his life force with Nikki had somehow improved his immunity. These days, it was only the hours between eleven and two that he had to avoid.

The men took a left at the first street and disappeared. He followed them with his vampire senses, all the while closing in. They were fast—even the human—but not fast enough.

He turned the corner and saw the two of them just ahead. One long and lanky, similar in appearance to Lenny, and the other bald and thickset like a boxer.

A slight hiss cut the air, approaching fast from his right. He dodged, but something hit his shoulder, the force of the blow spinning him around. Warmth flooded his back and side, and fire began to burn through his veins. It was no ordinary bullet he'd been shot with, but one made of silver.

Dizziness hit him. He staggered for several steps, then pressed a hand against the nearby wall. Sweat broke out across his brow and the pavement seemed to be doing a drunken dance. He blinked and looked ahead. The two men were dark shapes that danced as erratically as the pavement. But they were looming closer rather than running away.

He swore and spun round, only his feet wouldn't obey his orders and he found himself falling nose first to the pavement.

Pain smashed through the confusion, swamping his mind, swamping his senses.

As darkness closed in, two thoughts crossed his mind.

The bullet had been tipped with some sort of drug.

And he wasn't going to make his date with Nikki.

Three

MICHAEL'S PAIN CLUBBED into Nikki, the force of it dragging a gasp from her throat and driving her to her knees.

For too many vital seconds she couldn't move, couldn't think. Fire burned through every fiber of her being, and her shoulder was an explosion of agony.

Michael? She thrust open the link and called with every ounce of strength she had.

There was no answer beyond pain. Endless pain. *Oh God.* A sob tore up her throat, and tears blurred her vision. He *couldn't* die. Not now. Not when they were only just beginning their life together.

"Nikki? You okay?" Jake's question broke off as he swore softly and raced to her side. He knelt beside her, his grip fierce on her shoulders. "What's happened?"

"Michael," she somehow gasped. "Oh God—"

Jake shook her. "Break the connection, Nik. We have to get moving if we're going to help him."

She took a shuddering breath and forced a shield around her mind, blocking his pain as she'd been taught in psi lessons. "Okay," she said, as the pain eased to a muted, constant ache.

Jake helped her upright. "Where?"

She gulped down fear and swiped the tears from her eyes. "Outside. To the left."

He grabbed her hand and they raced into the corridor, then down the stairs. Her feet pounded as fast as her heart, but deep down she knew she was never going to be fast enough. Already her sense of Michael was being stretched, suggesting he was moving swiftly away. Given the pain and the curtain of darkness that billowed across the link between them, she didn't think he was moving of his own volition.

They raced down the pavement, slowing as they neared a side street. Nikki pulled Jake to the right, then came to an abrupt halt.

There was blood all over the pavement.

Her eyes widened, and she had to shove a hand to her mouth to stop her scream. She'd seen some horrible things in her time, but this was worse.

Because it was Michael's blood.

And because there was so damn much of it.

"Hell," Jake muttered. He squeezed her hand, then released it. "Wait here."

Nikki took a deep, shuddering breath. "No."

Jake's gaze was rich with concern. "You don't need to see any more than you already have."

"That's his blood, Jake. It might provide some clues." She hesitated and closed her eyes. Michael's presence was moving farther away by the second. If they didn't give chase soon, they might lose him. "Get the car. I'll look around here."

Jake studied her, as if trying to decide whether she was okay, then shrugged and jogged back around the corner. Nikki cautiously approached the blood and tried to keep a tight lid on the force of horror coursing through her. *Don't think about the blood. Don't react to it. Just find Michael.*

It was a mantra she repeated as she knelt beside the dark stain. *Lord, so much . . .* She took another deep breath and looked beyond the pool of wetness. No sign of a bullet, or whatever else had torn apart his shoulder. No sign of a fight. He must have gone down straightaway. She glanced back to the blood. Camille had once said that clairvoyance was a strange gift and often bore fruit in the oddest places. If she touched the blood, would her second sight spring into action? Would it be her psychometry that delved whatever secrets the blood might hold? Or would she simply end up with nothing more than bloody fingers?

There was only one way to find out.

She blew out a breath, closed her eyes and slowly, carefully, dipped two fingers into the warm, sticky pool.

For a second, nothing happened.

Then heat burned up her arm and her senses leapt away, following the trail that led to Michael. Shapes began to form in the darkness of her mind—human shapes, and strange-looking boxes.

She reached for them psychically—and was swept into Michael's presence. But unlike the previous times she'd used her psychometry, this time she didn't become one with him. Instead, she seemed to hover above him, a frightened phantom who could do nothing more than observe.

They were in a van that smelled of grease and metal. Michael lay on the floor, pale and unconscious. Rivulets of blood trickled from beneath his shoulder, pooling near his head, matting in his dark hair. Fear swelled through her, along with psychic energy, but in her phantom form, there was no release—and nothing she could do save observe.

Toward the front of the van, two men squatted near Michael's feet. One was brown-skinned, thickset and bald. The other reminded her of a scarecrow, with long, lank brown hair and ragged clothes.

She drifted forward. The driver was tall, with thinning hair and a face that looked to have seen more than a few harsh winters. The hands that clenched the steering wheel seemed oddly blurred, shifting between human fingers and something that definitely *wasn't*.

He was a shapeshifter, she realized, and she turned her gaze to the man in the passenger seat. He was of average height, with thick black hair that contrasted sharply against his pale skin. His features were thin, his nose long, and there was a sour, almost petulant twist to his lips. He was dressed in black, and his suit and shoes were clearly expensive.

He shifted, and suddenly she found herself staring into his eyes. Eyes that were a smoky, ethereal gray. Eyes that held no humanity whatsoever, only anger so deep-seated it could almost be called madness.

He raised an eyebrow, a smile touching his thin lips. "Well, who do we have here?"

A hand touched her shoulder. The vision disintegrated, and she jumped back to herself with a squeak of fright.

"Nik? It's me, Jake."

She put a shaking hand to her chest. Her heart

thumped so hard it felt like it was going to jump right out of her body.

"You all right?"

"Yeah." She rose and brushed her shaking, bloody fingers on her jeans. "I was just trying to find out where they might be going."

"With his blood?" Jake's voice was as incredulous as his expression.

"I haven't been sitting back and twiddling my thumbs during my lessons these last few months," she said tartly. "They're headed south."

"Then so are we."

They climbed into the Mercedes. Jake slammed the car into gear and took off with a squeal of tires. She grabbed the cell phone from the glove compartment and called the Circle, asking to be put through to Camille.

"What's happened?" The old witch's voice was nail-sharp.

"Michael's been shot and kidnapped. They're heading south in some sort of van." She hesitated, frowning as she tried to remember what she'd seen. Images rose—blood glistening to widening pools near dark hair. Her stomach curled. She swallowed heavily and added, "The van is gray. Probably a mechanic's van or something like that. We're following in Jake's car."

"We'll get people in the air immediately." Camille hesitated. "We'll get him back, don't worry."

No, they won't. A sob escaped. She bit her lip and hung up.

Jake leaned across and squeezed her knee. "He'll be all right. He's tough, remember that."

She nodded, not daring to speak lest she lose it

right then and there. She had to keep it together. Had to find him.

Because if she didn't, no one would.

She reached for the link between them again. There was no response from his mind, and the sense of him was growing more distant. "Left at the next street," she said. "And hurry!"

The car slid around the corner. The tires squealed in protest and the Mercedes fishtailed several times before Jake brought it back under control.

"They can't be heading for any of the airports," he said. "They'd never get an unconscious person past security."

She fought the urge to close her eyes as Jake wove in and out of the traffic. "Which won't be a problem if they're intending to use a private airfield. There are enough of them around . . ."

Ahead, the lights changed to red. Jake pressed his foot on the accelerator rather than the brake. Nikki tensed, her knuckles white with the force of her grip on the side of the seat. Cars moved into the intersection. Jake swore and slapped his palm against the horn. Then he gunned the engine, and the big car surged forward.

She closed her eyes and prayed that someone upstairs was looking out for them.

Tires squealed. Other horns blasted. Something hit the back of the Mercedes, and they slewed sideways. Jake swore, his hands slamming against the wheel as he fought to keep the car going forward.

Then they were through the intersection and speeding up the street.

She blew out a breath, but her relief was short-lived. A car flew out of a side street and arrowed toward them.

She barely had time to scream a warning before the car hit and blackness swamped her.

Nikki drifted in and out of consciousness, as if caught in a fragmented dream. Pain was a beat as steady as her heart, pounding through her veins like blood. Her throat burned and, for what seemed like ages, she couldn't swallow. She could barely even breathe.

Voices swam around her. Many voices . . . but none of them the one she really wanted to hear. Lights as bright as the sun burned into her eyes. She tried to blink and felt the touch of heat against her cheek and eyelid. She realized someone was holding her lid open, shining light into her eyes.

Something bit into her arm, sharp and stinging. Then the pain began to ease, and for a while there was nothing but peace.

When awareness returned again, it was to darkness. She opened her eyes, staring upward, seeing the white ceiling and wondering where the hell she was.

Then memory hit.

"Ohmigod," she said, jerking upright. "Michael! Jake?"

Hands grabbed her. She fought their grip blindly, desperate to get free.

"Nikki, it'll be all right." Jake's voice cut through the haze of fear. "Just calm down."

Her strength left in a whoosh and she collapsed into his arms. "No," she sobbed. "It won't." Michael was hurt—not so much physically as spiritually, and the ache of it pounded through her veins. And if he died, she would too, because her life was linked to his.

Not that she'd want to live without him now, anyway.

Jake hugged her tight. "Seline has assigned everyone who's free or on leave to find him."

It wouldn't help. She was the only one who could find him. The only one who could rescue him. Though whether that was intuition or just plain old fear, she couldn't say.

She sniffed, then asked, "Are you all right?"

"Bruised, but fine." He kissed her forehead and pulled back. "How are you feeling?"

"A little achy." She shrugged and swiped a hand at the tears on her cheeks. "Where are we?"

"The Circle's private hospital."

"Why?"

His gaze searched hers. "You don't remember?"

She frowned. "I remember the car."

He nodded. "It sideswiped us. Turns out they were working for the men who'd kidnapped Michael. Camille has been interrogating them, but she hasn't been able to get much information."

Nikki frowned. "So that means they were expecting us to give chase."

He grimaced. "It appears they were expecting a whole lot of things. Lucky for us, we were in the Merc."

"Meaning?"

"Meaning if it wasn't for the front and side air bags, you might be dead."

She stared at him for a moment, wondering what

he was talking about. She couldn't die. Well, technically, she could, but only through decapitation. "What do you mean?"

He reached forward and touched her neck. It was only then she became aware of the bandage.

"The impact of the accident shattered the windshield and sent glass flying everywhere. If the air bags hadn't taken the force off the piece that hit you, it might have sliced clean through your neck."

A chill ran through her. What were the odds of something like that happening by accident? What were the odds that it was *no* accident?

She swallowed, but it didn't seem to ease the sudden dryness in her throat. "How long have I been in the hospital?"

He hesitated. "Four days."

Her eyes widened. "Four days! God—"

Jake's hand clasped hers, squeezing lightly. "It's all right."

"It's *not* all right," she said furiously. "Anything could have happened to Michael! What in hell are Seline and Camille doing?"

"All they can, believe me. But there's more to this than you think."

"Like what?"

Jake's smile was weak and did little to remove the exhaustion and pain from his eyes. He knew, better than she, what losing a loved one meant. "I think I'll leave that for Camille to explain. You feeling up to a walk?"

"I think you know the answer to that."

He grabbed the robe off the end of the bed and held it out for her. She climbed out of bed, ignoring the aches that slithered through her limbs, and slipped her arms into the robe's sleeves. As she tied it together, she walked over to the mirror and studied her reflection. There was no puffiness or bruising from the beating Lenny had given her. And though the white bandage around her neck stood out starkly against her skin, there was no pain or soreness.

She'd healed very fast—yet another indication of her lost humanity. She closed her eyes and took a deep breath. Why was she even worrying about it? The only reason she was standing here today, on the verge of getting married to a man she loved heart and soul, was because of the fact she *was* no longer human. *Get over it,* she told herself fiercely, *and go get your man back.*

Jake tucked a hand under her elbow. "You ready?"

She nodded and let him lead her down the quiet halls. There didn't appear to be many people in any of the four wards they passed. Surely that was a good thing.

The double doors at the far end of the corridor swished open as they approached. Beyond was another corridor and four more doors. Jake led her through the last door on the right, and they entered a small conference room. Camille sat next to a phone at one end of the table, her vibrant green and orange sweater practically glowing in the surrounding whiteness.

Jake pulled out a chair for Nikki, then sat beside her. Nikki met Camille's bright gaze. "What's happened?"

"Lots of things." Camille's voice was grim. "But I'll let Seline explain."

The older woman pressed a button on the phone and Seline's harsh tones entered the room. "Nikki," Seline said. "I am so sorry I can't be there in person, but it's far too dangerous for me to be venturing out at the moment."

"Why?"

"To explain that, I'll have to give you a little history." Seline hesitated. "I don't suppose Michael has told you about Hartwood?"

Nikki snorted softly. Michael had a habit of telling her as little as possible, though he was certainly better than he used to be. "No, he hasn't."

"I can see I'll have to have a word with him." Seline's voice was tart, and Nikki smiled. She'd met the old witch only once, but she liked her more and more.

"Hartwood is where he and I first met," Seline continued. "He'd spent years tracking down a man by the name of Emmett Dunleavy—"

"Why?" Nikki asked. "What did Dunleavy do?"

Camille slid a sketch forward. "He made the mistake of killing a woman—Christine Marlow. A human Michael had a long relationship with."

The sketch showed a woman who was petite, pretty, with dark hair and green eyes. Except for the eye color, she could have been Nikki's sister, so alike did they look. His maker had been dark-haired as well. Obviously, Michael had always preferred brunettes.

But the fact that he'd had a long relationship with this woman *did* surprise her. The little he'd said about his past had led her to believe he hadn't really cared about anyone in those dark years. Obviously, that wasn't quite the truth. "And he found Dunleavy in this Hartwood?"

"Yes. Dunleavy was a sorcerer and worshipper of the dark gods. I'd been trying to stop him for years."

"Can I ask why?"

Seline hesitated. "Because I'm a big believer in the fact that those of us who have special gifts have a duty to protect those who don't."

The answer didn't surprise her, because that was the motivation behind the Damask Circle, and Seline had started the Circle. "Did Dunleavy kill friends of yours as well?"

"No. He simply killed, and that was enough for me."

"Were you working alone?"

"Yes. The Circle wasn't yet in existence."

But it had come into being shortly after—though exactly how it had evolved, Nikki wasn't entirely sure. "Did Dunleavy kill for the sake of killing, or was there a specific reason?"

"The dark gods grant great power in return for blood sacrifices. Dunleavy moved from town to town, kidnapping young women to torture before he sacrificed them on the night of the new moon."

"Sounds like a real winner," Jake muttered.

"Oh, he was a gem," Seline agreed drily. "The trouble was, Dunleavy was a special kind of shapeshifter— one who could take on the form of anyone he had killed. Unfortunately, it was a fact we didn't discover early enough."

Nikki frowned. "So he's more like one of those *manarei* Doyle was mentioning in monsters class?"

"In a sense, yes, though Dunleavy comes from human stock and the *manarei* don't."

"And he could take on either male or female form?"

"Yes, which made tracking him doubly difficult. The moment we thought we were on to him, he shifted form. Plus, he'd already kidnapped two women by the time we'd got there, and I wanted to rescue them first."

"I'm gathering Michael wasn't too happy about that."

Seline chuckled. "No. But nothing much frightens this old witch, even a vampire hell-bent on getting his own way."

"So what happened?"

"We rescued the women and caught the bastard, that's what happened."

"And Dunleavy? You killed him?"

Seline hesitated. "Yes, but not before Michael had exacted bloody revenge."

Meaning, she suspected, that Seline had killed Dunleavy only *after* Michael had tortured him. But from the sound of it, the creep had totally deserved it. "So what's this got to do with Michael being kidnapped?"

"What we didn't know at the time was that Dunleavy had a twin—Weylin. Although we have no idea whether he's a shapeshifter like his brother, he's not only a sorcerer, but a vampire. And he wants revenge."

"Then why not kill Michael straightaway?" The words made her heart shudder, but the question had to be asked. Simply kidnapping him made no sense. Not unless Weylin intended to torture him, and as yet that hadn't happened. She would *know*. She'd feel Michael's pain, if nothing else.

"Because he needs him for the ceremony."

Nikki blinked and glanced at Jake, who shrugged. At least she wasn't the only one not following Seline's train of thought. "What ceremony?"

"I fear Weylin intends to bring his brother back to life."

Nikki's gaze went from the phone to Camille. "Can you really bring someone back to life after he's been dead for a hundred years?"

"Yes," Camille said. "If the magic and your will are strong enough, you can do just about anything."

"But he's maggot food. How can he be raised?"

"A body is merely the vessel for the soul," Seline commented. "It's Emmett's spirit Weylin intends to raise."

"But . . . how?"

"To raise his brother's spirit from the hell to which it was consigned, he may have to replicate certain events leading up to the night of the new moon—the night Emmett was killed."

Meaning they had five days to stop him. "So he needs Michael." Nikki paused. "And you, Seline."

"Yes. A special-delivery letter came addressed to me this morning. He has a list of Circle operatives. I have one day to appear in what is left of Hartwood. If I'm not there, Weylin will start killing."

"Insanity obviously runs in the family," Jake muttered. "You can't go, Seline. It's suicide."

"I have no intention of going—or of letting anyone in the Circle get killed."

Nikki closed her eyes. If she had to go in alone after

Michael, she would—but she had a bad feeling it would all go to hell if she went without Circle help. "So what do we do?"

Seline paused and said, "I want you to go in my place, Nikki."

"What?" Jake half rose from the chair. "No way!"

Nikki touched a hand to his arm, squeezing lightly to stop his protest, and asked, "How? I might not have met you, Seline, but I know you and I look nothing alike. Besides, it's very likely that Weylin tried to kill me. He knows what *I* look like."

"Weylin may know a lot about what happened in that week, but I doubt he realizes I was using magic to hide my true appearance." She paused, and Nikki could almost hear her smile as she added, "The fact he kept referring to me as *Blondie* means he never really questioned my appearance as a voluptuous blonde. We'll use that same magic to hide your true appearance as well."

Using magic to make her a blonde was certainly a better option than stripping the hell out of her hair, that was for sure. "If he's a sorcerer, won't he sense it?"

"No. The spell will be similar to what he used to get Lenny in the building, but stronger. More deeply hidden."

"So you change my appearance, then what? I just waltz in there and get Michael back?"

"I wish it were that easy." Seline paused again, and unease crawled up Nikki's spine. "For this ceremony to work, he may need all the major players in place."

"How, when it all happened over a hundred years ago? Most of the major players will be dead, won't they?" But even as she said it, the image of the gnarled driver came to mind. She had a vague suspicion at least *one* of the major players was still alive. But whether he was still human was another matter.

Seline blew out a breath. "Yes, but all Weylin really has to do is get living replacements. His magic is strong enough to enforce some role-playing."

"So what will I have to do?"

"There are three huge problems." Seline's voice was grim. "The first being, if I *am* right, you must do what you can to disrupt the sequence of events. But we do not know which events Weylin knows about and which he will deem important for the ceremony. Plus, Michael and I were separated much of the time, and I don't know everything that he might have done."

"So tell me everything you remember, and I'll play it by ear."

"Yes." Seline paused again. "Then there is the sacrifice. Michael and I rescued the women on the night of the new moon. Weylin may or may not be using women—it may not be important in the scheme of things—but he *will* be sacrificing someone, if only to keep his power up. You must stop this from happening if you can."

"Will that be enough of a change?"

"To be honest, I have no idea. Maybe the mere fact of you going in my place will be enough to break the spell, but you will be playing my role, so it may make no difference. As I've said, I can't be sure—not of this, not of anything. If I went in and tasted his magic, I might know, but for everyone's sake, that is something I cannot risk."

"I don't suppose we have anything on the people he might have snatched, so I can try and trace them with psychometry?"

"Not a hope. He could have taken them from anywhere, and we haven't the time to try and track them down."

Nikki grimaced. She didn't think it would be that easy, but she had to ask all the same. "So what's the third problem?"

"Weylin has raised a protection barrier around the old town. We can't get anyone in."

"If you can't get anyone in, how am *I* going to get in?"

"He'll create a door at a specified time. If anyone tries to come in with you, he'll kill everyone in town except Michael. Then he'll start killing Circle operatives."

Nikki blew out a breath and slumped back in the chair. "He's got all the bases covered."

"He's had a long time to plan this. Beating him will not be easy."

Beating bad guys never was. "So, how many people are in town?"

"Hartwood was an old mining town. He'd have to have enough people to represent all the main players—barman, saloon girls, general store owner, preacher, people like that. At least a dozen, at a guess. And it *is* a guess, remember. I have no idea what path his magic has taken."

"How can he possibly manage all that magic and still control all those people? Surely it would sap his strength?"

"It will, which is why you must stop the sacrifices. As I said, he will use them to maintain his strength."

Great. She worried her lip for a moment, then asked, "What about Michael? He has a strong mind and strong shields. How on earth could Weylin force him to play this little game?"

"Michael may be strong, but Weylin has magic on his side. With the right spells and enough time, you can do anything. And if what we've discovered on Lenny and Nadia is any indication, you will discover symbols painted on and around Michael's spine."

"Meaning all I have to do is erase those symbols and he'll be free of Weylin's magic?"

"Again, I fear it is not that simple."

"Nothing ever is," she muttered.

Amusement filled Seline's voice as she said, "Not when it comes to magic, I'm afraid."

Nikki sighed. "So what's the problem in this case?"

"It's twofold. First, the symbols will be inked onto his skin, and they will need to be washed off with a special soap, which I can provide."

"And what if someone finds the special soap? Or if the magic prevents me from bringing it in?"

Seline chuckled. "Regular soap will work too. It'll just take a *lot* longer."

"Meaning we take a lot of baths?"

"This is a ghost town, remember," Camille commented, amusement touching her lips. "Most of it won't have running water, let alone hot running water."

"I guess that means electricity will also be at a premium?"

"Probably. The section where the rangers stay will

have power, but I doubt whether most of the old town would," Camille said. "And it wouldn't be necessary for any of Weylin's spells."

Nikki rubbed a hand across her eyes. She'd roughed it on the streets as a teenager, but her teenage years were long past, and she was well and truly used to life's little luxuries—water on tap, hot food and clean sheets. It was sounding like those were going to be a little sparse now. "How am I even going to recognize Weylin?"

Camille picked up a piece of paper and slid it across to her. On it was a sketch of a man—one she'd seen before. It was the man in the van—the one with the strange eyes. "That's Weylin?"

"Yes." Camille frowned. "Why?"

"Because when I tracked Michael to the van, he was there. He saw me." She pushed the sketch back. "If he could see me when I was little more than a spirit, would he not be able to recognize me even when I'm wearing the disguise of another?"

"I don't know," Camille said, voice troubled. "Seline?"

"It's possible," Seline said. "We have no idea what Weylin is capable of. I'm just basing everything on what I knew of Emmett."

Meaning *everything* could be off—including her suspicions about what Weylin needed to do to bring his brother back to life.

Jake swore. "For fuck's sake, you can't send her in there if there's any chance—"

"She is Michael's *only* chance," Seline cut in fiercely. "Believe that, if you believe nothing else."

Nikki touched Jake's arm, squeezing lightly. Jake

scowled at her, but didn't say anything else. She said, "Am I able to take anything in with me?"

"Weylin has provided a list of what can and can't be brought in. Candles, matches and a small camp oven are on the list. But we'll try and sneak some soap in, as well."

"What about food?"

"He has apparently stocked the general store, probably because I was spending a lot of time with the store's owner."

Nikki had a feeling she didn't want to know the exact details of that. "So what's the second problem with removing the symbols from Michael's back?"

"Michael himself."

Nikki's eyebrows rose. "Why?"

"He will be role-playing, remember, and will see you as me. He and I were never intimate, though my role as saloon girl meant we *did* share a kiss or three."

Seline paused, as if waiting for a reaction. Nikki shrugged, even though she knew Seline couldn't see the gesture. Michael had told her many times that he and Seline had never been *sexually* intimate, and Nikki trusted him. But he'd never said they hadn't kissed or touched, and she'd be a fool to think otherwise.

After another second of silence, Seline continued. "While instinctively he will be drawn to you, he will fight it, because deep down he knows that he and I never happened."

"So that's another way of maybe tripping the spell—dragging him into bed."

"Possibly. But one thing you should remember—

the Michael you meet in Hartwood will not be your Michael. He will be rougher, harder."

How much rougher and harder could he be than when she'd first met him? He'd been so close to the edge, so close to becoming one with the darkness, back then. And though he'd only really threatened her once, it was something she was never likely to forget.

"Is there anything else I need to know?"

"Plenty. But Camille will fill you in on the rest." Seline paused, then added softly, "Bring him home safely, Nikki."

She intended to.

After all, they had a wedding planned.

Four

NIKKI SQUATTED ON her heels and studied the ramshackle town sitting in the heart of the windswept hills of sagebrush that surrounded them.

Hartwood was bigger than she'd expected, and better maintained—though, in many ways, that wasn't surprising. The town and surrounding hills were a California State Historic Park—though what had happened to the rangers living here was, at this stage, anyone's guess. Maybe Weylin had forcibly enlisted them into his drama.

There were probably a good fifty or sixty houses that were in reasonable state—at least from this distance. There were another thirty or so that had either half or fully given way to the elements. Most of the buildings were wooden and the streets were dirt, though a couple of the streets still had wooden sidewalks that snaked past the buildings.

What was surprising were the people—there had to be at least twenty visible—some walking along the streets, some tending to horses, and others walking back from the skeletal mining structure situated halfway up one of the hills. If she didn't know better, she would have sworn this town was still functioning rather than having been abandoned a hundred years ago.

What she couldn't see was any form of a barrier.

She glanced at Camille. The older woman was standing several feet to her right, her red shirt clashing with the clear blue sky.

"Looks like I can walk right in."

Camille sniffed. "You can try, but I doubt you'd succeed. See those black stones near that sign?"

Nikki nodded.

"If you keep looking outward, you'll see more black stones. They're warding or protection stones, and they ring the entire town. When placed in certain sequences, they can provide protection against either magic, evil or, in this case, good."

"These are a hell of a lot bigger than any of the stones we've been shown in class."

"That's because the circle of protection needs to be a whole lot bigger."

Nikki studied the nearest stones for a minute, noting the way the black surface seemed to swallow rather than reflect the sunlight. "So why can't we just go down there and move the stones?"

Camille raised an eyebrow. "Didn't you say you studied that in class?"

"Yes." But she'd been half asleep, because Michael had whisked her off to San Francisco the night before to celebrate her passing the first section of the course. They'd partied, and then they'd made love all night . . .

Swallowing the anguish that swiftly rose, she let her gaze search the streets again. There was no sign of Michael anywhere—and no indication of where he might be. She clenched her fists, resisting the temptation to just go down there and start looking. There were still twenty minutes to wait before the so-called door opened.

"Then you'll know that—unlike smaller circles—it takes more than brute force or a well-placed silver implement to destroy a circle this size. And it takes time to do so by magic."

Meaning she was on her own for longer than any of them wanted. She bit her lip for a moment, then rose, her long skirt swirling around her booted feet, stirring up dust. "I'd better grab my packs and head down there, just in case the door opens early."

"It won't."

She knew that, but she couldn't stay here, doing nothing, for another second. Lifting her skirt a little, she walked down the long slope to the small camp that had been set up in the hollow between two hills. Camille followed her. There were probably a dozen people and tents down here, but there was really only one other person she wanted to see right now.

Jake glanced up as she approached. "I've packed everything that's on the list. I just hope the weather doesn't turn, because the sleeping roll may not keep you warm if it does."

Nikki shrugged and picked up the first of the packs. It felt like she was slinging a load of rocks over her shoulder. "Then I'm just going to have to convince Michael to keep me warm."

Jake's expression was worried. But then, he'd already lost one person he'd loved, and now *she* was willingly stepping into a trap. "Don't expect too much at the beginning. Remember what—"

"I remember," she cut in tartly. "But I just don't

think magic can ever entirely erase what we share."
Recognition would be there, even if it was buried
deep. And come hell or high water, she was going to
bring that recognition to the surface as soon as she
could.

"There's one thing that's got me puzzled, though,"
she added, glancing at Camille as she adjusted the
straps. "If Weylin needs to follow what happened a
century ago, how come everyone in town is wandering around in reasonably modern clothing?" Or at
least the men were. The one woman she'd seen had
been wearing an outfit that looked as if it belonged in
a bordello. She was mighty glad to have been allowed
a skirt and shirt once she'd seen *that* outfit.

"As Seline said, it's the location and the sequence of
events that are important."

"She also said she didn't know which events." Or if
they even mattered.

"True." Camille held out her hand. "Better give me
that ring."

Nikki glanced down at her engagement ring. Somehow, the act of taking it off felt like a betrayal, yet
wearing it might give away who she really was. She
tugged it off and placed it in the old witch's palm.
Her hand felt naked without it. "I'll be back for that
in four days."

"Make sure that you are." The ring disappeared
and a cell phone took its place. "Slip this inside your
skirt. Your bags will probably be searched the first
day, so keep the phone on you until after that happens."

"Will the phone work in there?"

"I don't see why not. Weylin couldn't afford to cut

off the town completely, or he'd have people out here investigating."

Nikki nodded and slipped the phone into her skirt pocket. Jake lifted the second pack, then pulled Nikki forward and hugged her fiercely. "Take care in there. I don't want to lose you."

"You won't." She hugged him back just as fiercely, all too aware there was a very real possibility she might never see him again if things went wrong in Hartwood. And she had to wonder if Jake was strong enough to survive her loss so soon after losing Mary. Right now their partnership seemed to be the only thing holding him together. After a while, she pulled back and added, "Not that either of you can do anything if the situation goes haywire."

"He won't kill you or Michael," Camille commented. "He needs you both alive for the ceremony."

"*If* he is trying to raise his brother. You have no real proof that's his goal."

"Seline says it is, and that's good enough for me." Camille grabbed her hand, her fingers like cold parchment against Nikki's skin.

"Here," she added, placing something cool and metallic into Nikki's hand. "Take this. We found it in the van."

Nikki's mouth went dry. It was the silver cross she had given Michael when they'd first met.

"It may help jog his memory—if you can get him to wear it."

Not trusting herself to speak, Nikki nodded. She wrapped her fingers around the chain and felt the tingle of energy run up her arm. The images from the cross came through muted, as if viewed from a distance and distorted by layers of dusty glass.

But she could feel him. Feel his anger. His despair. Seline was right. Deep inside, he thought her dead, and the agony of it was tearing him apart.

Tears stung her eyes. She blinked them away and spun around. "Let's get this over with."

The three of them walked down to the single white stone that indicated the entrance. Jake dumped the pack at her feet and shoved his hands in his pockets.

"Someone's headed this way," he commented.

Someone who looked a lot like the gnarled van driver, Nikki thought, eyeing the lean figure apprehensively. He walked like a man with the weight of the world on his shoulders, and even from this distance, the sense of his evil was something that crawled across her skin.

Goose bumps rose along her spine. Swallowing to ease the sudden dryness in her throat, she glanced at Camille. "You'd better retreat. The note said I was the only one allowed to be here."

"Yes." The old witch paused, and then she gripped Nikki's shoulder, squeezing lightly. "Good luck. And remember, once you enter that place, you are Seline, not Nikki. Never once can you say your real name, for fear that Weylin will hear."

Nikki nodded. "I'll remember."

"When you can, call me." Camille squeezed her shoulder a final time, then turned and walked back up the hill.

Nikki's gaze met Jake's. Neither of them said anything. Neither of them needed to speak. With a smile that was more a grimace, Jake kissed her forehead, then quickly followed Camille.

Nikki had never felt so alone in her life. Had never felt as frightened.

Crossing her arms, she watched the slow approach of the wizened figure. He stopped ten feet away and glanced at his watch. He didn't say anything, just stood there, waiting.

Given little other choice, she did the same.

After a while, energy began to buzz through the air, standing the hairs on her arms on end. The old man glanced at his watch again, then motioned her forward.

Nikki picked up the second pack and walked to the right of the white rock. The tingling in the air grew stronger, slithering across her skin with the warm stickiness of blood. Every step became an effort, and the buzzing grew so loud it thundered through her head, matching the rhythm of her heart.

Then it was gone, and she stumbled forward several steps before regaining her balance.

The old man snorted. "I would have expected a little more grace from an old witch."

She straightened and met his gaze. His eyes were the gray of ghosts. "Why?"

His gaze slid down her body, becoming heated. Disgust shimmied through her. *Old lecher* . . .

"I guess because I have a hard time imagining that someone so luscious could be so . . . clumsy."

The feeling of disgust increased. And while she was more than able to protect herself from lecherous old men, she had a feeling *this* old man might be more than he seemed. Might be her match physically *and* psychically.

She hitched the pack on her shoulder to a more comfortable position and said tartly, "Look, I can stand here and chat all day, but I thought Weylin wanted to see me."

The old man hawked and spat. The globule barely missed her boot. "Oh, he does. Thing is, you have to find him first."

"Meaning?"

"Meaning, Weylin's well aware that you intend to disrupt the sequence of events so that the ceremony cannot be completed. So he's given you an extra task, just to keep you occupied and on the right track."

As if she *really* needed something extra to do. "Won't giving me a task I didn't have back then disrupt the sequence?"

"Not when there are only two occurrences that really matter. You coming here is one of them. I'll let you figure out the other."

Seline had given her five events that she considered "markers." It could be any one of them. Or it could be something else entirely. Nikki scrubbed a hand through her hair. "What's my task?"

The old man grinned, revealing stained and rotten teeth. "There are eight rangers looking after this town. Two of them will be sacrificed at midnight—unless you can find and save them."

"And Weylin's going to let me wander around unhindered?"

"I never said that." His grin got bigger. "And can I add some friendly warnings?"

"Knock yourself out."

He hawked and spat again. "First, none of your magic will work in this place."

The only magic she had was the only one that was important, and it was obviously still working, because this old man was seeing Seline, not her.

"The barrier prevents that." She said it as a statement of fact, even though it was a guess.

The old man nodded. "Just as it prevents that vampire friend of yours from using his psychic skills. No messing with anyone's mind this time, I'm afraid."

Seline had warned her that this might happen. Whether it actually *had* happened, or whether the old man's words were just empty threats, was something she'd test later, when she was alone. But Seline wasn't supposed to have any psychic skills beyond telepathy, so she had to be careful.

"And?"

"And if you've snuck a phone in, be warned. We have a scanner in place. We'll catch anything you say, and if you say too much, someone will die."

"You and your master are sick, do you know that?"

He merely grinned. "Lastly, just let me warn you that it ain't just humans wandering around here now."

And *he* was one of those nonhumans. Though what he was, exactly, she wasn't sure. "Is that it?"

"For now." His smile faded, his eyes becoming almost luminous in the harsh sunlight. "I'll take you to your assigned accommodation. Just remember, the afternoon draws into evening, and the first two men will be sacrificed at midnight."

His voice had dropped several octaves, becoming rich and strong. It was the voice of the man in the van—the man with the ethereal gray eyes.

"You must think me quite a formidable enemy if you choose to speak through your servant rather than in person, Weylin," she said tartly.

The old man's eyebrow rose. "I will not make the same mistake as my brother. I will not underestimate you. The only time *you* will see *me* is when I take your life. Otherwise, I will continue to use intermediaries such as this to communicate."

There wasn't much she could say to that, so she waited. The luminous light faded from the old man's eyes and, after a moment, he turned and led the way down the slope.

"Do you have a name?" she asked as they passed a beautiful old wooden church that looked intact enough to still be in use.

"Kinnard." He glanced over his shoulder, his grin wide but his eyes cold. "You should know that."

She raised her eyebrows, feigning a casualness she didn't feel. "Why?"

"Because not only did you fuck me, but you almost killed me."

Had that actually happened? Or was he merely testing her? She'd met Seline once—and even then only briefly—but it had been long enough to know that she had far better taste in men than this. But then, she had no idea just how far Seline might be willing to go to catch a killer. A lot further than *she,* she suspected.

Still . . . her gaze skimmed over Kinnard again. Her gut said Seline *hadn't,* and right now, all she had were her instincts. "I may have tried to kill you, Kinnard, but we both know I didn't bed you. But, for the record, the next time I decide to kill you, I'll do a better job."

"There ain't going to be a next time." His eyes gleamed with maliciousness. "Because I'll have *my* revenge."

She had a feeling his form of revenge had nothing to do with killing her. Goose bumps ran across her skin, and she resisted the temptation to rub her arms. "That's only if Weylin wins. I wouldn't start counting chickens before they've hatched, Kinnard."

He snorted. "Blondie, we can't lose. Not this time."

Blondie was the nickname Weylin had used for Seline, too. Had Kinnard been around then, too? It was certainly possible given that he wasn't human. "And why would you think that?"

"Because, this time, all the odds have been stacked in our favor."

She'd been fighting the odds half her life, so that was really nothing new. This time, she had an added incentive—her wedding. And she had every intention of getting to that wedding and marrying Michael.

"We'll see," was all she said.

He led her down what once must have been the main street. Most of the old wooden buildings were still intact and, judging by the noise coming from them, occupied. She frowned, letting her gaze run past the dusty windows. If the yells, curses and slurred speech were anything to go by, most of the unseen men, and a good portion of the women, were drunk. Maybe it was easier for Weylin to control them that way. And if that *was* the case, then maybe her first duty should be to find a way to cut the supply of booze.

Though that would probably be useless. This was Weylin's game—and for the moment, he held all the cards. If she cut one booze supply, he'd just set up another.

Awareness skittered across her skin. She looked up quickly, her heart pounding as her gaze searched the second story of the nearest hotel. A shadow stirred the frayed remains of curtains in the solitary window.

Michael. Watching her.

She wanted to run to him and tell him she was all right, that she wasn't dead. But she couldn't. Weylin was undoubtedly watching, and right now, she couldn't afford to do anything that would give away the fact that she wasn't Seline.

But oh, how she longed to see him. To *hold* him.

She took a deep breath and let it out slowly. She had to maintain control. *Had* to. Otherwise their wedding plans might be put on hold—permanently.

But her gaze kept finding its way back to that window, and her skin burned with the intensity of his gaze. Yet there was no hum of awareness in the link between them. No indication that he had any idea who she truly was. Weylin had planted his magic deep.

"Found the boyfriend, then," Kinnard said.

She'd been so intent on trying to see Michael that the sudden sound of the old man's sharp voice made her jump. Her gaze swiveled to his. "He was never my boyfriend. He is, however, a friend, and that ultimately means more." She forced a sweet smile. "As you should know from experience. Or was that a lie, Kinnard? Another little attempt to catch me out?"

He gave her his stained and creepy smile again.

"And do you often fuck your friends? Because the two of you were at it like rabbits when you first met."

Obviously, he had no intention of this conversation getting sidetracked in any way—though she really couldn't see the point of *this* particular angle. Unless, of course, Weylin had sensed her presence. Seline's magic might be strong, but so too was Weylin's. He'd gotten his minions into the Circle's headquarters, after all. Her fear rose, but she forced it back and gave Kinnard a thin smile. "Then it's highly unlikely to happen this time, isn't it? We both know your master needs certain events to happen for his magic to work. Don't think I won't try my utmost to prevent those things from happening."

"Oh, you can try. Trouble is, you don't know which events—if any—he actually needs." His grin grew larger. "But the boyfriend? I'm right in that, if nothing else. The intense awareness I just felt confirms it."

She raised an eyebrow. "And how would you be feeling something like that when this place is supposedly a psi dead-zone?"

"Darlin', this may be a dead-zone, but you and I both know it doesn't stop personal magic. And to answer the question you were really asking, emotions are like blood to me."

"Meaning you're some kind of psychic vampire?"

He didn't directly answer, simply paused as they passed another bar and breathed deep. "Ah, anger. Sweeter than wine, that is."

As he spoke, a man came flying backward out of the bar, landing on his back at their feet. His nose was bloody, and he reeked of sweat and alcohol. Obviously, drinking was more important than bathing in this place.

Kinnard nudged the man with the toe of his boot, and without looking at either of them, the drunk climbed to his feet and staggered back inside. If the abuse and sounds of flesh hitting flesh were anything to go by, the fight was continuing right where it had left off.

Kinnard seemed to positively glow.

"Don't need to tell you that Hartwood is one hell of a lawless town, do I?" he asked, as he continued on down the dusty street.

"It was a hundred years ago." Seline had said Hartwood had the reputation of being one of the most lawless towns in the West, with death an everyday event. Nikki hoped like hell that Weylin intended only to imitate the feel of Hartwood. Surely he wouldn't want his captives killing each other—not until he'd finished the ceremony and raised his brother's spirit, anyway.

"A pretty girl like you could cause a hell of a commotion in a town like this," he commented.

She forced a smile. "A pretty girl like me *did* cause one hell of a commotion one hundred years ago. I can still protect myself, Kinnard, with or without the use of magic."

"I'm guessing we'll be seeing that boast in action all too soon. There aren't many women in this town, and the few that are here are finding themselves in demand."

That chilled her more than anything else he'd said. Everyone in this town—beyond herself, Kinnard and

Weylin—was here through force. Those women had no choice. They were merely playing a role, and in many ways, what Weylin was doing to them was more despicable than the threat of killing the rangers.

Kinnard stepped onto the wooden sidewalk and walked toward a small house. She followed, eyeing the old building somewhat dubiously. It was in much the same condition as the surrounding buildings, but it seemed to have a definite sag in the middle. The old wood was gray, much of it gaping and splintered, though at least the roof looked fairly solid. The door and one front window were also intact, and the cracked and peeling paint of the door was a bright yellow that contrasted starkly against the gray. The concrete steps leading up to it were broken and wobbled dangerously under her weight.

"Your boudoir," Kinnard said, opening the door with a rusty key and stepping to one side.

She held out her hand. He gave her another smile and placed the key in her hand, his fingers clammy as they brushed hers.

She repressed a shudder and said, "I'll take it from here, thanks."

He glanced at his watch. "Dinner is served nightly between six and seven over at the Hollis Hotel. Miss it, and you don't get nothing unless you buy something from the store."

She'd brought money, so that was no problem. "So Weylin's intending to make a profit in addition?"

"Why the hell shouldn't we?"

It was interesting that Kinnard said "we" rather than "he," because it suggested that he was somehow connected to Weylin rather than being the mere gopher she'd taken him to be.

"Fine, then. 'Bye."

"Oh, this ain't goodbye, darlin'. I'll be seeing you around."

The anticipatory look in his eyes sent another chill down her spine. She watched until he'd disappeared around the far corner before walking into her house. It was everything she'd expected it to be—filthy and uncomfortable.

Two walls were a red-brown timber and the other two either mud or plaster, decorated with peeling strips of flowered wallpaper. They rustled softly in the breeze coming in through the broken side window, with a noise like the sighing of ghosts.

In one corner there was a small metal stove, and beside that, a wooden rocker. A picture frame hung above the chair, but the picture was long gone, replaced by dusty spiderwebs. In the opposite corner was what once must have been a breakfast nook. The table was sturdy, but only two of the four chairs were useable. A new candle sat in the middle of the table, looking out of place amid all the dust.

She dropped her packs in the middle of the small front room and walked through the next door. It turned out to be the bedroom. There was only one small window, but at least it was solid. The blind covering it was tattered and torn, sagging unevenly. The bed was metal-framed and, like the house, seemed to sag in the middle. The old mattress had definitely seen better days. She wouldn't be surprised if it was infested with vermin. Sitting beside the bed was an old blanket chest, and beside that was a sturdy red-

wood dresser. In the corner nearest the door was a
small metal tub, and on a nearby hexagonal table,
a porcelain basin and jug. The bathroom, obviously.
There was even a chamber pot sitting under the table,
meaning that toilets were an outside affair.

She'd lived in places worse than this as a teenager.
She could survive for a few days.

She glanced at her watch and saw it was nearly
four. Time to start finding those rangers. Hopefully,
it wouldn't be too hard. After all, there wasn't much
of Hartwood left, so surely there couldn't be too
many hiding spots.

But first, she had to find Michael.

Five

MICHAEL CLATTERED DOWN the old stairs and strode through the hotel's small main room and bar. As usual, it was full of people, smoke and noise. The miners were drinking hard after a day underground, and the scantily clad saloon girls lustily plied their trade, alleviating the miners of their cash. Some of them didn't even bother going upstairs—much to the enjoyment of the surrounding men.

He shook his head. He'd never been one to enjoy such exhibitionism, though he'd seen plenty of it over the centuries he'd been alive. Had even taken part in such acts during his early years as a vampire, although never willingly. For him, the pleasure came from one-on-one intimacy, not voyeurism.

His gaze swept over the crowd. The blonde wasn't here yet. Maybe she'd been taken to one of the other hotels, or even down to the whorehouse at the end of Main Street. There'd been four extra women brought in over the last few days, and they'd been hustled into the bars and into work pretty quickly—mainly because there were far more men than women in this town. The whorehouse was finding it hard keeping up with demand.

A miner reeking of sweat and alcohol stumbled toward him. Michael did a quick sidestep, but the fool still managed to hit his shoulder, sending pain washing through his body in sickening waves. For some reason, the bullet wound was slow to heal. Why, he had no idea. He'd been shot often enough in the past, and the wounds had healed within a day or so. But four days after receiving it, this wound still festered.

Not that he could even remember getting shot in the first place.

Frowning, he thrust the drunk away, cannoning him into the backs of three other men. The miner recovered quickly and swung around, fists flying. Michael snorted contemptuously, ducking the first blow and catching the second in his fist.

Wrapping his fingers around the other man's grubby hand, he squeezed tightly. Bone cracked. The other man screamed and dropped to his knees. Michael's gaze went to the men gathering behind the screaming drunk. "Don't even try it," he warned coldly.

They swallowed, backing away, their sudden fear evident in the rapid rise of their heartbeats. The darkness in him rose, needing to taste the sweet life that coursed through the veins of these men. He clenched his free hand, fighting the desire to feed, wondering why the darkness was so strong now when he'd spent years successfully ignoring it.

He tossed the miner away from him and strode from the hotel. Though he needed to feed, he hesitated on the edge of the wooden sidewalk, his gaze going to the old house two buildings back from the whorehouse. He switched to the infrared of his vampire vision and saw that the blonde was alone in the back room. Relief slithered through him, followed quickly by surprise. He'd never been into blondes, and he certainly wanted nothing to do with any of the women who'd made this hellhole their home. And yet . . .

This blonde had caught his interest, but it wasn't so much her looks—which were stunning—but something else, something he couldn't really define. He'd felt her coming long before he'd seen her, and the awareness that surged when his gaze met hers had nearly burned his senses. His physical reaction had been just as intense, almost suggesting a familiarity with her curvaceous body.

Impossible, of course. He'd been with Christine for ten years, and there'd been no one else. Memories rose like guilty phantoms, and suddenly he was kneeling in the Chicago street yet again, with Christine in his arms, her life draining as fast as the blood that pulsed from the bullet wound in her chest. Reliving the moment as she lay there, gasping for breath. She'd touched his cheek and declared her love—a love he'd never been able to return, despite all his caring.

He closed his eyes, forcing the images away yet again but not denying the anger that surged through his veins. He would find Dunleavy and he would kill him. Maybe then Christine's ghost would finally rest in peace. He turned away, walking toward the nearest stable. He had a killer to hunt down. Dallying with a whore, however winsome he might find her, could play no part in his mission.

He slid open the barn door. The scent of hay, horse and dung drifted out to greet him, and in the semi-darkness beyond, eyes gleamed as horses shifted nervously. They could sense what he was. Most animals could. He smiled grimly. Humans could certainly learn a thing or two from the beasts they used and abused.

He walked down to the end stall and unlatched the door. The brown mare snorted warily, tossing her head. He spoke soft words of encouragement, hypnotizing her with his voice as much as with his gaze. When she was still, he sank his teeth into the soft flesh under her neck and drank his fill.

He'd barely finished when he heard the footsteps. He wrapped the shadows around himself, stepping into the corner of the stall. For several seconds, there was no sound beyond the tremulous beat of a heart and the restless stirring of the other horses.

Yet without even looking, he knew who it was. The blonde. And the amazing awareness that seemed to surge between them was even stronger this close, surging through his veins like life itself.

"Michael?"

Her voice came out of the dusky shadows that hovered near the main entrance, her tone soft, warm, and somehow familiar. Heat chased the awareness through his veins, and suddenly he wanted this woman with a fierceness that had him shaking. Why? What was it about her that had him responding so intensely?

Or was it nothing more than some sort of magic? Emmett Dunleavy *was* a sorcerer. Michael had.found that out the hard way—and still bore the healing scars down his back. Maybe his reaction to this woman had nothing to do with desire, and everything to do with some sort of trick.

"I know you're here, Michael. We need to talk."

She hadn't moved. Though he could taste her tension, hear the rapid beat of her heart, he couldn't feel fear. Which was strange, because if she knew his name, she probably knew what he was.

He flicked the curtain of darkness away from himself and exited the stall. Her glorious green eyes widened slightly, and as her gaze raked him, then came to a halt on his shoulder, he'd swear he saw the brief sheen of tears.

As if she knew he had a wound under his shirt.

After relocking the stall door, he took several steps toward her, then stopped. This close, her eyes weren't really green but a strange green-brown, as if the green was backlit by a warm amber. Right now, those strange-colored eyes were filled with such promises that the ache in his groin became even more painful.

He crossed his arms, resisting the pull as he watched the warmth flush across her cheeks. Her full lips pursed, then opened slightly, as if she couldn't drag in enough air. Perhaps the intense attraction went both ways.

He let his gaze slide down. Her breasts were voluptuous, their peaks hardening through her tightly buttoned checked shirt even as he watched. Her skirt was brown, and though it swirled lightly around her feet, it was slit up the sides to her knees and would undoubtedly reveal tantalizing flashes of leg when she moved. He ached to explore what was still hidden, to slide his hand up the silky flesh of her thighs and discover paradise . . .

"What do you want?" His voice came out harsh, roughened as much by need as anger at his own reaction. Good lord, he wasn't so starved for sex that he'd take his ease on a *whore*. He hadn't been that desperate for a long, long time.

She studied him for a moment, then licked her lips. Like a lamb caught in the stare of a wolf, he watched as if hypnotized.

And that only succeeded in making him angrier. There *had* to be magic involved. What else could account for such a strong and instant attraction?

"We need to talk," she repeated eventually.

"So you said. About what?"

His voice was still harsh, but if she sensed his anger, she wasn't showing any fear. Either she was as stupid as a mule or she was more capable of looking after herself than she appeared. Or, as he'd originally thought, she was protected by some form of magic. He could probably discover the truth if he stepped closer, but instinct suggested he shouldn't. He didn't know why, but for the moment, he was following that instinct.

"I know why you're here in Hartwood," she said softly.

"Do you now?"

She shifted, affording him a glimpse of lightly tanned leg and thick boots. Not the shoe of choice for a whore, normally. "You're here to hunt down and kill a man by the name of Dunleavy."

He continued to glare at her. She shifted again, yet still there was no sign of fear in her mannerisms—no tremor in her voice, no avoidance of his eyes, no fluttering, nervous movements. Maybe the little fool didn't even realize he could snap her neck in the blink of an eye.

"What makes you think that?" he asked.

"Because I'm hunting him, too."

He couldn't stop the laugh that escaped. "You? Hunting a man like Dunleavy? Sweetheart, he'd eat you up in half a second."

Her eyes darkened imperceptibly at the endearment. "No, he won't. Nor will you."

"You think?"

"I know."

Maybe it was time to show the little idiot she was playing with fire. At the very least, if he managed to scare the wits out of her, she'd run so far and so fast he actually might be able to concentrate on what he had to do. With dusk fast approaching, he could ill afford to be standing here exchanging verbal blows with a lady of ill repute.

"What if I tell you that I could be by your side in the blink of an eye, drinking your blood while you moaned in ecstasy? What would you say to that?"

"I'd say that if you tried, I'd knock you on your ass so fast your head would ring."

He smiled slightly. The woman had spirit, that was for sure. "Then perhaps I should try."

She didn't say anything, just flexed her fingers and continued to watch him. He couldn't help admiring her courage.

He stepped to the right, deep into the gathering shadows, and wrapped the cloak of darkness around himself. Then he ran toward her so fast the wind of his approach flung her smoky-blond hair backward, as if offering the long column of her neck in supplication.

Though he had no intention of tasting *any* human, the darkness still rose. *If* there was a spell on this woman, then maybe it was not one of seduction, but one designed to court the darkness within him. Maybe Dunleavy sought to shatter the bonds Michael had secured around his demon, hoping it would send him back to the hell from which he'd emerged long ago.

He stopped close to her, and her scent spun around him—honey, sunshine and cinnamon. A warm, somehow familiar, scent that stirred him in ways that went beyond the physical.

She sidestepped him and placed a hand on his chest, even though he was still wrapped in shadows. That surprised him. Few humans could do what she'd just done.

He threw off the cloak of night and reached out, wrapping his fingers lightly around her neck, caressing the warm pulse that fluttered so rapidly with a thumb.

"I could break your neck so easily."

Her eyes widened a little, and the flutter under his fingers grew quicker. "Do that, and you destroy your future."

He raised an eyebrow. "How so? You are nothing but a whore."

Something flashed in her eyes—an amber fire that did strange things to his breathing. "Are you so sure of that that you're willing to kill me?"

"Perhaps." After all, what future did he really have to look forward to? The years that stretched before him were as endless and as dark as the ones behind.

He stepped closer. Her breath caught, yet the look in her eyes was more anticipatory than fearful. "Who are you working for?" he asked.

"No one."

He closed the remaining distance between them. Her rapid breaths caressed his cheek with warmth, and her breasts pressed against his chest. Awareness surged across his skin—an elemental force that was all passion, all heat.

"I don't believe you."

"I'm here to stop Dunleavy—nothing more, nothing less." Her strange-colored eyes searched his, and heat bloomed fiercely in her cheeks. She licked her lips, and it was all he could do not to taste their moistness for himself. Lord, he didn't know what it was about this woman, but she'd hooked him in her web faster than a spider's caught a fly.

"But," she continued softly, breathlessly, "I'll need your help, if I'm to succeed."

"You could be right," he murmured and gave in to temptation, briefly kissing her sweet lips. It felt like he was dipping a toe into heaven. It felt like he was coming home. "But I have no intention of helping you."

"I could make it worth your while."

"Oh, I'm sure you could." He slid his hand down her back. Even through the thick woolen shirt he could feel the heat of her skin. Like him, she seemed to burn. "Only I do not need a partner. Dunleavy is mine to kill."

"Dunleavy is more than you think he is. And he intends to sacrifice two men in a ritual tonight. We have to stop him."

He caressed the firm cheeks of her rear. A quiver ran through her, and her pupils widened slightly, evidence of the desire he could almost smell. Holding her gaze, daring her to stop him, he slid his hand back up to the band of her skirt and began to tug her shirt free.

"There is no 'we' in any of this, and I do not care if Dunleavy sacrifices a hundred men—not if the bloody trail leads me to him."

"That is a very selfish and unproductive attitude."

Smiling coldly, he undid the bottom button of her shirt and moved up to the next one. "I am a very selfish man, and I'm prone to taking what I want, when I want."

"And right now you think you can just take me?"

Another button gone; two more to go. His anticipation rose. "Yes."

"You'd be wrong, you know."

He raised an eyebrow, but his attention was more on what was about to be revealed than what she was saying. "You're the one who said you could make it worth my while."

"Only if we work together. I don't believe in free samples before the agreement."

The last button came undone, and he pushed her shirt open. Her breasts were far smaller than they'd appeared, but as glorious as he'd imagined. Yet it was the scar at the base of her neck that held his gaze.

"What is this?" he said, wondering at the anger that surged through him.

"A cut."

"I can see that. How did you get it?"

"By being stupid." She shrugged, her gaze on his, as if searching for something.

He frowned, forcing himself to concentrate on getting rid of her rather than trying to understand the puzzle she represented. He skimmed his fingers up her flat stomach, his gaze holding hers as he cupped her breasts, but he didn't quite touch their hard, pebbled centers.

"I can feel your desire, little one. Do not try and deny it."

"I'm not." She moved with a suddenness that surprised him, pushing him backward as she hooked her foot around his leg. He ended up on his ass at her feet, just as she'd warned he would.

He couldn't help laughing. "The whore has spirit."

She crossed her arms but made no attempt to cover her breasts. "Just why do you think I'm a whore?"

He rose and dusted the hay from his butt. "Because the only women in this town are whores, and because no decent woman allows a complete stranger to undress her."

One dark blond eyebrow winged upward. "What if that woman knows the man in question will play a major role in her future?"

He laughed again. Maybe he *should* keep this woman around, just so her inane comments could lighten the darkness of his life. "I do not need, nor do I want, a woman in my life. Not as a partner, not as a lover, not even as a short-term bedmate." Not until he'd avenged Christine's death, anyway. He owed her that much.

Her gaze skated down his body, and a smile tugged her lush lips. "Sections of your body are denying that statement."

"Something no decent woman would say out loud."

Her smile grew. "I never claimed to be decent, just that I wasn't a whore."

"Then, Miss Whatever-you-are, I suggest you return to your house and lock your doors. Night is approaching, and this town can get mighty unpleasant."

"As I told you before, I need to rescue the two men."

"Then do it on your own." He half turned away, then stopped. He couldn't let her go without tasting her again, even if every instinct said it was wrong. Wrapping a hand around the back of her neck, he pulled her roughly into his arms and claimed her mouth as fiercely as he wished he could claim her body.

Then he released her, spun and walked away.

Nikki wasn't sure whether to throw something at Michael's back or run after him. *Damn it,* every inch of her thrummed with desire—a desire that was obviously shared—and yet he was walking away.

She took a deep breath and released it slowly, but it did little to ease the ache.

Seline had warned her this would happen—not so much the frustration, but Michael refusing her help. Apparently, he'd done much the same one hundred years ago. Which meant she was following the chain of events rather than breaking them.

But, damn it, she hadn't really expected him to refuse to help her. She had expected the love they shared to transcend the spell and make wanting her seem as natural as night following day. Yet he was resisting even that. Obviously, the spell that held him was strong, and she was going to have to work a *lot* harder to get him to accept her in any way. Still, at least he *had* recognized the scar, so the spell wasn't as all-encompassing as Weylin might have hoped.

She sighed and buttoned her shirt. Now what? Part of her wanted to follow Michael, but she sensed this would only anger him and make him even more reluctant to help her. Somehow, she had to prove she could be useful to him—though that was hard to do when the shield around this town had smothered most of her psychic gifts.

Or had it?

Frowning, she glanced at the nearby pitchfork and reached for her kinetic energy. There was no response, and the fork stubbornly remained where it was. Yet *some* of her gifts were working. She'd been able to sense that Kinnard wasn't human, and she'd known where Michael was without looking. Maybe the shield around this town resembled the magic that had been in the Circle's testing room—and if that were the case, it meant she at least had her flames for protection.

She hoped so, because the only weapons she'd dared to sneak in were two sets of knives—one set strapped to her wrists, the other currently strapped to her thighs. She hadn't dared risk anything else, just in case her packs were searched. But as good as she was with her knives, she really didn't want to depend on them. Nor did she want to depend on the maneuvers she'd learned in self-defense. She had a feeling Weylin Dunleavy would be able to counter either source of protection easily enough.

She tucked the ends of her shirt back into her skirt and walked to the rear door. Dusk was settling in across the sky, painting the clouds a vibrant red. No rain tomorrow, at least. She let her gaze slide across the houses that remained in the small back street, but she couldn't sense life in any of them. That didn't mean there *wasn't* life, just that there was no no-longer-human life, such as vampires. Given Kinnard's earlier warning, there could be shapeshifters and God only knew what else in the half dozen sad-looking buildings dotting the street, and she wouldn't sense those until she got closer to them.

Michael wasn't anywhere close, but that didn't surprise her. He was here for one reason—to reenact past events. And she was here to disrupt them and stop Weylin—if she could.

She thrust *that* thought away. Of course she'd stop him. She had a wedding half-planned, and she had every intention of finally going out to buy her wedding dress.

Her gaze roamed beyond the buildings. The night crept shadowy fingers across the hills, and nothing seemed to be moving.

Where would Dunleavy sacrifice the two rangers?

Seline had told her that the sacrifices on the night of the new moon would be performed in a side shaft in the main mine, but Nikki doubted Dunleavy would risk using that site for these minor sacrifices, if only because some ritual sites needed purifying before reuse, and he wouldn't want to be doing that every night.

So, where else?

In its prime, Hartwood had had close to one hundred and fifty working mines. She'd never be able to search all of them, but then, many of them would undoubtedly be sealed up. This place was a State Park, and neither the rangers nor the local authorities would want people wandering into unsafe or unsound mines.

Which meant that, maybe, all she had to do was look for signs of recent use around the mine entrances. But where to start?

She bit her lip for a moment, then swung left. Dust stirred under her boots, swirling through the air. She sneezed.

"Bless you," a cold voice said to her right.

Nikki jumped and swung around, resisting the impulse to flick a knife into her palm simply because she recognized the voice.

"You spying, Kinnard?" She eyed the old man warily as he walked from the shadows of a small lane alongside the barn.

"Of course." He hawked and spat. Nikki quickly shifted her boot to avoid the blob, and suspected he did it purely to piss her off. Kinnard grinned. "The emotion of sexual excitement is almost as potent as anger. You and that vampire of yours fairly set the air alight."

"I'm happy for you," she muttered. "What do you want?"

"I came to remind you that dinner is being served."

He came to spy, more likely. Obviously, he was Dunleavy's eyes and ears, and he had probably followed her simply to see whether she was playing the game or not.

And maybe following Kinnard should be her plan of attack once she'd rescued the rangers. It might be the only way she was going to figure out where Dunleavy was. *If* he was a vampire, as Seline had said, then she should be able to sense him the minute she got near him. But he was also a sorcerer, and would probably be wearing some form of concealment—if he hadn't totally changed shape. After all, his twin had been a shapeshifter. There was every chance that Weylin was, too.

"I'm not eating tonight, thanks," she said.

"Ain't much but beans in the store, you know. And they're worth a king's ransom." His gaze skated down her. "Of course, for a pretty thing like you, I'll do a special price."

Revulsion stirred. "No, thanks."

Kinnard raised an eyebrow. "Too good for me, huh? Well, that'll change. It did last time."

"The only time it happened was in your dreams, Kinnard." She stepped back. "If you'll excuse me, I have rangers to find."

"Ah, yes." Humor lit his pale eyes. "That reminds me—I've been sent to give you a hint and a warning. Wolves prowl the eastern rim. Get past them, and you might just find your rangers."

Might not, too, she suspected. "And when I free the rangers, Weylin promises to release them?"

"Gotta like a woman with confidence." He gave her a stained smile. "They can join the miners in the bar, but they can't go free."

No one can. The unsaid words hung in the air between them. Nikki swallowed to ease the dryness in her throat. "He'd better keep his promises, Kinnard."

He snorted. "And what are you going to do if he doesn't, girlie? This is our game, and you're playing by our rules."

"Rules can change." *Would change,* if she had anything to say about it. "And remember, old man, neither you nor your master knows as much about me as you think you do."

Chew on that, she thought, spinning around and walking away. His gaze burned a hole into her back long after she'd turned a corner and headed for the nearby hills.

Once she'd passed the last of the old buildings, she stopped. The hills rose above her, dark and silent expanses of dirt and sage bush. To her left, halfway up one of the hills, stood the Standard Mill, which had once processed ore from the Standard Mine, the largest and most profitable of all the mines in the area. A series of wooden poles led from the mill to the hilltop—the remains of a gondola system that had once carted the ore from the mine to the mill. She couldn't see the mine entrance from where she stood, and she had no intention of going there tonight. But that was where she'd have to go come the night of the new moon.

Her gaze came back to the mill. Kinnard had suggested that the rangers were being held in the eastern section, but she didn't believe him. The mill was certainly far enough away from town to hold prisoners, but as one of the few almost whole structures that remained outside the town, it was also a very obvious hiding spot.

Would Weylin do the obvious? Probably not. But instinct was pressuring her to check out the mill and, right now, all she really had to go on was instinct.

Picking up her skirt, she walked toward the mill. The wind stirred, brushing cold fingers across her cheeks even as it teased long strands of hair away from her ponytail. It was still somewhat jolting to see blond hair rather than brown, and she was damn glad there'd been no mirrors in the old house. It was an unreal sensation to look in the mirror and see someone else's reflection staring back.

She wondered why Seline and Michael had never been intimate. While she knew, from comments that Camille had made, that Seline was dark-haired, Nikki very much suspected that the rest of the image the spell used was pretty much the real Seline. Put dark hair with the green eyes and voluptuous figure, and it was amazing that *any* man, vampire or not, had resisted her. And from comments Michael had made in the past, she knew Seline was not one to shy away from intimate situations if the chance presented itself. So why had the two of them never been more than friends? It was curious, to say the least. And though she'd asked Michael, she'd never got more than a simple "because I never saw her that way."

Maybe *this* was her chance to learn more about him and the past he was still reluctant to talk about. While she could hardly talk to him about Seline, there was a lot of other information she could mine. Centuries of it, in fact. The Michael who'd been in the stable was the Michael she loved—and yet, at the same time, he wasn't. Seline had warned her that he'd be rougher, darker. Harder. And in some respects, he'd been all of those. But he'd also seemed a whole lot more talkative. *Her* Michael played his cards very close. Maybe it was something he'd learned from Seline. Maybe they'd had no other choice once the Circle had begun taking the bad guys out in earnest.

The mill loomed, and Nikki slowed and swept her gaze across the nearest buildings. There were a good half dozen smaller buildings surrounding one larger cluster, which she guessed would probably be the main mill works. Most of the buildings were clad in sheets of corrugated steel, but there were a few that were all wood. It was to one of these that she found herself walking.

That fact brought her up short.

Was it instinct that had brought her here, or something else?

She stood still and listened. Sheets of metal rattled on the roof of a nearby building, and the wind whispered through shattered windows—a forlorn sound that chased goose bumps across her skin. A takeout container rolled along the well-worn path that ambled through the buildings, blown in from God knew where.

No one seemed to be here, and yet . . . something was.

She licked her lips and took a step back.

A rumble of sound rose from the night behind her.

She froze, knowing she'd fallen into Weylin's trap.

The wolves weren't patrolling the eastern perimeter. They were right here in this mill. With her.

Six

MICHAEL STRODE DOWN the center of Main Street, scanning each hotel with the infrared of his vampire vision. For a town that only had a small number of inhabitants, there seemed to be an overabundance of drinking holes.

Unfortunately, Dunleavy didn't appear to be in any of them. Vampires had a slightly different glow under infrared, and all the people currently in the hotels were human.

So where was Dunleavy? While the fiend was young in vampire years, dusk had settled across the hills, and it would be safe enough for him to start moving around. Yet he was nowhere to be found. Again.

Maybe he was hiding in one of the mines—though given Dunleavy's preference for the high life, it was hard to imagine him putting up with the dark, dank tunnels for any length of time. The rat *had* to have a hole somewhere. It was just a matter of finding it.

His gaze went to the blonde's home, and he frowned when he saw the blur of life inside. There was no way she could have gotten past without him noticing, so it couldn't be her. And besides, the red blur was smaller, and it seemed to have an odd energy pattern. It wasn't a vampire. In fact, it wasn't anything he could remember seeing before. It was almost as if the creature in that house wasn't even something that lived and breathed, in the normal sense of the word.

Frowning, Michael quickened his pace, striding beside the old boardwalk rather than on it to mute the noise of his steps. The red blur froze anyway, head cocked to one side as if listening. Then it scurried toward the rear of the house. Michael smiled grimly and blurred into the night, racing around the buildings to the back of her home.

He was just in time to catch the sneak climbing out of the rear window.

"Well, well," he said, grabbing the man by the scruff of the neck with his good hand and dangling him above the ground. "What have we got here?"

The felon squawked, his wizened face screwed up in fear, scarred hands and booted feet swishing wildly through the air. "Nothing! Let me down."

"Not until you explain what you were doing in this house."

"It's *my* house," the man said. "I can damn well do what I want!"

Michael gave him a shake. Though he was holding the felon tightly enough to almost choke a normal man, it seemed to have very little effect on *this* particular man. Maybe the fool was too frightened to realize he was being choked, though his actions suggested anger rather than fear.

Reaching telepathically, Michael tried to read the old fool's thoughts, but nothing happened. For some reason, his telepathy skills had deserted him since he'd walked into this place. Either that or the old man had shields stronger than anything he'd ever come across—which meant, perhaps, that he was a whole lot more than he seemed.

Maybe he was connected to Dunleavy in some way. It was logical that Dunleavy would have someone to do his bidding during the daylight hours, when he was restricted to the shadows.

"If this is your house, then why were you climbing through the back window?"

"I heard steps. Thought it might have been one of the miners coming after the money he's owed."

"So you're a cheat as well as a thief?"

"I ain't." But it was sullenly said.

"Then stop waving your hands and empty your pockets."

The old man glared. Michael shook him hard enough to rattle the old fool's teeth. With a soft curse, the thief slowly emptied his pockets. Fine silk underclothing fell to the ground.

Michael's anger rose thick and fast, and suddenly it was all he could do not to kill this creature right then and there.

"A cheat, a thief, *and* a pervert. Perhaps I would do this town a great favor if I rid it of your presence."

"Whores don't need undergarments," the old man muttered, his sullen words at odds with the strange flame of anger and anticipation in his pale eyes.

"And you do?" Michael retorted. "Tell me what you were doing in this place, or I *will* kill you."

The old man regarded him for a moment, his expression shrewd rather than fearful. Which was decidedly odd given that Michael only needed to apply a tiny bit more pressure and the fool would be dead.

"I was sent here to search the whore's things," he said eventually. "I had to make sure she brought nothing dangerous into the town."

"Who sent you?"

The old man hawked and spat. Michael dodged the glob and squeezed his hand a little tighter. It made no more difference than before.

"Dunleavy," the old man said eventually. "He runs this place."

"And the undergarments?" Michael asked.

"A gift for the other whores. This one probably isn't going to live out the night, so it won't matter if I take them for others to use."

Michael's grip tightened even further. Any other man would have died right then and there, his neck snapped. Yet there was no bone under his fingertips. Impossible, surely . . .

"What do you mean?" he asked, voice harsh.

"Listen to the wind, vampire. It howls for blood."

As if the old man's words were a trigger, the howls of wolves suddenly sang on the night breeze. It was a sound that spoke of hunting and the need for blood. A sound that stirred the darkness in him, despite the fact that he'd fed only a few minutes ago.

He frowned, his gaze searching the darkening hills. The blonde was in trouble.

The desire—no, the *need*—to go to her aid pounded through his blood and itched at his feet. Yet she was nothing to him, just a luscious stranger he wouldn't have minded spending some time with had the moment been right.

So why did his heart freeze at the thought of *not* helping her?

He shook the old man, hard. "I don't care if the wind or the wolves howl for blood. I have other business to attend to. What's your name?"

"Kinnard." The old man regarded him for a second, then added, "And this is something I didn't expect."

"What? Being caught?"

Amusement flitted through the old man's eyes. "Oh, there's more than one of us caught right now, but *only* one of us realizes it."

"Enough with the riddles, Kinnard. Where can I find Dunleavy?"

"I don't know."

"Then how do you get your orders?"

The old man gave him a strange smile and tapped his head. "I hear him. He tells me, I do it. Simple."

Michael shook him again. "You *must* have seen him sometime, Kinnard. An invisible man cannot run a town."

A strange sound that might have been a laugh, or might have been a gasp for air, rumbled up Kinnard's throat. "I cannot help you in your quest, vampire, because I do not know. But I *can* tell you that what you seek is right under your nose."

And then he laughed—a high, cackling sound edged with insanity. Michael tossed him away in disgust. "Do not let me find you raiding this house again," he warned.

The old man picked himself up, dusted off his clothes and sniffed. His expression was an odd mix of disdain and madness. "There are many forces at work here, vampire. Until you are aware of the value of all the players, I suggest you do not waste lives needlessly."

"Then *I* suggest you take my advice and stay away from this house."

Kinnard snorted softly and walked away. Michael watched until he'd disappeared around the corner of the whorehouse, then he picked up the undergarments and tossed them back through the window.

The wind that stirred his hair and caressed his face was full of the scent of wolves. He frowned and glanced toward the hills. As much as he wanted to continue his search for Dunleavy, he simply couldn't leave the blonde in trouble. Especially if *she* was the prey the wolves hunted. He sighed and ran toward the distant howling.

He wasn't all that surprised to find both the wolves and the blonde at the mill.

What *did* surprise him was the fact that she was standing quite calmly in the middle of the snarling pack.

He stopped ten feet away from the tableau and crossed his arms. The wolf closest to him looked over its shoulder and gave him an almost human once-over. *Shapeshifter,* he thought, and glanced at the other four. Three were normal wolves, while the fourth was another shifter. *Interesting.* Shifters didn't often mix with their animal counterparts.

His gaze went back to the blonde. "And here I thought you might need assistance."

There was no sign of fear in the amazing green-brown depths of her eyes, though there were hints of amusement and frustration. The woman was definitely odd.

"They haven't been sent here to hurt me." Her voice was a low caress that stirred memories he couldn't quite catch. "Just to harass me. Dunleavy doesn't want me to find those two men I mentioned."

He swept his gaze across the nearby buildings. "There's no life in any of these buildings."

"I figured there wouldn't be."

"Then why come here?"

"Because I had to check. Dunleavy might have hidden the prisoners here just because it *was* too obvious a hiding spot."

Only a woman would think like that. "Do you want assistance?"

She gave him a deadpan look. "Hell, no. I'm enjoying myself too much."

He held back a smile. "Two of these wolves are shifters, and as they'll understand every word we're saying, it might be best—"

"They won't understand," she countered, "because they're under Dunleavy's spell and following his orders."

"And you know this because . . . ?"

She hesitated. "I'm a witch."

She was a witch as much as *he* could fly. Then he frowned, wondering why she was lying. But if she wasn't a witch, then how did she know the shifters were spelled?

"Then why don't you magic your way out?"

She sniffed, her look so haughty he couldn't help smiling. God, she looked so damn cute he could kiss her. He quickly quelled the thought. Where was his mind? He was here to avenge Christine, not dally with another woman.

"Magic cannot be raised willy-nilly," she said, her

voice bordering on disdain. "And it should always be used with care."

"That doesn't really answer my question."

She hesitated again, then said in a more normal tone, "I can't raise the magic here. The conditions aren't right."

He had a feeling the conditions were never going to be right for her. And that begged an interesting question. Why did she claim to be a witch when she could not raise magic?

"So, as I asked before, do you need to be rescued or not?"

"Yes, please," she said, a touch primly.

He couldn't help smiling again—and three times in one day was something of a record. It seemed to have been forever since he'd last felt so relaxed with someone. He'd even been guarded with Christine, though he'd known her for close to ten years.

He looked past the blonde again, searching the buildings closest to them, looking for one that was long, with exits at either end and few windows. He found one to the side of the old wooden shack. It had windows, but they were high up and not big enough for a wolf to jump through.

"Do you think the shifters would shift shape if they were trapped?" he asked.

"Not until the spell wears off, and I doubt that'll happen until after midnight."

"Midnight being the time Dunleavy intends to kill his prisoners?"

She nodded. "So, what's the escape plan?"

"Prepare to be swept off your feet," he said, blurring into the night.

He swept her into his arms, ignoring the twinge in his shoulder as he raced toward the building. She gasped, her heart a wild tattoo against his chest as she snuggled closer. He couldn't help noticing again that she was not as voluptuous, not as soft, as she appeared. Yet in many ways, he found that more appealing.

Behind them, the wolves stirred, howling their anger as they lunged after them. He opened the door of the building and ran through the cobwebbed darkness, his footsteps a whisper that barely stirred the thick dust. Behind them came the clatter of claws as the wolves entered.

He opened a second door and ran on. The exit wasn't that far away—but neither were the wolves. Given the fierceness of their snarling, he wasn't relying on her assertion that they didn't intend to harm her.

He opened the last door, glanced over his shoulder and saw a big gray wolf launch itself at him. He slammed the door shut, heard the thud and saw the door tremble.

He placed the blonde back on her feet. "Hold this tight," he said, indicating the doorknob.

Her fingers slid warmly across his. "Where are you going?"

"To lock the other door."

She nodded. He ran around the building and closed the other door. Then he hunted around the nearby buildings for something to secure the doors. Eventually, he found some long lengths of rope in what looked to have been a toolshed. He lashed the handle and tied it back to a rocky outcrop. Then he raced back to the blonde.

She looked around as he approached. "You took your time." Her words were punctuated by thumps against the door.

He showed her the rope, then began lashing the door. "Do you have a name?" he asked, realizing he couldn't keep referring to her as "the blonde."

She hesitated. "Seline."

He looked at her as he began securing the other end of the rope to the door handle of the building directly opposite. "Really?"

"Really." She crossed her arms and looked somewhat defensive. "Why?"

"Because you don't look like a Seline."

She raised an eyebrow. "Then what do I look like?"

He shrugged. "Something softer."

A smile twitched her lips. "Softer? Do I look like the soft type to you?"

His gaze did a tour down her body, then rose to meet hers again. Heat touched her cheeks, and awareness and longing burned in her amazing eyes.

"I think you're cotton candy with a steel core," he said softly.

She smiled. "You could be right." Her gaze lingered on his for a moment, then she glanced down and frowned. "You're bleeding."

A fact he knew, as he could smell the blood. It wasn't much more than a trickle, though, and would undoubtedly dry up soon. He shrugged. "Got shot a few days ago. The wound is taking time to heal."

"You'd better let me look at it."

"It's fine."

"But it might get infected."

"I said it's fine."

She still persisted. "But if it was silver—"

"Damn it, woman, I do not need or want your help—with anything."

Her expression closed, yet her green-tinted eyes filled with anger and frustration. "Fine. I'll continue my search for those men, then."

He frowned. "Alone?"

"Yeah. Why not?"

"Because you are a woman, and this is a rough town. And because wolves come in all forms."

She shrugged. "I can protect myself."

"So you've said before." And he was no more inclined to believe her now than he was before, despite the fact that she'd tipped him on his ass earlier.

He glanced at the town below them. Lights shone warmly from the hotels and the whorehouse, but there seemed to be little activity anywhere else. Dunleavy hadn't been down there at dusk, and previous night searches had proven useless. He had a feeling tonight's search would prove just as useless.

And as much as he didn't want this woman's help, he also couldn't bear the thought of her wandering out here alone. Why, he had no idea. It wasn't as if she meant anything to him. Lord, he'd only *just* met her. Yet, at the same time, it seemed as though he'd known her forever.

He met her gaze again. "Perhaps I should accompany you on your endeavor."

She raised her eyebrows. "Why? I thought you didn't want my help."

"I don't. But if you insist on wandering out here

alone, then I shall accompany you. I intended to search beyond the boundaries of the town tonight, anyway."

"So this is not so much an offer of help as a way of protecting me while you continue your own search."

"Precisely." He turned and offered her an arm. "May I escort you away from this mill? The paths tend to be uneven."

"My sight is as good as yours, vampire." She brushed past his offered arm and strode away, as if to prove her point.

He chuckled softly. He'd never met such a fiercely independent woman before, and while it was annoying, it was also extremely refreshing. Would she be this feisty in bed? Somehow he suspected the answer was yes.

He followed her, enjoying the sway in her walk, the flash of calf. She hitched her skirt up as she reached the longer grass, revealing lithe, well-muscled legs. Not a woman who spent most of her time on her back, that was for sure.

He lengthened his stride to catch up with her. "So what does the witch do when she is not hunting killers?"

"I do not spend my time whoring." She cast him a sideways glance. "What does the vampire do?"

"For the most part, try to stay out of trouble."

"Some things never change," she muttered. "Vampires, no matter what the age, are a close-mouthed lot."

He raised an eyebrow. "You've associated with vampires previously?"

"Yeah." She looked at him, and there was something in her eyes that stirred him. "You might even say I love one."

"If the feelings are returned, then why are you here alone?"

She ducked her gaze away from his. "Because my vampire went away."

"Ah. I'm sorry."

She shrugged. "It doesn't matter."

It mattered a lot, if the sense of hurt and frustration he was picking up from her was anything to go by. Though *why* he was picking such things up from her was something he didn't know. "Would it help if I say vampires rarely stay in relationships for long?"

Her gaze came back to his. Amusement touched the amber-lit green depths. "So I've been told." She hesitated. "Have you had many long-term relationships?"

"Very few."

"How many is very few?"

"That is none of your business."

She smiled, and he couldn't help feeling her amusement came from a joke he should be able to share.

"You called me a whore, but I can count the number of men I've had on a couple of fingers. Can you say the same, vampire?"

He studied her for a moment, wondering why this seemed so important to her. Wondering why the thought of her having had a couple of lovers tore at him so. "That depends on what you term a relationship."

"More than just sex. And more than a few nights."

"Ah, well." He paused, thinking back through the long years of aloneness. "Maybe three."

She looked surprised. "Really?"

"Really." His voice was a little sharper than he'd intended. "Watching someone you love grow old and die is never easy. Mostly, it's better not to love."

"Then why not make your lover a vampire?"

"Are you always this damn nosy, woman?"

"Yes. And I tend to nag when I don't get the answers I want."

"All women nag. It's an ability you're born with."

Amusement touched her eyes. "And it seems men are born with the innate ability to sidestep questions."

"Then let me answer yours. Turning your lover into a vampire almost never works, because the fledgling stage of vampirism is basically a madness that can last ten or twenty years."

They skirted the old pump house situated at the southern edge of the pond and continued on. The scent of another person touched the air, and he raked his gaze across the night. The same old man was rustling about in the bushes lining the far edge of the pond. Hunting or spying? Or something else entirely? Maybe he should check out those bushes once day broke. He wasn't sure why he thought daylight would affect Kinnard when he wasn't a vampire, especially because he'd seen Kinnard moving about in daylight, though admittedly not during the midday hours. But intuition was suggesting that Dunleavy's right-hand man was a whole lot more than he seemed, and he wasn't about to ignore it.

"And that," he continued firmly, returning his thoughts to the blonde and her questions, "is all you're going to get out of *this* vampire."

She arched an eyebrow, amusement rich in her eyes.

"You're very touchy when it comes to personal matters."

"You don't know me, so you can't say what I am or am not."

"I wouldn't bet on that, Michael."

Actually, he wouldn't bet on it either. He had a vague suspicion this woman knew him better than anyone else alive. Maybe she *was* a witch.

"Any idea where this so-called ceremony might take place?"

She shook her head. "I suspect it's happening in one of the mines, but there are so many, we could never check them all in one night."

He could. Or he could at least check which of the mines currently had life in them and go from there. But Dunleavy would sense his presence the minute he got anywhere near those mines, and the fiend had proven adept at disappearing in the past. Which again left him with the woman and the possibility of using her as a decoy.

An option he didn't like, and one that had not worked well in the past.

His gaze went back to the bushes. Kinnard had gone. *Interesting.* "Does Dunleavy intend to kill the men in some sort of ceremony, or does he merely execute them?"

"There's no 'merely' about an execution."

He glanced down at her. "If he merely kills them, it could take place anywhere. If he intends to perform a ritual, wouldn't that lessen the search area? Don't such ceremonies require specific locations?"

She hesitated. "Yes."

Again, he got the impression that *he* knew more about magic than she did. "Such as?"

She bit her lip, her expression one of fierce concentration. It was the sort of look an unprepared student might have when asked a question by a teacher. "It would need to have limited access. And depending on the type of ritual he performs, it would need to be big enough to contain not only the protection circle, but a ritual fire and perhaps a table."

Michael nodded. "Then that cuts down our search area. There are five mines that are big enough to cater to those requirements. One of them is the Standard Mine, which we just left."

"It won't be that one. He intends to use that the night of the new moon."

He raised an eyebrow. "Couldn't he use the same place twice?"

"He could, but I doubt that he will. He has to follow a set pattern."

"Why?"

Her gaze slid from his. "Because he has a ceremony to perform on the night of the new moon, and the lead-up to that ceremony does not include killing anyone else on the site."

"You're sure?"

"Yes." She hesitated, then grimaced. "No. Not really."

He half smiled. "There is one way we could easily find out."

She glanced at him inquisitively. "How?"

"Vampires can move with the speed of the wind. I could very easily check out the five mines for the presence of humans, then come back here." And, in the process, he could check out Kinnard's disappearance while keeping her at a safe distance from trouble, should it arise.

She stopped, crossing her arms as she looked up at him. "We both know you could have suggested that when we were standing in the middle of the mill, so what's suddenly made you change your mind?"

"I merely wish to make your search easier."

"Crap. You've seen something, haven't you?"

The woman *had* to be a witch—either that, or she had some form of telepathy that somehow breached his shields, allowing her to read his thoughts. "If we continue as we are, we will not have time to search all the mines before your midnight deadline."

"Fine." Her voice was flat, angry. "Go."

He caught her hand and raised it to his lips, inhaling her intoxicating scent as he kissed her fingers. "I won't be long."

"I believe that as much as I believe the reason you're going," she replied tartly.

He smiled, stepped back, and let the night cover him.

For several seconds, Nikki glared at the spot where he'd been standing and silently cursed him. She'd forgotten just how frustrating he could be—which really only showed how much he'd changed in the time they'd been together. Now, thanks to the spell he was under, he was back to telling her nothing and trying to get rid of her the minute anything dangerous appeared on the horizon.

While she had no doubt he *would* check the mines,

she also suspected he was going to check what Kinnard had been up to. If she'd noticed the old man foraging around in the shrubs, Michael surely had.

And he was about to learn yet again that she wasn't going to be left behind, where it was supposedly safe. She hitched up her skirt and walked back toward the pond.

Just as she reached the old pump-house building, a scream rent the air. She froze, a chill racing across her skin as she stared toward the town. It had come from the direction of the whorehouse and had been a sound of sheer terror. Someone was dead. Horribly dead. Of that she was certain.

And Seline had warned her . . . *There will be five people killed,* the old witch had said, *two on the first night. Stop them, if you can.*

Nikki had fallen into a trap, all right, but it wasn't the wolves. It was believing what Kinnard had said about the rangers and thinking that the rangers were the two who would lose their lives tonight. God, she was a fool!

She turned and raced down the hill. People were out in the streets, some simply standing there, some running toward the whorehouse.

She pushed past the small crowd standing in the doorway, then hesitated, glancing around. Sobbing was coming from the room to her left, but it was the stairs that drew her attention. Blood that was fresh and bright dribbled slowly down each step, its source an unknown well at the top.

Nikki swallowed, then lifted her skirt higher and carefully made her way up the stairs. It wasn't until she reached the landing that someone tried to stop her.

A big man with red hair and matching cheeks stepped forward, one large hand outstretched. She sidestepped the pool near the top stair then came to a halt, her gaze unwillingly following the trails to the doorway on the right. The door was closed, but that wasn't stopping the blood. God, what had happened in there?

"Sorry, Miss, but it's better if you don't go any further." His voice was gravelly but gentle. "It's not very pretty."

There was a sheriff's badge on the left pocket of his khaki shirt, but it was the plastic kind they sold in toy shops. His pants were also khaki, and Nikki very much suspected she'd just found one of the missing rangers. But did that mean the others were also in this crowd, or was this another of Dunleavy's little games?

"I've had medical experience," she lied. "I might be able to help."

"There's no one left alive in there to help, Miss. Best you go back down the stairs."

"Sorry, but I can't do that."

She tensed, expecting him to react, to try and force her back down the stairs, but all he did was shrug and step back. "Then on your head be it."

Nikki's gaze went from the ranger to the door and her stomach clenched. She didn't want to step through that doorway—no sane person would—but she had to do it. She was here to do a job, to stop a killer, and something in that room might provide a clue.

Gathering her courage, she stepped to the door and

wrapped her fingers around the handle. After taking a deep breath to calm the churning in her stomach, she carefully opened the door.

For a moment, she simply couldn't believe what she was seeing. It looked for all the world as if some youngster had gone crazy with a can of paint. Red was sprayed across the walls in insane patterns and dripped steadily from a thickening blotch on the ceiling. Actually, there was *too* much blood. The human body contained a finite amount, and one body couldn't have provided enough blood to do what had been done here *and* drip down the stairs. Weylin—for she had no doubt he was behind this atrocity—had to have gotten extra blood from another source. She hoped that source—be it human or animal—had died faster and cleaner than this woman.

Two men were covering body parts with white sheets, a tough task when there were so many parts, many of them no longer resembling anything human.

Her gaze went to the window. When she saw what was sitting on the sill, she put a hand to her mouth, holding back a scream that seemed to stick somewhere in her throat. Then her stomach rose, and all she could do was run—from the horror of the room, from the overripe smell of blood and from the grotesque remains on the sill.

Remains that were the image of *her*.

Seven

NIKKI GOT AS far as the side of the building. Once there, she lost what little she'd eaten over the course of the day. When there was nothing more than dry heaves left, she stumbled to the back of the building and sank to the ground, leaning her head back and closing her eyes.

Dunleavy was sick.

Though she'd never doubted it, she now had proof positive. What manner of man could do something like that? God, he *had* to be insane. Inhuman . . .

The thought stopped her cold. Dunleavy *wasn't* human, and he couldn't be judged by those standards. He was a vampire, a worshipper of dark gods and a shapeshifter.

A monster.

And monsters didn't think like the rest of humanity. Jasper had certainly proven *that*.

"Are you all right?"

Michael's voice rose out of the night, soft yet filled with concern. *Wishful thinking*, she thought. He was probably too busy tracking down Kinnard to worry about what she was doing right now.

"Are you all right?" he repeated, his voice, and his concern, nearer. Sharper.

Suddenly he was beside her, his fingers pressing warmth into her cheeks as he held her face. "What's wrong?"

She opened her eyes. He knelt in front of her, eyes rich with worry. She touched his lips with her fingertips, trailing them down his chin and neck and pressing them against his chest. His heart beat a rhythm that could only be described as erratic for a vampire.

She smiled, remembering another time, another place, when she'd echoed those exact same thoughts and actions. Something flickered in his eyes and, just for a moment, she thought she saw a touch of recognition. Then the spark died, leaving only normal concern.

But perhaps there lay part of her answer—by following patterns of the past and forcing memories to surface, maybe she'd undermine the spell.

"Damn it, woman, will you answer me?"

Her gaze jumped to his. The concern in his eyes was stronger. As much as the spell was trying to force him to, he wasn't treating her as a stranger.

"Can't you smell the blood?" she answered.

"Its sweetness rides the air," he said. "But right now, the source of that nectar is not my major concern."

His words made her heart do strange things. Lord, how she loved this man! "I'm okay. I just need a drink."

"Then you shall have it."

He rose and disappeared, but he was back within minutes with a small bottle of water. He must have raided the store to get it, because she couldn't imagine the hotels selling plastic bottles of water. Surely it wouldn't be in keeping with the feel Weylin was trying to achieve. Although, as she'd admitted to Michael, no one was really sure what was and wasn't important. Not even Seline. In the end, it was all guesswork, and she had a very bad feeling that whatever game plan Weylin was following, it wasn't one that would take a normal, rational path.

Michael handed her the water and sat beside her on the ground. His arm brushed against hers, and warmth pulsed through her body, erasing the chill, calming the churning.

"What happened in there?" he asked, thumbing toward the building at their back.

"I made a major mistake."

He frowned. "What do you mean?"

She took a gulp of water, swished it around her mouth, and then spat it out. "I was told Dunleavy would sacrifice two men at midnight if I did not rescue them. I stupidly presumed they were the two people I knew would die tonight—"

"How did you know two people would die?"

She hesitated. "The same way I know this is all leading up to a sacrifice on the night of the new moon."

"A vision?"

"Yes."

He studied her for a moment, making her wonder if he'd sensed that she wasn't telling him the *exact* truth. "Who told you two men would be sacrificed?"

"Kinnard. He's Dunleavy's gopher."

"So I discovered." Michael's voice was grim. "I

caught him searching through your belongings earlier this evening."

"Looking for items I wasn't supposed to bring into town, no doubt. Bastard!" She gave him a sideways glance. "Although the obvious question is, what were you doing at my place?"

"I was passing and saw his blood heat." He met her glance. "I have no interest in either your possessions or you."

Uh-huh. That was why he was still sitting next to her. Weylin's magic might control his mind, but it wasn't stopping the pull between them. "Anyway, I thought the two destined to die would be the two Kinnard mentioned, which is why I was looking for them."

He gave her another speculative look. "This town is full of men. How did you intend to define the search?"

She hesitated again, not sure how much she could safely tell him. Dunleavy had probably guessed she'd try and tell Michael the truth, and he would have factored some sort of counter into the spell holding Michael's memories hostage. "The missing men are rangers."

"Ah." He considered her a moment longer, then said, "So, if two were to die tonight, was it their bodies in that room?"

Images of blood and gore and shredded body parts flitted through her mind. She shuddered and took a hasty swallow of water. It only seemed to stir her agitated stomach more.

"It's hard to say how many bodies there were, but I

only saw one head." And that head had resembled *her*. Not the disguise she wore, not Seline. *Her*.

And that begged the question—did Weylin suspect who she really was? And if he did, why was he not reacting to it? Did he not care, or didn't it matter?

Or had the sight been aimed at Michael? That would probably make more sense, especially if it was a means of further torturing a captured mind.

Michael frowned. "Why could you not tell how many bodies there were?"

"Because there were bits everywhere."

"He tore the body apart?" There was no surprise in Michael's voice. But then, why would there be? She knew he'd seen far worse in his time, though he'd never really discussed the details with her.

She nodded.

"That doesn't make sense if he needed the body for a ritual."

No, it didn't. She frowned, forcing herself to look beyond the gore in her memories. "He left the head on the windowsill. For a minute I thought it was—" She hesitated, barely catching herself in time. "My sister."

Michael wrapped an arm around her shoulders, pulling her close. Warmth leached from his fingers and body, chasing away the chills that still ran through her. "He's trying to scare you."

"He damn well succeeded."

"You're tougher than that. It's merely the shock of it that got to you." It wasn't *just* shock. It was also horror, combined with the realization of just how far Dunleavy was willing to go.

"So you didn't see a second head?" he continued.

"One is more than enough, believe me."

"Not if two were meant to die tonight."

"There was lots of blood. And blood dripping from the middle of the ceiling." She paused, swallowing more water before adding, "The roof."

"The roof," he repeated, and removed the warmth of his arm from her shoulders. "You stay here while I check."

"Like hell." She scrambled upright, all awkward arms and legs compared to his elegance. "I'm here for a reason, too, remember, and like it or not, you and I have to be a team on this."

He gave her a look that said, *Yeah, right*. But he didn't try to stop her from following as he turned and made his way around the back of the building.

The stairs were around the far side—an old, rickety bleached-wood structure that barely seemed capable of supporting a gnat, let alone the two of them.

"Don't say it," she warned as Michael glanced at her.

"One at a time, then."

With the whole structure seeming to sway in the barely existent breeze, she could hardly disagree. He turned, running up the stairs so fast his feet barely seemed to touch each step. She followed more warily, trying to ignore the shudder that went through the wood as she climbed.

Unlike many of the other buildings that still remained in the old town, the whorehouse had a flat wooden roof. The sides of the building rose a good three feet above the roofline, providing a nice amount of shelter from prying eyes in the street or nearby buildings. Shelter someone had obviously needed.

She stopped on the last step, her gaze on Michael rather than what lay in the middle of the roof.

"Here's your ritual killing," he said, squatting on his heels. "Complete with pentagram."

She took a deep breath and let her gaze drift left. Compared to what lay in the room below, this killing was almost sterile. A black star had been etched onto the roof, and a man lay in the middle of it. Candles sat on each point of the star, their bluish flame shooting odd-colored shadows across the surrounding walls and lending the man's skin a weird, almost luminous glow. He was naked, his body white and flaccid. His hair was dark and still looked damp, and his cheeks and chin were free of stubble, as if he'd cleaned up before coming here to die. This impression was reinforced by the fact there was no terror in his face, and his eyes were closed. He would have looked asleep were it not for the two-inch wound in his chest and the tiny trickle of dried blood that ran from the cut and down his left side.

"There's not enough blood," she said.

Michael glanced at her. "The knife went in through the chest and out through the back. Gravity took care of the blood, I'm afraid."

"So it's his blood dripping from the ceiling below?"

He nodded. "There's a lot more than blood missing from this body, though."

She stared at him for a moment, silently debating whether she really needed to hear the rest of it. "What do you mean?" she asked reluctantly.

"I mean, he has no heart. It's been sucked out of his body. As has his brain."

She gave him a sharp glance. "How do you know that?"

"The death is fresh. The blood has not settled yet."

"Oh." Her stomach threatened to rebel again as her gaze went from the small wound in his chest to his hair, and she realized it wasn't water that dampened his hair. Yet there was no obvious cut near his head that she could see—not from this angle, anyway. And she wasn't about to change angles. Her stomach couldn't take such a discovery right now.

She added, "Why would he do that?"

He glanced at her, one eyebrow raised. "You're the witch. *You* tell *me*."

Had she been Seline, she probably could have. As it was, she didn't have a clue. "Dunleavy worships the dark gods."

"The pentagram has been drawn in black soot, and the candles are black. There's definitely black magic at work, so possibly he was sacrificing to his gods."

"And they answered the call, taking the heart and the brain."

"Either that," he replied grimly, "or Dunleavy has a taste for the brains and hearts of his victims."

"Vampires can't eat."

"My point exactly. So why was Dunleavy sacrificing to his gods?"

"To help maintain his strength, and therefore the strength of the barrier," she said, frowning as she studied the man's feet. They were burned in the arch—and the burn marks oddly resembled lips.

"Barrier? What barrier?"

Her gaze jumped to Michael's, and she suddenly realized what she'd said. There was no reaction from him other than puzzlement, yet the tingle of energy seemed to touch the night air.

Was it the spell on Michael reacting to her words, the pentagram, or just her imagination?

Could spells even work like that? It was so damn *frustrating* that she didn't know. Playing it by ear, when there was so much at stake, was not something she wanted to do, and yet she had very little choice. She couldn't risk calling Camille—not out here in the open and so close to the town, anyway. She had no idea what the range of the scanners was, but she wasn't about to risk someone's life to discover it. Especially when Camille probably couldn't tell her anything more about the spell on Michael without actually seeing the runes on his back.

She softly cleared her throat and answered his question. "There's a magical barrier around this town, preventing anyone from getting in or out."

"Really?" His expression was neither believing nor disbelieving, and his voice was flat, which, in the past, had always meant skepticism.

"Really."

"Then how did you get in?"

"Dunleavy wants me here. You're not the only one in this town out for revenge, you know."

He raised an eyebrow. "And knowing this, you still came here?"

"I had no choice."

"There is always a choice when it comes to death."

"Not always. Sometimes the choice is taken from us." She kept her gaze on his and filled the link between them with images of the time he'd snatched the choice from her, giving her a piece of his life force, oining them spiritually and forever altering the direction of her life.

Something flickered in his eyes, and just for an instant, annoyance surged through the link. The spark died as quickly as it had begun, but her hopes soared. It was a breakthrough, minuscule maybe, but nevertheless something she could continue to work on.

"Sometimes the choice is taken for a very good reason," he said, voice clipped.

"I know that."

He stared at her for a moment longer, and the buzz of energy riding the night got stronger. He shook his head and returned his gaze to the body. "What do we do with the body and the pentagram?"

"Leave it." She didn't have the skill to deal with the pentagram, and until the pentagram had been deactivated, or de-spelled, or whatever, she wasn't about to touch it. Or the body within it.

"Is that wise? It might yet be feeding strength to Dunleavy and his gods."

"I don't think we have any other choice right now." She rubbed her arms against a sudden chill, unsure as to whether it was from the cold night air or a premonition of worse to come.

He rose and moved toward her. "I'm going downstairs to check the room. I suggest you go back home—" He broke off, frowning a little. "If Dunleavy *did* invite you here to exact revenge, it might not be wise to remain alone."

She raised an eyebrow. "You're offering to move in with me?"

"I'm here to find a killer, not babysit."

"Then what are you suggesting? That I move in with another man?"

"No."

It was sharply said, and she smiled. The magic might have forced his memories away, but his territorial instincts were well and truly intact.

"What, then?"

He thrust a hand through his dark hair, and she noted the blood on his shirt again.

"You're still bleeding."

"It is of no consequence—"

"You were shot with silver," she cut in. "That wound needs special attention."

"And how would you know I was shot with silver?"

"I know a lot more than you do right now, vampire. Instead of trying to get rid of me, you might want to sit down and listen."

"What I need to do right now is to get downstairs and see what Dunleavy has done."

"Then I'll come with you."

He challenged her. "Can you stomach a return to that room?"

"No. But I want to question the woman who found the victim."

"Why?"

"Because I want to find out what form Dunleavy was wearing when he entered that room." She turned and carefully made her way down the stairs.

"Dunleavy's not a shapeshifter. He's a vampire."

She gave him a sharp glance over her shoulder, then remembered that neither Seline nor he had known until near the end that Emmett was a shifter. Obviously, Michael's knowledge now was equivalent to what he knew when he first came to this town. "His twin brother was a shapeshifter who could take the shape of anyone he'd consumed. There's no reason why Dunleavy can't be a shapeshifter as well as a vampire, is there?"

"No." The stairs quivered as Michael moved behind her. His warm breath caressed her ear as he asked, "Dunleavy has a twin?"

"A dead twin he intends to bring back to life."

Even without looking at him, she could feel his confusion as clearly as she could feel the heat of his body against her back. On some level, the link was beginning to function, magic or no magic.

"No," he said.

"Yes."

"I have chased Dunleavy a long time. I know him well, and there *is* no brother."

"You don't know him as well as you thought. Not then, and not now."

"Woman, you speak in riddles."

"I have a good teacher."

"That makes as much sense as your previous comment."

She grinned up at him as they strode toward the front of the whorehouse. "You'll understand it sooner or later, believe me."

"I doubt it." His dark gaze met hers. "I'm here to catch the bastard who killed my lover—nothing more, nothing less. Whatever it is you are truly up to, I cannot—and will not—get involved any more than I am."

Energy rippled across the night again and he rolled his shoulders, as if to ease an ache. It definitely had to be the spell on him she was sensing. And if what she'd just witnessed was any indication, that spell was attempting to force him into her arms. But why? Did Dunleavy truly believe Seline and Michael had been lovers? Or was it yet another indication that he suspected who she really was under this disguise?

If the latter, it provided her with something of a quandary. Making love to Michael might help free his mind from the chains of magic, but, by doing so, she'd confirm Weylin's suspicions and play into his hands.

But even the former presented problems. Michael was fighting both his attraction to her *and* the spell because he saw her as Seline and knew the wrongness of what the spell was trying to enforce. Which meant that *she* would have to be the aggressor when it came to making love.

And yet, if that was what Weylin wanted, it was the one thing she *couldn't* do. Kinnard had suggested there were only two events of any real importance, and while she knew Seline and Michael had not been lovers the first time, if Weylin believed otherwise, dare she take the chance on it being one of the two events?

Or was Kinnard's assertion that there were only two key events yet another lie, just like the one about the rangers?

That, she thought sourly, was the problem with not knowing a goddamn thing.

The crowd was gone from the doorway, and even though the entrance hall was lit with nothing more than candlelight, it was obvious someone had cleaned the stairs, because the blood no longer stained the wood. But no amount of cleaning could take the smell of death from the air.

Her gaze went to the small room to the left of the door. The sobbing woman had gone, but a big, black-haired man was sitting at the desk, his large frame squeezed into a wooden chair. Since he was wearing the same sort of khaki outfit that the red-haired man had worn, it was likely he was another ranger. He looked up from his notes as they neared, his gaze sweeping the two of them before he pushed to his feet.

"I'm afraid we've had to close this place down until we sort out what's happened," he said. "The Hollis Hotel is offering you ladies free accommodation in the meantime."

Nikki opened her mouth to state yet again that she wasn't a whore, but Michael put a hand on her arm, squeezing lightly. Power spun through the air, a familiar energy that caressed her senses like a summer breeze. Michael was trying to enforce his will on the big man. But there was no reaction from the ranger, confirming Kinnard's earlier threat that Michael's psychic abilities would work no better than her supposed magic.

Michael frowned, but all he said was, "We're here to investigate the murder."

The ranger didn't object, which again suggested Dunleavy wanted them to investigate. Though why wouldn't he? The more time they spent on this, the less time they had to find and stop him.

"I'd advise the lady to stay down here, though," the ranger said. "It's not very pleasant up there."

Michael glanced at her. "You'll wait here?"

Knowing it was said more for the ranger's benefit, she nodded. He slipped his hand down her arm and lightly squeezed her fingers before he moved away. She knew it was more a warning to behave than a gesture meant to comfort. Smiling slightly, she glanced back at the ranger. "Do you have any suspects?"

The big man shrugged and sat back down. "The client she had booked was late arriving, and the last man she saw left her alive and well. Ain't no telling what really happened."

She frowned. "So it was the late client that found her?"

He nodded. "And Maggie, the owner, who was taking him up to the victim's room."

That must have been the woman she'd heard sobbing. She wondered if the two women had known each other—and if Dunleavy had chosen his victim simply because of the woman's resemblance to *her*.

"So no one was seen going in or coming out of her rooms after her previous client left?"

"No one. Maggie saw her go to the bathroom to clean up, but she returned to her room a few minutes later." He shrugged. "Maggie runs a fairly tight ship here. No one would have gotten in or out without her noticing."

Obviously, this man also believed that they were in the past, because whorehouses weren't legal anymore. "But someone obviously did." Or maybe that should be some*thing*.

"Yeah." The big man frowned. "I checked the window. Nothing came in that way—it's stuck half open, but a kid wouldn't have fit through that gap, let alone someone strong enough to—" He cut the rest off, glancing at her apologetically. "Sorry."

She shrugged. She'd already seen the gore, and there was nothing this man could say that could be worse than the images still haunting her subconscious. "So no one went in or out or even near the room until Maggie took the client up there?"

"No."

"And no one heard anything?"

"No."

"Don't you find that a bit odd?"

He frowned. "Why would I?"

Because there should have been noise. Should have been screaming. Should have been thumps as the various body parts were flung about . . . Her stomach twisted threateningly, and she thrust the thought away. But then, why would anyone in this town find the lack of those things odd when they were all under the spell of the man who'd probably committed the crime?

Goose bumps ran up her arms. Who was next on Dunleavy's list? And did they even have a hope of stopping him?

"You should go home, Miss, and light a fire. The night is going to be a cold one."

"Right now, I don't feel particularly safe in my house." She met the big man's gray eyes. "Where are you staying right now?"

He raised an eyebrow. "That an offer, Miss? Because if it is, I'm on duty—"

What was this fixation Dunleavy seemed to have about whores? Was that how he saw *all* women, or had some whore rejected him, and this was his way of getting vengeance? Not that *that* made much sense, but they weren't exactly dealing with a sane mind here. "It's just curiosity, nothing more."

"Ah. Well, I'm staying at the Wheaten Hotel."

"Don't you have a house here in Hartwood?"

"Yeah, but the Wheaten is closer to the . . ." He paused and frowned, as if trying to remember why he wasn't staying in his own home. Nikki wondered if Dunleavy needed them close to keep control. It would probably be hard to pull the strings of your puppets if they were spread far and wide.

"I have to stay close, what with the murders happening and stuff," he finished eventually.

"And all the rangers are staying here?"

"All but Jimmy. Haven't seen him for a couple of days."

Meaning Jimmy was probably dead. "Which house is Jimmy's?"

"The yellow one at the junction of King and Prospect streets."

Which, if the map Seline had drawn was correct, was about where she'd seen the light coming from. "So where is your place?"

"Five houses down from Jimmy's, on King Street. Number Nine."

"And it's currently vacant?"

"Yeah."

"If you're staying here, I don't suppose you'd mind renting me your house for a few days, then, would you?"

The big man blinked, looking lost for a moment. Dunleavy obviously hadn't considered her asking *that* question.

"I guess." His voice was hesitant. "It ain't much of a house, though."

It would have to be better than the place Kinnard had dumped her in. And if the rangers were living here over the summer and autumn, it would surely have hot water and good heating.

"We don't need much," she said, almost stumbling over her words in her hurry to get them out. Dunleavy might not have realized she'd ask this question, but he could still stop her if she wasn't fast enough. It just depended on what sort of spell he'd bound this man with—and how much of a link he had with his puppets. "Is it okay if Michael stays there as well?"

"Michael?"

"The man upstairs."

The ranger's bewilderment increased. "I guess."

"You don't mind Michael stepping over the threshold of your home anytime he pleases?"

He frowned, obviously puzzled by the odd request. "No, I guess not. But like I said, it ain't much."

Relief slithered through her. She wasn't sure if the invitation worked secondhand like this, but if it *did* work, it couldn't be recanted.

And if Dunleavy was holding everyone in this section of town to keep them close and accessible, that suggested having them stay at their own homes made them *in*accessible. Being a vampire, he couldn't cross a threshold uninvited, and even though he controlled their minds, he couldn't force that invitation, because it had to be freely given.

So possibly they were safe from Dunleavy when they were in that house. Whether they'd be safe from Kinnard was another matter, yet her instinct suggested they might be. Why, she wasn't sure. But right now, instinct was about the only thing she *could* depend on.

She reached into her skirt pocket and pulled out a couple of bills. "Advance payment," she said, handing them over.

The ranger visibly brightened. "I was running low on drinking money. This will come in handy."

"I thought you were on duty."

"I am. But I'm off in another hour or so."

She frowned. "Will anyone take over your post here?"

"Don't think so. Won't be a need, will there?"

"What about the body?"

"It'll be taken care of."

She raised an eyebrow. "By whom?"

The ranger waved a hand. "By people."

"What people?"

"Undertakers, and the like."

So, Dunleavy was intending to hide the evidence? Why would he bother when he had no intention of letting any of them out of here alive?

She crossed her arms and leaned against the wall. "When are you next on duty?"

"Tomorrow."

"What about the other rangers?"

"Also tomorrow."

"What time?"

"About noon." He shrugged. "Ain't nothing going to happen before then."

Did that mean Dunleavy didn't intend to kill anyone before then, or was the information another red herring?

"And is Jimmy the only missing ranger?"

"Yeah." He frowned. "I haven't seen Harry for a few hours, though."

Was Harry the man on the roof? Probably. She wondered how many other bodies they'd find in and around Hartwood before the new moon dawned. She rubbed her arms and glanced toward the stairs. Michael was taking a long time.

As if he'd heard the thought, he appeared at the top of the stairs. The barely glowing candles lining the stairwell threw a yellow light across his features, even as they allowed the rest of his body to get lost in the darkness. His face was expressionless, as were his dark eyes, but his fury hit her with the force of a cyclone, almost flattening her against the wall.

"I need you to come up here—if you think you can handle it again." His voice was as flat as his expression.

She pushed away from the wall and slowly walked up the stairs.

"What?" she said when she'd reached the top.

He merely pointed her into the room. She took a deep breath, gathered her courage and went inside. It was just as bad the second time. Worse, perhaps, because all the white sheets only emphasized the utter mutilation that had occurred.

She stopped several paces inside the door, clenching her hands against the need to turn tail and run. "What did you find?"

"Look at the windowsill."

She closed her eyes. "I've seen what's sitting on the sill, remember? I don't need to see it again."

"Then do you remember what you said?"

What on earth was he going on about? "Of course I do."

"Then tell me," he all but exploded, "how the hell you could be a sister to someone who had *no family*?"

Eight

MICHAEL GRABBED THE witch's arm and spun her around. Her face was pale, her odd-colored eyes a mix of confusion and panic. Part of him wanted to do nothing more than wrap his arms around her and offer the comfort she so obviously needed.

But he couldn't. Dunleavy had been playing him for a fool for some time now, and until he was sure who was friend and who was foe, he couldn't afford to trust *anyone*. Even a woman who affected him in ways he couldn't even begin to describe.

"What game are you playing? Or was this simply an attempt to gain my sympathy?"

"I'm not playing *anything*." Yet her gaze slid from his, confirming her lie.

"Then why did you make the statement that *that* woman is your sister? I know for a fact the only siblings Christine had were brothers."

She blinked. "Christine? You think that head belongs to Christine?"

"I do not think; I *know*."

Her eyes flashed with anger, the green fired by an inner amber glow. It was a glow that called to something deep inside him.

"Then you know *wrong*."

"Listen, witch—"

"No, I won't, because what you see is *not* reality. It's not Christine, and it's not—" She stopped abruptly, clearly swallowing back something she had intended to say. He wondered what it was. "Besides, I said I *thought* that woman was my sister, not that she *was*."

She was lying. He knew what he'd heard, and it certainly wasn't *that*. And yet, why could he sense no lie in her words?

"Please," she added, "just trust me for a few more minutes. I'll explain when we're somewhere where there's less chance of being overheard."

He snorted. "Why would it matter if we're overheard? And why would you think I trust you?"

"I think you want to," she replied. "And I *know* you need to."

She was right. He did want to trust her, but how could he when she was so very obviously lying? Not only about being Christine's sister, but so many other things. The most sensible thing to do right now would be to just walk away. He had a killer to find, and no matter what this woman was up to, he could not let it interrupt his hunt. But something in her eyes and her manner held him to the spot. He dropped his gaze to her lips and, almost against his will, he leaned forward and kissed her. She tasted as sweet as the finest wine and, somehow, so very familiar. *Damn it, no!* It was yet more lies. It had to be.

"I can taste your schemes on your lips, witch," he murmured. Her breath was enticingly warm against his mouth, but he resisted the urge to kiss her again. "Whom do you work for? Dunleavy?"

She swore and pulled away from his grasp. "I'm here to *stop* Dunleavy. Believe that if you believe nothing else." She glared at him, her hands on her hips and fury in her eyes. "If you really *do* want answers, vampire, you'd better start listening to me. We both know you cannot force the answers from me, because your telepathy isn't working right now."

"And how would you know that?"

"Because the same magic that has robbed you of your psychic skills has robbed me of my . . . skills."

Skills? Why would she use that word rather than "magic"? "Meaning this barrier you mentioned earlier?"

She nodded, her nostrils flaring, as if she was as acutely aware of the smell of blood and death that surrounded them as he. She ran a slightly trembling hand across her forehead and said, "Look, can we take this discussion elsewhere?"

"In a moment." He wasn't quite ready to go, simply because he wanted to keep her unnerved. He had a feeling it might be the only way to get those answers she kept going on about—even if he wasn't sure they were answers he'd actually need or want.

She glared at him, and he could have sworn he heard her swearing, even though her lips never moved.

"If I have to stay here," she muttered, "then how about you tell me if you found anything? Do you have any idea how the murderer got in?"

He knew he should keep pushing her about Christine, and yet he found himself oddly reluctant to do so. "There's a connecting door that leads into another whore's room. And there's the window. Either could have been the entry point."

"Nothing else?"

"Other than the fact there didn't appear to be a struggle of any kind."

"How . . ." She stopped, swallowing. "How can you tell that in all . . . this?"

"No blood or skin under the fingernails."

"Oh." She went even paler, if that was possible. "Can we go now?" she asked quickly.

He relented and stood to one side. She ran out. He caught up with her as she stopped in the middle of the road, sucking in great gulps of night air.

"You don't appear to have a strong enough stomach to be hunting the likes of Dunleavy."

Her smile was slightly bitter. "Monsters don't bother me as much as some of their deeds."

"Then why hunt monsters?"

She snorted softly. "Because the man I love insists on hunting them."

"And he lets you? The man is a fool."

She looked at him, a strange sort of smile touching her lips. "He's not a fool. He just made a good choice."

"If you were mine—" He stopped abruptly. He had no right to be saying such things when Christine lay rotting in the ground, her death not yet avenged.

"Let's get you back home," he said coldly.

Her gaze searched his for a moment, and then she picked up her skirts and began walking. "I'm not staying in that house tonight."

The thought of her staying at one of the hotels had ice running through his veins. "Where, then?"

His voice was sharp, and when she looked at him,

amusement played across her lush lips. "I've arranged to rent a room from one of the rangers."

"And will the ranger be there?"

"No. He's staying at the Wheaten Hotel."

"Good."

She chuckled softly. "For a man who doesn't trust, and who claims to have no interest, you're acting a little proprietary."

He was, and he had no idea why. "You appear to be the only decent woman in this town. I have no wish to see you hurt, that's all."

Her eyes twinkled almost merrily in the darkness. "Then after I've picked up my belongings you'll accompany me to my new lodgings?"

His gaze went to the surrounding hills. Dunleavy was out there somewhere. As was Kinnard. If he was escorting this woman, he couldn't be out there finding them and exacting revenge. But, on the other hand, she appeared to have at least some of the answers he needed. Answers that just might help in catching the fiend.

He met her gaze again. "If you promise to answer my questions."

"I'll answer them, but I don't promise that you'll like or understand the answers."

More riddles. This woman could have been vampire-trained. He glanced at her house, noting there was no movement or life inside. "It's safe," he said, stopping at the door. "I'll wait here."

She didn't argue, and was back within a few minutes with two heavy bags. He grabbed them both, slinging one over his shoulder and carrying the other. "Where to?"

"Five houses down King Street from the corner of King and Prospect."

Which was about as far away from the center of town and the drunken miners as you could get without straying into the hills. At least then he wouldn't have to worry about louts harassing her while he was off hunting Dunleavy.

They walked through the dark streets in silence, though the night itself was far from quiet, with the miners' revelry rolling through the darkness.

The ranger's house was in better shape than most in this town, though like the rest of the houses on this street, it could have used a good coat of paint. He followed her up the steps and stopped.

"I cannot go inside," he said, offering her the bags.

"The ranger gave his permission for you to cross his threshold." She opened the door and tossed the bags inside.

He raised his eyebrows. "I'm not sure it works secondhand."

"There's only one way to find out." She stepped to one side and waved him through.

He frowned, but walked forward. Nothing slapped against him with the force of a hammer. Energy *did* caress his skin as he walked through the door, but it was a warning that the barrier was in place, nothing more. And at least it meant other vampires could not cross this threshold without invitation. He walked into the middle of the room and turned around.

"I have lived several hundred years and never knew an invitation could be granted from a distance."

She smiled as she closed the door and flicked on a

switch. Brightness bit into the gloom. "Proving that even old vampires can learn something new." She picked up one of the bags and made her way toward the dust-covered table. "You want to take off your shirt so I can tend to that wound of yours?"

"I came here for answers, not medical help."

"You'll get your answers while I tend to the wound." She patted the back of a chair. "Sit."

"I will not sit, and I do not want the wound tended. Why did you say Christine resembled your sister?"

She sighed and gave him the sort of look a wife would give a stubborn husband. "Look, I'm using magic to cover what I truly look like—"

"Yet," he cut in, "you said your magic won't work in this town."

"This type of magic does."

He studied her, not sure whether to believe her or not. "I feel no magic."

"Yet it is here, working. On me and on you."

The woman was definitely mad. Either that or she was trying to drive *him* insane. "There is no magic at work on me."

"No?" She raised an eyebrow, her gaze challenging. "Care to test that?"

"How does this magic work if I cannot see or feel it?"

"The magic I speak of comes in the form of symbols and pictures entwined around our spines."

"There is nothing on my back but the scars I received from the last time I met Dunleavy."

"Want to bet those scars aren't scars?"

"How?"

"You take off your shirt, and I'll take off mine."

His gaze swept down her lush form, and longing surged through his veins. He clenched his fists against need and said, "Did Dunleavy send you here to seduce me? Is that your game?"

She rolled her eyes. "If I wanted to seduce you, I think I'd be offering to show you something a little sexier than my back."

Back, front, it didn't matter. It was a part of her and innately seductive. "So you're not trying to seduce me?"

"Right now, no. Later, yes."

He couldn't help a smile. "I thought you didn't believe in free samples?"

She gave him an arch look. "I don't. Before this night is out, you'll agree to work with me."

He didn't bother refuting her statement. He'd probably only be wasting air anyway, as she wasn't likely to believe him. Stubborn and this woman were old friends, he suspected. He glanced at the door, with half a mind to walk out and leave this crazy woman alone. Yet he couldn't, and he didn't know why. That made him wary—of her, and of his own attraction. And of the way it seemed so right, so natural, and yet so wrong.

"You *are* crazy, aren't you?"

She merely smiled. "Go close that blind for me."

She pointed toward the window to his left, and after a moment, he obeyed. Her reflection filled the grubby pane of glass, and he watched, mesmerized as she began undoing buttons. A moment before her creamy flesh was revealed, he yanked down the blind and took a deep breath. It did little to cool the fever of his imagination. The itch to caress her warm skin once again . . .

"Okay," she said.

He turned around. She had her back to him, and he let his gaze drink in the slender curves for a long moment before he noted the weapons strapped to her wrists.

"The witch is well protected," he said softly, fiercely glad of that fact.

"I told you I could defend myself." She glanced over her shoulder, eyes sparkling with amber fire in the bright light. Odd how the green had completely disappeared. "And I certainly did not strip to show you that."

"No." He dragged his gaze to her spine. "There's nothing there."

"Come closer. It can only be seen at certain angles."

He obeyed, touching her creamy shoulders, turning her toward the light. Something glowed briefly along her spine—Celtic symbols, combined with images that resembled goddesses of old. He held her still and ran his fingers across the drawings. Her skin was warm under his touch, the needle-fine lines even warmer. Power tingled across his fingertips, a heat that was somehow pleasant, almost welcoming.

"There is nothing like this on my back," he said, allowing his fingers to trail down to the base of her spine. A quiver ran through her, and he snatched his hand away from the temptation to explore further.

"Take off your shirt and let's take a look." She pulled her shirt back on but didn't fasten the buttons, so when she turned around, the folds of heavy fabric stirred, revealing tempting glimpses of paradise.

He pulled off his shirt and turned around. Her touch played across his shoulder for a moment, pressing lightly against the rough bandages he'd placed there earlier. He winced. "I did not strip so you can investigate a wound that will heal well enough by itself."

"It may heal, but you'll have a scar if you don't let me treat it."

"I don't care about scars."

"I do." Her touch trailed to his spine, her fingers so warm, and somehow so familiar, against his skin.

"No symbols," he said, voice rough, "as I said."

Her hands were tracing patterns along his back, sending longing surging through his veins. He'd never reacted to a woman this strongly before. This was more than desire, more than mere lust. This was need.

It was almost as if her touch were as vital to his life as the blood he drank every other day. In time, his need for blood would lessen even further, and he'd be able to go days without it. He suspected the same could not be said about his desire for this woman.

He didn't know her. It *had* to be a spell of some sort. Had to be.

He stepped away from her caress and spun around. "Now that you've seen the truth, how about telling me the truth?"

She crossed her arms. The action caused the top of her shirt to puff out, and his gaze was drawn to the revealing swell of her breasts. God help him, he wanted to caress those creamy mounds. He wanted to caress *her,* kiss her, taste her—but it was wrong.

So wrong. He had no idea why. He only knew he couldn't give in to this craziness.

"I've seen the truth," she said, her voice soft and so sexy it seemed to tease his blood into a fever. "But, obviously, you can't. Come with me."

She foraged in her bag and pulled out a small mirror. Then, without another glance, she walked toward the door at the back of the table and disappeared down a hall.

He glanced at the front door. He'd never considered himself a coward, and he had never run from any challenge. But right now, he was beginning to think that was exactly what he should do. This woman called to him in so many ways, and on so many levels, that it was almost frightening. He'd lived a long time, had served his time in purgatory more than once and had long ago resigned himself to companionship rather than love. A few hours in this woman's company had him thinking that his heart might not be as far out of reach as he'd thought. And yet, instinct insisted he couldn't touch her, no matter how powerful the attraction.

He'd survived many a dark and dangerous time by listening to his instincts. He wasn't about to abandon them now.

"Michael?" She appeared in the doorway again, her expression questioning. "Do you want the truth or not?"

He wanted the truth, but he had a feeling he wouldn't be getting it. Or at best, he'd get only part of it. But he followed her down the hall and into a small bathroom that held a bathtub, a basin and a mirror.

"Turn around so that your back is facing the mirror."

He did so, and she handed him the small mirror she'd pulled from her bag. "Now use this to look at your back."

"All I see are scars."

She nodded. "But watch what happens when I touch them."

She placed a finger against his skin and began to trace the outline of one of the scars. Her finger was warm against his skin, her touch sending waves of energy tingling across his nerve endings. After a moment, the black and blistering skin began to disappear under her caress, becoming lines and symbols similar to what had been on her back. Her hand moved on, revealing the symbols entwined around his spine. As her touch moved, the symbols faded, becoming ugly scars once more.

"What game is this you play?"

"No game—or at least, it's not my game, but Dunleavy's."

"If Dunleavy had been near me, I'd have killed him. Or he would have killed me."

"Really? So how long have you been in Hartwood?"

He hesitated. "Four days?"

"And how did you get here?"

He frowned. He couldn't honestly say. Just as he couldn't say how he got the bullet wound. "What has this got to do—"

"Everything," she cut in. "Dunleavy wants you here for the same reason he wants me here. You and I killed his brother. He wants his revenge, but he also wants to bring his brother back to life, and to do that, he may need a repeat of certain events and the main players in place. You and me."

Her words were nonsense. Utter nonsense . . . and yet, memories stirred. An image of this blonde, a knife held high above her head as lightning arced around her. The press of flesh against steel as he hacked off Dunleavy's extremities one by one, until there was nothing left but a screaming, bloody shell of a man for the blonde to kill. A spew of blood that faded into the images of two men—one long and lanky, the other bald and thickset, like a boxer. Men he'd seen here, in Hartwood, and somewhere else. Somewhere he should remember, but couldn't. Pain hit him then—searing, blinding pain—and suddenly he was falling to his knees as fire burned into his shoulder and blood pulsed down his arm and spread like a river across the pavement . . .

Darkness surged, taking his sight, trying to take his mind. He hissed, closing his eyes, fighting the darkness, fighting the pain.

"Michael." Her voice was soft, insistent. He couldn't see her, but the fire and the darkness weren't stopping her voice. Nor did it take away the sensation of her touch as her hands pressed into his shoulders, as if she tried to hold him down and keep him still. "You have to fight the spell. You have to remember!"

"Remember what?" he ground out. "That Dunleavy killed Christine? I remember that, and I will kill him for it."

"Did you truly love Christine?"

"Yes." *No.* He'd cared, as much as he could care about anyone these days. But Dunleavy had taken her life, and for that, Dunleavy would pay. "What does it matter to you?"

"Christine has been dead for close to a century, Michael. It is not her death you mourn."

"No?" He laughed harshly. "Woman, you don't know what you're talking about."

"Don't I? What does Christine look like?"

"Brown hair, warm amber eyes, slender—"

"Really? And here I was thinking Christine had dark hair and green eyes."

He frowned, trying to shake off the darkness, the pain, the impact of her words. "No—"

"Yes."

"*No.*" He pushed her away violently, heard a thump and a slight gasp of pain. Her pain hit him like a club, filling him with remorse, filling him with anger. But with her closeness gone and her words silenced, the blackness receded. He took a deep, shuddering breath and opened his eyes.

She was in the hall, struggling to rise. Her gaze met his, amber eyes filled with wariness and anger. Yet, oddly enough, he sensed that her anger wasn't aimed at him.

She puffed out her cheeks, expelling air, and wiped a hand across her forehead. It was then he saw the lump, and the bruise already beginning to darken her fair skin.

Cursing his own carelessness, he rose and walked over to her. "I'm sorry," he said, offering her a hand. "I did not mean to lash out at you."

"Yes," she said, placing her hand in his. "You did."

He grimaced and helped her rise. He didn't release her hand immediately, because he suddenly needed her touch the way a drunk needed his next drink, and her hand was safer than anything else. "Well, yes, but it wasn't so much at you as at the pain."

"That's the spell inked onto your back at work. He doesn't want you to remember anything more than what he's given you."

"Even if I believe everything you say, how would my remembering what happened affect Dunleavy's plans?"

She sighed and rubbed her forehead wearily. "I honestly don't know."

There were dark shadows under her eyes and redness in them. He touched a hand to her cheek, gently running his finger down to the lips he longed to sample again. "Perhaps you should sleep. We can talk more in the morning."

Her gaze searched his for a moment, and a sweet smile touched her mouth. "I don't want to sleep alone tonight."

Her breath whispered across his hand, her lips warm and moist against his fingertips. The scent of cinnamon and honey and life teased both his senses and his memories, but those memories remained tantalizingly out of reach.

"I cannot," he said softly, releasing her hand and stepping back. "It would not be right."

With little more than a fingertip against his chest, she stopped his retreat and drew him back just as easily. "Why wouldn't it be right? It's what I want, and it's what you want."

"I came here to avenge Christine. Nothing more, nothing less."

"You avenged Christine a long time ago. This is about you and me, nothing else."

The pulse at her neck was little more than a wild flutter, a rhythm that called to the darkness in him. A rhythm that called to the man. Her nipples were pebbles pressing against his chest, her skin so warm that sweat formed where their bodies brushed.

He wanted her, there was no denying that. But he'd spent a lifetime denying desire, and this was no different than the need for blood. He might want her, but it wasn't right to take her.

Still . . . He wasn't made of stone. He was flesh and blood, and even after all these years, there were some desires that could not be completely repressed.

He leaned forward and kissed her sweet mouth—softly, seductively. "I cannot," he whispered, his lips so close to hers he could taste her every breath.

"I am not who you think I am," she said, her voice a husky whisper that tore at his resolve.

"I do not know who you are," he replied, stepping back. This time, she didn't try to stop him. "Right now, I'm not sure of anything more than the fact that Dunleavy is out there, and I have to find him."

"Dunleavy will find *us*."

"Perhaps he will. But for tonight, it's best if I continue my search. You will be safe enough here alone."

For one brief moment, he allowed himself the pleasure of simply looking at her, letting his gaze travel down the long length of her neck, taking in her small but perfectly formed breasts, the sharpness of her breathing, the thunder of her heart.

He had a sudden image of loving her, of losing himself to pleasure deep inside her, feeling the warmth and love and hunger of her response. The fierceness of his own response. He clenched his fists against the need to reach out, to make the image a reality. He quickly turned away, leaving behind both her and the emotions she seemed to raise.

The woman was definitely a witch. There was no other explanation for what was happening between them.

Was there?

He wasn't sure, and that was perhaps the most frightening aspect of this entire night.

Nikki took a deep breath and somehow resisted the urge to scream in frustration. She wanted Michael so desperately she ached, yet at the same time, part of her rejoiced at his resolve. He wasn't seeing her, but Seline, and despite the intense attraction, he was resisting. She wanted to think it was just as much an innate desire to remain faithful to *her,* to the love they shared, as the deep-down knowledge that he and Seline had never been lovers.

She would have to crack his resolve soon if she was to have any hope of breaking the pattern of events. She should have pushed more tonight—and would have, if it hadn't been for the spell and the horrible effect it seemed to have on him.

And yet she still couldn't escape the niggling notion that this was exactly what Weylin wanted. That maybe Seline was wrong, and all Weylin really needed for his ceremony was vengeance on the man who'd killed his brother.

She didn't know, and dared not contact anyone to

ask. Weylin might be content to play his games for now, but if she started asking questions like that, who knew what he'd do? And there was a whole town of people here under his control—more than she and Michael could handle.

Michael. What the hell was she going to do with that man? How was she going to break the spell that held him? Seline might have given her soap, but if her efforts to force his memories to the surface tonight had caused such a violent reaction, what the hell would attempting to erase the runes on his back do?

She yawned, leaned her head back against the wall and closed her eyes. He was right about one thing—she needed to sleep. It had been a long, frustrating and very tiring day, and she had a feeling tomorrow wouldn't be any better.

But she couldn't go to sleep just yet. Not until she'd investigated the neighboring house belonging to the ranger known as Jimmy. If he was dead in his house, it had to mean he'd invited Dunleavy into his home. While she wasn't absolutely certain Dunleavy had a telepathic link with everyone who wore his spells, she couldn't risk the possibility that he didn't. She had to presume he'd know, sooner or later, that the big man had told her about Jimmy. Had to presume that if there was evidence in the house, he'd make sure it was quickly destroyed.

She pushed away from the wall and did up her shirt as she made her way out to the main room. After digging out a jacket from her pack, she pulled it on and headed out the door. She didn't bother locking it. The only two people likely to come here right now were the only two people not likely to be stopped by locks.

She just had to hope the threshold would stop Dunleavy, if not Kinnard.

The night air was colder than it had seemed half an hour ago. She shivered and shoved her hands into her pockets as she made her way down the steps and up the dusty road to the house on the corner.

The light still burned brightly, shining out the windows like a beacon. She glanced at the door, then moved to a side window and peered inside.

The room was small and neat, the cream-colored walls bare of decoration. There were a couple of wooden chairs sitting around an old table, and to one side of that, a leather sofa. She shifted a little and saw the small TV. *Buffy the Vampire Slayer,* she thought, and smiled at the odd appropriateness of it. Obviously, even though Hartwood was a living museum, the rangers who looked after the town on a daily basis were not expected to forsake modern-day appliances. Well, not before Dunleavy had come to town, anyway.

She pulled away, letting her gaze roam across the darkness. The sensation that the night had eyes rippled across her skin, yet she couldn't actually sense anyone out there. Not that she would if the barrier was preventing the psychic talents she'd long depended upon from working. Maybe it was just nerves.

And maybe it wasn't.

She pushed up the sleeves of her coat, ensuring she had easy access to the knives strapped to her wrists. Then she walked around to the front door and tested the handle. It wasn't locked.

"Hello?" she said as she pushed the door open.

No one answered—not that she expected anyone to

answer, even if there was anyone alive in the house. She listened to the silence for a moment, then stepped inside.

The smell hit her immediately. It was the smell of death. The smell of decay.

She closed her eyes, fighting the instinct to just turn around and leave. She'd seen death plenty of times before, and nothing she'd see here was likely to be as bad as what she'd seen in the whorehouse earlier tonight. *That* death, she suspected, had been designed to shock and torture Michael as much as it had been a warning for her. But here it would be a calculated death, a death designed either as a booster for Dunleavy's own strength or that of his dark gods.

She walked over to the TV. The back of the unit was hot, indicating it had been running for some time. She switched it off and walked across to the sofa. The newspaper sitting on the sofa was Wednesday's news, and the coffee cup sitting on the floor was half-filled with congealed milk.

Her gaze drifted to the doorway to her right. Death waited for her down that small hall, and there was no use putting off the discovery. Not if she wanted to get some sleep tonight.

She'd barely taken three steps into the hall when the sense of wrongness hit her. She froze, listening to the silence, to the creaks of the old house, to the sound of her own breathing.

And knew she was no longer alone.

Something, or someone, was here with her.

And suddenly she remembered what else Seline had said about that first night in Hartwood. Two men had attacked her, one human, one not.

Two men waited for *her* in the darkness ahead.

One was human. One wasn't.

Michael had rescued Seline that first time, but Michael couldn't rescue her here, because he couldn't cross the threshold uninvited.

She took a step back, and all hell broke loose.

Nine

MICHAEL SQUATTED TO study the footprints in the sandy soil. These prints were far heavier than those leading up to this point, which indicated someone had stopped here for some time. He swept his gaze over the surrounding darkness. This was roughly where he'd seen Kinnard, so the question was, what had Kinnard been watching?

Or, perhaps, waiting for?

He couldn't have been spying on them—the pump house was in the way, and he wouldn't have seen them until they'd come around it.

So why stop here? There was nothing else here but the old reservoir and lots of weeds. He rose, scanning the ground for more prints. Kinnard had disappeared very shortly after Michael had spotted him, but he couldn't have done so without leaving some trace. Even vampires, who could move with the speed of the wind, left footprints.

But there was nothing. It was as if Kinnard had disappeared into thin air.

Maybe he *was* a shapeshifter. The glow of his body's energy hadn't suggested any type of shape change Michael had ever come across, but he knew better than to think that, even in all his years of existence, he'd come across every type of shifter there was.

Frowning, he followed the fall of the ground away from the pond. The weeds were still relatively thick here, providing ample protection for a rat like Kinnard. He pulled free a long, thick handful, holding them by the roots as he walked on.

The ground around him rose until he was walking into a small valley. Hartwood had disappeared from sight, and the darkness here was deeper, though the sounds of drunken singing carried easily on the still night air. It was amazing anyone in that town was still in a fit enough state to look at a whore, let alone carouse with them.

He switched his sight to infrared, scanning the ground as he walked. After a few minutes, he saw a scuff in the soil that looked like half the heel of a boot. A few more steps and he saw two deep prints. Kinnard had not only stopped here, but if the odd impressions just in front of the boot prints were any indication, he'd knelt down.

He stopped, sweeping his gaze across the ground directly in front of him. Something was here; he was certain of it.

A crack in the dirt caught his attention. It was too straight, too perfect, to be caused by weather or the natural drying of soil.

He squatted beside the crack and ran his fingers across the dirt. Soil shifted beneath his fingertips, revealing a hardness underneath. Wood. He ran his fingers along the crack until he found a junction of two corners, then he retraced the crack until he found a similar junction on the other side. A trapdoor, here in the desert. It had probably once been the entrance into a mine, but now it was obviously a rat hole.

He glanced skyward. The night was far from over, and he wasn't foolish enough to confront Dunleavy on his own ground. He'd wait until dawn, when the sunlight drove Dunleavy into sleep. When it came to the likes of such a fiend, it didn't pay to play fair. He'd already tried that, and Christine had paid the price for his stupidity.

He followed his own steps back, using the long weeds to brush over his prints as he retreated. Hopefully, it would disguise the fact that he'd been here. Once back at the pond, he tossed the weeds into the murky water and watched them sink.

What now?

His gaze drifted to the warm lights to his left. And even as he fought the desire to go to the witch, pain hit, flaring down his thigh as sharply as the kiss of a knife. And he knew, without knowing how, that it was *her* pain he was feeling.

With a curse, he spun and raced toward her.

Nikki backpedaled as the two men came at her. She had to get out of here, out of this house, get free of the threshold restriction so that Michael . . .

Damn it, what the hell was she thinking? She *wasn't* helpless; she had never been helpless, even without her gifts. And since joining the Circle, she'd been trained to defend herself, trained to fight. She didn't need Michael to protect her. She'd always been able to look after herself, one way or another, even before the training or his arrival in her life.

So why the hell was she suddenly running?

Or was it more a case of magic than instinct? Was there something in the barrier holding them captive that brought to life her worst fears, the very fears she'd thought long conquered?

It was a possibility she'd have to be wary of, but there was one thing she *was* certain of—Dunleavy couldn't kill her. Not until he either killed Michael or hacked off her head, at any rate. Therefore, she could fight with everything she had.

She flicked her knives down into her palms, holding them in front of her as she retreated into the middle of the room. The shifter paused, his brown eyes widening slightly, as if he recognized the fact that both blades were silver. The human merely laughed and launched at her.

She slashed at him with a knife, felt the slight resistance as the sharp point tore into flesh, then dove out of his way, hitting the floor with a grunt and rolling back to her feet.

Air stirred, and too late she saw the shifter's fist. The force of the blow against her chin sent her sprawling over the back of the sofa and onto the floor. One of her knives flew from her grasp, clattering across the floor, and her breath left in a whoosh of air as stars danced drunkenly before her eyes.

The air stirred again, warning her. She rolled to one side, barely avoiding the booted foot that crashed mere inches from her head. She twisted, lashing out with her legs, striking the thin man's feet and sweeping them out from underneath him. She scrambled upright as he crashed to the floor.

The shifter launched himself at her. She dodged

and pivoted, smashing her heel into his side, driving him back against the wall. He hit the floor with a grunt, but he shook his head and quickly picked himself up.

She didn't give him time to recover, but simply threw the knife at him. At the last moment, he saw it and dodged. The knife hit the wall with a thud, burying itself hilt deep into the old wood.

The shifter leered at her. "That makes the fight a whole lot easier."

"You think so?"

She ducked the blow of the human and punched him hard in the gut. Too late, she saw the knife in his hand. She swung away, but not fast enough. The knife slashed through her skirt and bit deep into her thigh.

Both men chuckled.

"Nice start," the thin man said, "but I've got a hankering to see a little more flesh than that, girlie."

"You've seen as much as you're going to," she muttered, grabbing the hand that held the knife even as she kicked him in the nuts.

He dropped with a hiss of pain. She pulled the knife from his slack grip and spun, slashing with the blade as the shifter came at her. The knife scored his chest, cutting both shirt and flesh as easily as butter.

He roared in anger, lashing at her with a clenched fist. She ducked the blow and heard the crash of glass behind her, the scream of air. Not knowing what was happening, but certain retreat was better than valor at this particular moment, she dropped to the floor and rolled away.

The shifter hit the ground and didn't move. She

climbed to her feet and saw why. Three feet of wooden railing was sticking out of his chest, the rest of it buried deep inside. He'd been dead before he hit the ground.

There was a gargled cry, and she swung to see the second man scramble to his feet. He dove at her, his eyes wide with shock and grief, his mouth open in a scream that never passed his thin lips. She sidestepped him and stabbed with the knife, feeling the brief resistance of flesh before the knife slid deep. The thin man dropped and didn't move.

She took a deep, shuddering breath and looked at the window. Michael stood there, his dark eyes filled with a fury she could feel through the link.

"What the hell are you doing here?" he said, his voice flat and all the more deadly because of it.

"Investigating what happened to the ranger who owned this house." She bent and retrieved her knife, wiping the blood from the blade on the dead man's shirt while trying not to think about the fact that she'd killed him.

"And you didn't think to mention this need earlier?"

She shrugged. "You ran before I could."

"So you were intending to mention it after you'd seduced me? Somehow, I seriously doubt *that*."

The anger she could feel from him edged his voice this time, and she couldn't help smiling. The spell might have taken his memories of her away, but deep down, some part of him remembered how she usually acted.

"I wasn't thinking of anything much beyond seduction," she said honestly. "But given that I wasn't successful, I turned my mind to other things."

"You could have turned it to sleep."

"But there might be some clue here to find. I didn't want Dunleavy erasing it before I got the chance to investigate."

"Given those two men were in the house, waiting to attack you, it's a fair bet that any clues that were here are long gone."

"Not necessarily." She retrieved her second knife and shoved it back into her wrist sheath. "Is there anyone else in this house?"

He frowned, his gaze narrowing slightly as it went beyond her. "No. Only a dead man."

"Then that's where I'm headed."

"You are the most frustrating, annoying woman I have ever had the displeasure of knowing."

She raised her eyebrows, trying to hide her grin and not being very successful. "It's a trait that'll grow on you, believe me."

"I doubt it," he muttered, stepping back from the window. "I'll keep watch out here."

Her grin broke free. "Like you have any other choice."

"If the death was a few months old, I would. Unfortunately, it takes time for the restriction to dissipate." He scowled at her. "Just hurry up. That leg of yours needs attention."

"No more than your shoulder does," she bit back. Then she spun, heading down the hall. The truth was, she could feel the blood running down her leg. While she couldn't exactly bleed to death anymore, blood loss could still weaken her, and she certainly couldn't afford that.

The dead man waited in the room at the end of the hall. She stopped in the doorway and turned on the light. He was lying on his bed, as naked as the day he was born. Unlike the man who'd been sacrificed on the roof, though, this man had obviously fought to survive. The signs of a struggle showed in the tangle of the bed covers, the bruising on his body and the shredded remains of pajamas on the floor. They told a story of violation as much as death, and bile rose in her throat.

She swallowed heavily and forced herself to step closer. There were bite marks on his neck and deep bruises around his mouth, indicating a hand had been clamped over it for a long time. Her gaze skated down his body and rested on his feet. She thought of the odd burn marks on the soles of the other man and shifted slightly to see better. This man, too, bore the mark of lips. And if they *were* lips, then whoever did this did not cause the bite marks on the neck. The mouth sizes were totally different.

Either they were dealing with someone who had enough strength to hold down a man fighting for his life, or two men were involved.

And suddenly she remembered Kinnard's reaction as he'd sucked in the anger of the miners, the way his body seemed to flesh out and glow with renewed health.

Kinnard fed on emotions. He'd fed on the man on the roof, and she was suddenly certain he'd fed here, holding the ranger down as his master brutalized the man and sucked away his life.

They were *both* monsters.

The question was, had this ranger been killed purely for pleasure, or was it done to help boost the strength of the barrier around them? Why kill one man within a pentagram and not the other?

It was so damn frustrating that she didn't *know*!

She turned and studied the rest of the room. There was nothing here that jumped out at her and said "evidence," so she backtracked and went into the other rooms leading off the hall. One was a bathroom and held the ranger's shaving gear, a couple of towels and some shampoo. The other was a second bedroom. The bed was messy, indicating someone had slept there. Was that how Dunleavy got in? Had the ranger invited him to stay the night?

She'd never know for sure, but it was certainly possible. She walked around the bed, but she didn't find anything that seemed out of place, so she headed back into the main room. Stopping in the middle, she looked around again. Maybe Michael was right. Maybe Dunleavy—or Kinnard, given he was Dunleavy's patsy—*had* cleaned up. Yet . . . her instinct itched. There was something here, something Dunleavy had missed. She was sure of it.

Her gaze came to rest on the small mat in front of the door. She hadn't noticed it when she'd come in, having been more interested in what lay beyond the silence of the room.

It was full of mud, but it didn't look as if it had rained in this area for some time, so where had the mud come from?

She knelt beside the mat and picked up a clump. It was more clay than soil, and darker in color than what was around here. Possibly, it had come from one of the mines. But if that were the case, why wasn't it caked with the reddish soil that surrounded the town? Vampires couldn't fly, she knew that much for certain, and while it was more than possible that both Kinnard and Dunleavy were shapeshifters, if Dunleavy was anything like his brother, then he'd take on another human form rather than that of an animal.

So how did he get so much mud on his feet and yet not pick up any dirt from the street?

She shoved the clump into her pocket and opened the door. Michael was standing just beyond the threshold.

His gaze slid down her body to her leg. "You're dripping blood onto the floor."

She looked down and saw that he was right. "Damn."

"And are you intending to bleed to death in the doorway, or will you step over the threshold so I can take you home and tend to your wound?"

"I can look after my own wounds, thanks."

He simply gave her a look that said *Of course you can, but you won't,* and held out a hand. She placed her fingers in his and stepped over the threshold. He immediately swung her into his arms and raced her back to the house. She closed her eyes and enjoyed the ride. Enjoyed the momentary closeness.

Yet, this close, she was aware of the tension growing in his limbs. The quivering in his muscles that spoke of desire, but not sexual desire. If the spell that contained them brought to life the worst of her fears, wouldn't it also be working on Michael, causing his darker desires to surface?

"What do you have in the way of salves and bandages?" he asked as he placed her on the sofa.

She studied him, seeing the tautness in his shoulders, the strain around his eyes. "You are not tending my wounds until you let me look after yours."

"Woman, I am not bleeding to death—"

"Neither am I." She placed a hand against his lips, felt the slight elongation of his teeth. They weren't fully out, meaning he was retaining some control, but still, she dared not risk it. If he drank from her, he could kill her. He might have made her all but immortal, but he could also *unmake* her. If he drank her blood and his hunger got out of control, he could very easily do just that. "You hunger for my blood, Michael. You can't tend to my wound until you tend to the need surging through your veins."

He scowled at her. "I am not a monster who is driven to lust at the sight of blood."

"I know. But the spell placed on you is trying to force that very reaction. Trust me. Go feed, then come back and let me fix your shoulder."

He pushed away from her. "If I go, I will not be coming back."

He'd be back. Because of the spell and because of the bond they shared—a bond and a love that couldn't be erased as easily as memories.

"That's your choice. I'll be here if you change your mind."

He didn't say anything, but simply turned and walked out. The door slammed shut with enough force to rattle the windows. She winced and slowly pushed to her feet. After treating and bandaging the knife wound, she hobbled into the bedroom, dumped her bags on the bed and dug out the T-shirt and sweatpants she intended to sleep in.

Once changed, she swept back the covers, fluffed the pillow—and stopped. She didn't want to go to bed alone. She didn't care if it was precisely what Weylin wanted. *She* wanted to go to bed with Michael, to go to sleep with his arms wrapped around her, his breath whispering warmth past her ear and his body hugging her with his heat.

God, it seemed like *ages* since she'd been with him. She gave a huge yawn, then shook her head. She was not sleeping alone, damn it! She just couldn't. She'd spent far too many years alone, and she wasn't about to do it again when the man she loved was only a stone's throw away.

She grabbed a blanket off the bed and trundled back into the main room. As she switched on the TV, she wondered what Michael's reaction would be to it. After all, in his mind he was living in the past, and TV certainly hadn't been around one hundred years ago. But then, the past wasn't being perfectly created, so there was every chance he would simply accept what didn't fit. She turned the sound down to a murmur, then made herself comfortable on the sofa and tucked the blanket in around her.

Michael would be back, of that she was certain. All she had to do was wait.

And figure out a way past his admirable but annoying reluctance to get into bed with her.

* * *

Michael strode down the street, annoyed at himself as much as with the witch who seemed to know him so well. *Damn it!* He had better control than this. He'd fed earlier tonight and shouldn't have needed to feed again for a least another day or so.

But the need for blood thrummed through his veins, and not just any blood. He wanted *her* blood, wanted to taste the sweet life that flowed under her creamy flesh. His teeth elongated further at the thought, and he swore.

Maybe she was right. Maybe there was a spell on him. There could be no other explanation for the desire that raced through his veins. He'd spent too long denying the darkness to have it raise its head this easily, this quickly.

And if it *was* some sort of spell, maybe she would know how to stop it.

Darkness swirled around him and pain hit, a blinding jolt that had him stumbling and falling. He shook his head free of the pain and climbed back to his feet. He frowned and tried to catch the trail of his thoughts but couldn't. His gaze hit the stable. That was where he'd been heading.

He drank his fill from a brown mare, then retreated. He stopped in the street, his gaze sweeping the darkness. The drunken revelry had eased, and though he could see life and movement in a few of the rooms above the various hotels, most of the miners had apparently collapsed into an exhausted and drunken sleep. He couldn't see the strange blur of energy that was Kinnard. Couldn't see Dunleavy. But they *had* to be here, somewhere.

Or did they?

He frowned and glanced under his feet. Maybe the rat was back in his hole.

And maybe *his* reluctance to search that hole had nothing to do with the desire to wait for the day, and everything to do with the spell the witch insisted lay on him. He'd certainly never worried about cornering a fiend on his own ground before, and he certainly had nothing to lose by doing so now—or did he?

The nagging sense that he *did* wouldn't leave him alone. Yet the only one he truly cared about these days was his brother Patrick, and Patrick was still on a ship on his way here to America.

He strode down the street, but his gaze went to the blonde's house as he came out of Main Street. Light still shone from her window. She wasn't asleep yet. Part of him wanted to go there and discover what she was up to, but he resisted the temptation. He was here to kill Dunleavy. It was high time he began concentrating on that.

A short time later, he arrived at the trapdoor. The sandy soil was still free of footprints. He wedged his fingers under the wooden hatch, feeling along the edge until he found the catch and released it.

Soil puffed skyward as he dropped the hatch to the ground, revealing a set of stairs leading down into a deeper darkness. He could feel no sign of life within, but the smell coming out was of dank earth and sour, unwashed human. Kinnard, not Dunleavy. Switching to infrared, he slowly entered the rat's hole.

And it *was* a hole, not the tunnel he'd half expected. It was round, small and shored up with wood that had bent under the weight of the earth. There was a bed covered with several foul-looking blankets, a small table on which sat a candle and some matches, several cases of booze stacked next to this and little else. Except pictures. They were everywhere, filling almost every inch of the rough-hewn walls.

Unable to see just what the pictures were with his infrared, he switched back to normal vision, swept several photos off the wall and moved back toward the entrance. At least there, the stars provided a little light.

The pictures showed a woman with shoulder-length brown hair that shone with auburn highlights in the sunlight. A woman with pixie features and rich amber eyes. *Christine,* he thought, then frowned. No, it wasn't. It was someone else, someone he knew and loved, as he'd never loved Christine . . . Pain hit again, sending him staggering backward. He hit the wall hard, then shook his head, trying to clear it.

His gaze fell on the photos again and rage swept through him—a rage unlike anything he'd ever experienced before. He spun, sweeping more photos off the wall, bringing them to the light. Kinnard had obviously been watching her for some time. There were photos of her laughing. Photos of her eating with an older man. Photos of her in a large, bubble-filled tub with a dark-haired man whose face he couldn't see. Photos taken through her window as she changed clothes.

His rage grew, until every muscle shook with the need to find Kinnard and kill him. To rip his body limb from limb, as Dunleavy had ripped that woman's.

Instead, he turned, tearing the remaining photos from the wall and piling them all on the filthy bed inen. When the last of the photos had been taken down, he grabbed the matches and set the pile afire.

The rat would know he'd been there, but Michael didn't particularly care. He waited until the bed-clothes had caught, then he climbed up the stairs and slammed the hatch shut on the smoke.

And stood there, scanning the night, shaking with anger and wondering why.

There was still no sign of Kinnard or Dunleavy, but rats usually had more than one hole. And as much as he needed to find them, he suspected he needed answers more. There was only one person in this town who seemed to know what was going on. And, oddly enough, that woman had eyes the same color as the woman in the photo. He suspected it was more than coincidence. Suspected that there was a hell of a lot more happening here than what he'd originally thought.

His simple need to kill Dunleavy suddenly didn't seem so simple anymore.

He ran swiftly to her house and entered, only to stop just inside the door. She lay on the sofa, wrapped in a blanket, her pretty face serene in sleep.

He couldn't wake her. She needed sleep more than he needed answers.

He took a deep breath and released it slowly, trying to calm the turmoil and anger still surging inside. He closed the door and walked across to her, tucking his arms under her body and carefully lifting her.

She stirred, murmuring something he couldn't quite catch, and snuggled closer to his chest. God, it felt so right holding her like this.

Pushing the thought away, he found her bedroom

and placed her gently into bed. She didn't stir as he tucked the rest of the blankets around her. In the darkness, her blond hair looked almost brown, but her face was nothing like the woman in those pictures. So why did he have the certainty that somehow the two were related?

It was so damn frustrating, this not knowing. He turned and pulled down the blind, determined that Kinnard would not be spying on *this* woman. Then he stripped and lay down beside her, under the top blanket but not the rest. A possibly dangerous move, given her earlier attempts to seduce him, but the need to simply lie here and hold her close was one that would not be denied right now.

Nikki woke to the realization that she was no longer on the sofa. And no longer alone.

Michael lay with her, his arm wrapped around her waist and his body pressed against her back, warming her spine despite the layer of blankets between them.

She smiled. Sometimes love could *not* be ignored, no matter how strong the magic or the will.

She shifted slightly and realized then she was still in her T-shirt and sweatpants. *Damn!* Seducing him when she was naked would be a hell of a lot easier. And she had a feeling that if she took time to undress in the middle of the action, he might take off again. He was determined to be honorable, which was absolutely wonderful in one respect but not what she wanted right now.

She slipped free of his arm and carefully got out of

bed. He stirred and she froze, watching as he turned onto his other side. He flung out a hand, as if searching for her, but quickly settled back to slumber. She stripped, then carefully pulled back the first blanket and climbed in beside him.

Knowing she couldn't allow him time to think, only react, she pressed herself against the length of him. His heat flowed around her, through her, burning her skin, stirring the desire long held at bay. She'd always found it a little weird that he was so warm given he was a vampire, but as he'd often said, he was undead, not *dead* dead.

She slid her hand down his firm, flat stomach and touched him intimately. His response was immediate. Instinctive.

As his body leapt to life, he made a sound that was almost a growl and turned around, pulling her into his arms. Then he was kissing her as if his very life depended on it, and whatever slivers of control she'd had were totally and irreparably smashed by the force of it. By the passion behind it. God, she loved this man. And right now she needed him more than she needed to breathe.

His hands seemed to be everywhere, urgent yet gentle, leaving her shuddering with pleasure and yet aching for more. He kissed her, caressed her, until need, deep and primal, rushed through her, and all she could think about was getting him inside, feeling him fill her, complete her.

She pushed him onto his back and climbed on top, claiming him in the most basic way possible. He groaned, his hands sliding to her hips, pressing her down harder.

Then they began to move, and thought became impossible. All she could do was savor the sensations flowing through her. There was nothing slow, nothing gentle, about this lovemaking. It was all passion and heat and desperation, and she'd never felt anything so damn good in her life.

The fever burning between them became a furnace that made breathing difficult, and deep inside the pleasure built, until her whole body burned with the need for release. She clung to him, clung to that edge, staring deep into his beautiful dark eyes, willing him to remember this, remember her. For a moment, she thought she saw a response—a spark of joy, a spark of love.

Then pleasure spiraled beyond her control and her climax hit, the convulsions stealing her breath and tearing a strangled sound from her throat. He came a heartbeat later, his body slamming into hers, the force of it echoing through every fiber of her being.

Once the shudders had subsided, she leaned forward and gently kissed his lips. He wrapped his arms around her waist, holding her in place as he lengthened the kiss.

"You do not play fair, woman," he said eventually, eyes sparkling as amusement touched his lips.

"I never said I intended to."

"This does not mean I will work with you."

She grinned. "You won't have any other choice, because you won't be able to keep your hands off me."

He chuckled softly, then rolled them over so that he was lying on top. "Nothing like being comfortable with your own sexuality."

She kissed him again, soft and lingering. "It's more a case of being comfortable about *us*."

"There *is* no us—not beyond this, anyway."

She didn't bother disputing his claim. Until more of his memory returned, or until she was able to soap away some of the spell on his back, there wasn't much point. "Why do you smell of smoke?"

The amusement and tenderness died in his eyes, the dark depths becoming hard. Furious. "Because I made a bonfire of some pictures I discovered in Kinnard's rat hole."

She frowned. "What sort of pictures?"

"Photos of Christine." He ran a finger down her cheek, sending warm tingles of desire shooting through the rest of her. Desire hadn't finished with her yet— but then, that wasn't exactly unusual when they made love. "Her eyes in the photos were rather like yours."

The thought that Kinnard had been not only watching her, but taking photos of her, left her cold. But the fury so evident in Michael's dark eyes, and the fact that he'd burned every one of those photos, made her heart sing. Deep down, he knew her, spell or no spell.

And if he could now see her eyes were amber, did that mean the spell concealing her identity was fading, or that he was beginning to see beyond it?

"Christine's been dead for a long time, Michael. Kinnard couldn't have take photos of her."

Something flickered in his eyes—recognition of her point, perhaps. Then his expression shut down and he shrugged. "He must have been following her *before* she died."

Damn it, she *had* to get rid of the spell on him. "Kinnard will know you did it."

"I don't care."

She smiled. "So where was this rat hole?"

"Near the old reservoir." His voice was distracted as he slid a little farther down her body and began to trace the outline of her breasts with a soft fingertip.

"Near where he was hiding in the bushes?"

The look in his eyes set her pulse racing again. "You don't miss much."

Neither did he. Especially when it came to getting her aroused. His touch was moving in on her breasts in ever-tightening circles, sending goose bumps fleeing excitedly across her skin. "No."

It came out breathlessly, and he chuckled—a throaty sound as seductive and as arousing as his touch. "You may have started this, woman, but I intend to finish it—and a lot more leisurely this time."

She had no problem at all with that, and normally she would have been right there with him. But there was the situation and the spell to consider as well. "Stinking like a bonfire? That's not at all seductive, you know."

His breath was warm on her skin as he dropped a kiss on a nipple. "Didn't seem to bother you a few moments ago."

"That's because my sense of smell was still half asleep."

"So what will it take to get you concentrating on the business at hand?"

"A bath." She grinned. "We can share, if you like."

"I like." He shifted back up, kissed her fiercely, then rolled out of bed. "I shall go prepare it."

"And I'll get the soap and the salve for your shoulder."

"I knew there was an ulterior motive," he said, amusement evident in his voice as he walked out.

"Yep. I went to all the trouble of seducing you just so I can tend to your wound."

"I wouldn't be at all surprised."

Grinning at the dry edge to his voice, she climbed out of bed and grabbed the second of her packs. The salve for wounds was there, but the soap Camille had given her to help wash the symbols off Michael's skin was gone. She swore. When he'd gone through her things, Kinnard must have recognized what it was and stolen it.

"And if you intend to treat all my wounds with seduction first," Michael continued, the sound of running water almost smothering his voice, "then I might be tempted to get wounded a little more."

She grabbed the salve, some clothes, a towel and a washcloth, and headed for the bathroom. Steam was beginning to fill the room, and she reached for the small window, intending to open it.

"Don't." He caught her hand and pulled her close against him. His body was warm and hard against hers, and he was more than ready to play again. She couldn't help smiling. Vampires certainly had great stamina. And, thanks to the fact that she now shared his life force, so did she.

"Keep your windows and blinds closed at all times," he continued softly. "I don't want Kinnard spying on you."

She kissed him, then reached past him, opening the small cabinet above the hand basin. Sitting right beside the toothpaste and toothbrush was a cake of soap. She grabbed it and tossed it into the water. It was better than nothing. "If you don't turn it off soon, that water is going to overflow."

He turned off the water and stepped into the bath. "What about your wound?"

"It wasn't bad, and I heal fast." She unwound the bandage and shifted her leg so he could see there was little more than a pink scar on her thigh.

"Unusually fast," he commented and offered her a hand. "Coming in?"

She tossed the washcloth into the water, placed her fingers in his and stepped in carefully. The water was almost too hot. She eased down, sighing softly as the water lapped at her breasts and began to relax her muscles.

He pulled her back against him, then grabbed the soap and began washing her breasts and belly. When she could stand the torturous pleasure no more, she grabbed the soap and cloth from him and turned around.

"Your turn," she said, and made a swiveling motion with her fingers. "Back first."

The black markings on his back were thick and ugly, and more intricate than what she'd been told to expect. And the wound on his shoulder was red and angry-looking. She took care of that first, easing away the scab and washing away the infection. Though he didn't say anything, he flinched a number of times, indicating the wound was sorer than he'd admitted. Once both ends of the wound were clean, she began working on his back, carefully scrubbing at the drawings.

He didn't give her long enough, though. Maybe it was the spell protecting itself and forcing him to move out of her reach, or maybe it was just desire. Either way, he turned around and took the soap from her, putting it on the edge of the bath. Then he grabbed her legs and slid her forward until she was sitting between his thighs.

She wrapped her legs around his waist and her arms around his neck. "This is nice," she said with a grin.

"Not as nice as this," he murmured, placing his hands against her butt and pushing her forward just a little more.

The heat of him slipped deep inside, and from that moment on, there was no more talk. He loved her long, stroking deep as he caressed and nipped and kissed. The pressure began to build low in her stomach, fanning through the rest of her in waves as warm as the bathwater, until it became a molten force that flowed across her skin. It was a heat far warmer than the turbulent water, a heat that made her tremble, twitch and groan.

His breathing became harsh, his tempo more urgent. His fierceness pushed into her, into that place where only sensation existed, and then he pushed her beyond it.

He came with her, his lips capturing hers, kissing her urgently as his warmth spilled into her and his body went rigid against hers.

For a moment, neither of them moved. Then he sighed and kissed her neck. "Ah, Nikki," he murmured. "Eternity may come and go, but I will never be able to get enough of you."

She froze, holding on tight to the elation that wanted to race through her soul. "What did you just say?"

Even as she asked the question, energy stirred, tingling across her skin where they still touched. The spell enforcing itself once more. Obviously, Dunleavy had set the spell to react to certain words, and maybe even certain thoughts.

He pulled back, blinking slightly. "As much as I am enjoying myself, I am here to catch a killer. I really should be going."

Damn, damn, *damn!* "Not until I put some salve on that wound."

"I'm a vampire. It'll heal." He climbed out of the bath and grabbed a towel.

"That wound was caused by silver. The salve will help with the infection the silver caused."

"And how would you know the wound was caused by silver?"

She followed him out of the water and began drying herself. "I'm a witch. We know these things."

He cupped a hand to her cheek, his fingers warm against her skin. "You're a witch all right. I'm just not sure you're the kind that performs real magic."

She turned her face, pressing a kiss into his palm. "No?"

"No," he said softly. "Though I'm tempted to think there's something close to magic happening between us."

"That's not magic. That's something far stronger."

He raised an eyebrow. "And what might that be?"

"Love."

"Love?" A smile touched his lips. "Woman, I barely even know you."

"You've known me far longer than you think. And why can't you remember my name?"

He frowned, dropping his hand. "I told you, it doesn't sound right."

"It sounds a hell of a lot better than being called 'woman' all the time."

"This conversation is getting ridiculous. And I have a killer to hunt down before the sun gets too high." He began to dress.

She snatched up her shirt. "*We* have a killer to hunt, you mean."

"You cannot—"

"I will *not* be left behind." She thrust her hands on her hips and glared at him. And damn if it didn't feel like old times. "No matter what you do or say, I'm going, so quit arguing and just accept the fact."

Something flashed in his eyes. Anger perhaps. Or maybe even recognition. They'd certainly had *this* argument more than once in the past.

"I will not be responsible for your safety."

"I'm not asking you to be responsible for me."

He met her glare with one of his own, but after a few moments he shook his head and stepped back. "On your own head be it, then."

"Fine." She hesitated, then added, "The sun being up won't make a bit of difference to Dunleavy, you know."

"Why not? He's a vampire and younger than me."

"But he's also a sorcerer. He's using his magic to move about in daylight."

"Then why can't he be found—by day or by night?"

"I don't know. Maybe he's shifting into other forms."

"Even in other forms, I'd see him with infrared. Shapeshifting would not alter a vampire's basic heat pattern."

"Then maybe he's using magic to hide his form."

"Magic to create the barrier that supposedly confines us. Magic that apparently controls me as well as everyone else in this town. Magic to hide Dunleavy's own form, and magic to feed his dark gods." He raised an eyebrow. "Even for one as young and strong as Dunleavy, that's an awful lot of magic happening at one time. I doubt there'd be much left of him right now."

"Maybe that's why you can't find him. Maybe he can't move. Maybe Kinnard is not only the creepy sidekick, but Dunleavy's eyes and hands."

"Kinnard wouldn't be able to perform the sacrifice ceremony in Dunleavy's place, though."

"No. So maybe Dunleavy is conserving all his strength for the ceremonies, and Kinnard is doing everything else." Which might mean it was Kinnard, not Dunleavy, who had torn that woman apart. Goose bumps fled across her skin, and despite the air's warmth, she shivered. She had a feeling the true extent of Kinnard's evil had yet to be revealed.

Michael studied her for a moment, eyes slightly narrowed. "Which would mean Dunleavy would be somewhere unlikely to be found very easily."

She nodded and zipped up her skirt. "Like deep inside a mine." She hesitated, frowning. "You haven't searched any of the mines yet?"

He hesitated. "No."

She didn't bother asking why, because she had a suspicion the answer was simple: Dunleavy had no intention of being found by Michael, so he'd put some sort of diversion magic in the runes on Michael's back.

Which would explain why they were so intricate—
they had an awful lot of ground to cover.

"Then perhaps that's where we should start our
search."

His frown was deepening, and the tingle of energy
was beginning to caress the air. She wished she understood exactly how the runes worked, and whether
the magic was built to regenerate, or whether the energy needed for the runes to perform was siphoned
from Dunleavy, as needed. Seline had been unable to
help her on that one, simply because there were so
many variations. All she'd been able to suggest was
that Nikki keep pushing, because no magic was ever-
lasting. Even blood magic—the most powerful of all
and the one Dunleavy was probably using to sacrifice
to his dark gods—had its limits.

"We don't know for sure," Michael said.

She remembered the mud she'd found on the mat in
the ranger's house. "Wait a minute."

She ran into the bedroom, strapped on her wrist
knives and dug the dirt ball out of her jacket pocket.

"Here," she said, dropping the mud into his hand.
"What do you make of that?"

"It's clay from the mines," he said immediately and
met her gaze. "What of it?"

"It was all over the ranger's doormat last night."

"So?"

"So, if the ranger walked from the mines to the
house, how come there's no reddish soil in the mix?"

His gaze went back to the clay. "Because he didn't
walk from the mine to the house."

"Exactly. Either he was carried, or there's another
way to get from the mine to that house."

"The rat has a hole. Maybe he has a tunnel or two as well." His gaze met hers again. "It was very observant of you to notice this."

She grinned. "I'm an observant sort of girl. Shall we go investigate?"

He hesitated, and in the silence, the buzz of energy was as loud as the whine of a mosquito. He dropped the clay to the floor and brushed his hands. "Let's go look," he said, voice flat yet full of determination.

She shoved on her shoes and headed for the front door. "Since the mud was on the mat near the front door, the tunnel entrance has to be very close to the steps."

He opened the front door and ushered her through with a gentle press of his hand against her spine. "Well, he can't have flown in."

The day was almost overly bright, the sun hot despite the earliness of the hour. She squinted up at the sky. Despite the warmth, dark clouds gathered on the horizon. "Could he be using the mines to get around?"

But why would he bother if he could walk around in daylight unharmed?

"Probably. It would certainly explain why I've been unable to find him."

She glanced at him. "Meaning?"

"Meaning, I can't see through earth. No vampire can."

She raised her eyebrows. "Why not?"

"Why can't we cross thresholds uninvited?" He shrugged. "It's just one of those things that is."

As they approached the ranger's house, she returned her gaze to the sandy soil, briefly scanning for anything that seemed out of place. "How come, when all vampires know the rules, no vampire knows *why*?"

His smile made her heart do a little dance. "How come some women just can't seem to stay out of trouble?"

"It's not polite to answer a question with a question."

"It is when I don't have the answer to the question."

She grinned. "If you're not careful, I'll hit you with questions you *can* answer."

He touched her arm, gently stopping her. "Like what?" He squatted down and swept his hand across the dirt. Red dust puffed, revealing wood.

"Like asking about your brother."

"How do you know I have a brother?"

His voice was distracted as he ran his fingers along the edge of the wood. After a moment, there was a faint click. He opened the door, revealing the darkness of a tunnel. Red dust flew as he let the door drop to the ground.

She twitched her nose, fighting the urge to sneeze as she stared into the foul-smelling darkness. There was no sound, no hint of life coming from the mine. Not that she really expected there to be. "I know you have a brother the same way I know you turned him."

"I wasn't the one responsible for turning him. I merely nursed him through it."

Surprise rippled through her. "Really?"

"Really."

"Then where is he now?"

"On a boat, on his way here from England."

She wondered how long he'd lived in America before Jasper killed him. And *how* Jasper had killed him, when Jasper had to have been little more than a fledgling at the time. "Why is he coming here?"

He glanced at her. "Because he misses his baby brother."

"Really?"

A smile touched his lips. "Really."

"Are you supposed to be meeting him, then?"

"Yes, in San Francisco, once I take care of this mess." He frowned, and shadows crossed his eyes. He didn't say anything, yet she felt the surge of anger and sorrow. Deep down, he knew Patrick was long dead, and all these years later, he still quietly grieved for him.

"Was Patrick much older than you when he was turned?"

Michael scrubbed a hand across his jaw and, for a moment, looked as if he wouldn't answer. Then he glanced down at the hole and said softly, "No. He took the ceremony to become a vampire on his death earlier than I. But he wasn't in such a hurry to die, and he didn't turn until his heart gave out when he was in his forties."

"He had a heart attack?"

"No. Living was tough back then, and forty was fairly old."

"And you were by his side?"

He nodded. "By then, I had reasonable control of my bloodlust, and I had left Elizabeth. Patrick had caught sight of me a few years earlier, and he told me he knew what I was. He made me promise to be by his deathbed, because the man who had turned him was dead, and he didn't want to hurt or kill anyone while in the fledgling stage."

She raised her eyebrows. While a man being turned by a man didn't *actually* mean either man was gay, she had a suspicion that in *this* case it was the truth. Was that why Patrick had been headed for San Francisco? Was the city so liberal in its thinking way back then? She didn't know, but even if it wasn't, it surely wouldn't have bothered a vampire all that much.

"So who turned him?"

"I don't know. He never told me."

"But it was a man?"

He looked at her again, answering what she hadn't asked rather than what she had. "Patrick's bisexual. He's the reason the Kelly line still lives on in Ireland."

"Then you never had kids?"

"No." He raised an eyebrow. "A fact I suspect you already knew."

She grinned. "Just confirming these things while you're under the influence."

"Of what?"

"A spell that has apparently frayed your natural reticence when in comes to speaking about your past."

"Woman, you speak in riddles."

"Yeah, makes a nice change, doesn't it?"

He shook his head. "Enough of this ridiculousness. Wait here while I check to see what waits below."

She didn't argue, just watched him disappear down the hole. "It's not a very wide tunnel," he said, after a few minutes.

"Rats don't need wide tunnels," she commented, squatting down. The sunlight filtering into the tunnel barely lifted the gloom, and Michael was little more than a shadow. "Is it safe enough?"

"It appears so."

"Then move aside, because I'm coming in."

She hung her legs over the edge and eased herself down. Hands grabbed her hips, catching her weight and lowering her the rest of the way. It was farther down than she'd first thought. He didn't release her immediately, his gaze burning into hers. "You will do what I tell you to down here, won't you?"

"Always."

He gave her the sort of look that said he didn't believe her. Grinning, she rose up on her toes, gave him a quick kiss and said, "After you."

For a moment, he did nothing more than simply look at her. Even though the sunlight filtering in from above barely lit the shadows, she could see the questions in his eyes. See the doubts. It didn't really matter whether those doubts were of the situation or of her. The mere fact that he doubted was a start.

And while there was no response in the link between them, he'd said her name while making love. Somewhere deep inside him, the spell was beginning to fade. All she had to do was keep pushing. Keep doing and saying things that were echoes of times past. Keep trying to wash the runes from his back.

"That end of this tunnel probably runs down to the town," he said, pointing to his left. His soft tone echoed around them, mingling with the insistent buzz of energy. "If Dunleavy can't move far, he might need to be near his food source."

"I was told the ceremony he'll perform to bring his brother back to life will be done in the Standard Mine. If that's true, and he can't move far, then he won't be far from there."

"I doubt—"

She raised an eyebrow. "Do you actually have doubts, or is it the spell on your back making you think that way?"

"I do feel a pressure to go down rather than up the tunnel." He hesitated. "So, up it is."

He caught her hand, his fingers warm and strong against hers as he tugged her forward. The darkness surrounding them quickly faded as her eyes adjusted. It was as if she were looking at a negative—the air was black, everything else various shades of gray. And while this allowed her to see in darkness almost as well as Michael, she wasn't about to let go of his hand. The last time she'd been in a tunnel like this, the damn thing had collapsed on her and she'd almost died. And while sharing his life force now meant she couldn't really die unless he did, or unless she was beheaded, she wasn't about to go through a repeat of the pain.

She pushed the memories away and peered past Michael. The walls of the tunnel were rough-hewn, the roof supported by aging beams of wood that were darkened by moisture and time. From a distance up ahead came a soft but steady dripping, and while the ground beneath them was dry, the air was stale and damp.

There didn't seem to be any sort of incline, suggesting the tunnel was burrowing deeper into the hill. The creaks and groans of the supports seemed to be growing louder, as if they were having trouble bearing the weight of the earth above them.

She shivered and somehow resisted the urge to glance upward and inspect the roof.

Michael stopped abruptly. "I smell blood."

The air smelled no different to her, but she wasn't as attuned to blood as he was. Nor did she ever want to be. "Old or new?"

He hesitated. "Both."

"A sacrifice site?"

"Possibly. It seems to be coming from the right, which means there's probably a junction in the tunnel up ahead."

"So let's check it out."

Something sparked through the link between them—a brief surge of resignation and amusement combined. She reached out, trying to touch that spark, trying to bring his awareness of her out into the open. For a moment, their thoughts combined, wrapping her in joy and love, then energy surged between them and the spark died.

But not for long, she suspected, barely able to resist the urge to dance. *Her* Michael was closer to the surface than ever before.

"You should stay here," he said, looking over his shoulder. "But I'm guessing you won't."

"And you'd be guessing right." She squeezed his fingers lightly. "Can you sense anything else?"

"At this stage, no."

He tugged her forward again. They'd barely walked a dozen steps when they reached a T-intersection. There was nothing to be seen in either direction but more rough-hewn tunnel.

"Still nothing?" she asked.

"There's a heartbeat. It's faint, but very fast." He frowned at her. "Its beat is more one of pleasure than pain."

She raised her eyebrows. "There's a difference?"

His smile was slow and sexy and made her heart do a dance.

"Oh, yes."

"How?"

"Now is not the time for an explanation," he said, voice dry. "Perhaps we should see what's going on ahead, first."

"Then let's do it."

They moved quickly down the right-hand tunnel. The air became thick and chilled and slapped wetly across her skin. Water splashed into the silence, growing ever louder the closer they got to the source. The rough-hewn walls gave way to natural rock, and the beams supporting the roof became few and far between.

The tunnel opened into a cavern. Her footsteps seemed to echo, lending the cavern a feeling of vastness. Michael stopped, and his anger boiled through the link.

"What?" she said, her eyes following his upward gaze.

And seeing what he saw.

It wasn't water dripping.

It was blood.

Ten

NIKKI COULD ONLY stare, wondering if she'd stepped into some macabre version of *The Twilight Zone.*

A woman hung from the ceiling. She was naked. Her torso was unmarked and her skin had a bluish tint and was covered with goose bumps. She was hanging upside down, her feet somehow roped to the ceiling. Her arms were free, hanging limply past her ears. Her wrists bore several small cuts, but the blood dripped rather than pulsed down the woman's fingers. Some of the cuts had scabbed over, some hadn't, indicating, perhaps, that the wounds were being monitored and opened when necessary. The woman's eyes were wide open but unfocused, almost dreamy-looking, and barely audible moans pushed past her bloodless lips.

They weren't moans of pain, but rather of pleasure.

Nikki swallowed, forcing her gaze away from the obvious bliss on the woman's pale face, and studied the *thing* covering half of her body. It was almost sluglike in form, and it stretched from breast to groin, where its body joined with the woman's. It was squirming in what looked like ecstasy, its actions matching the woman's groans.

"What is *that*?" Though Nikki kept her voice soft, the words seemed to echo harshly around the cavern, again hinting the space was larger than it looked.

The slug creature obviously wasn't bothered by the fact that it was no longer alone. If its movements were anything to go by, the prospect of being watched seemed to excite it.

She swallowed back bile and pulled her gaze away from the sight.

"I have no idea what that is," Michael said, his voice flat and cold.

But there was something in the way he said it that made her look at him sharply. He shook his head almost imperceptibly and walked farther into the cavern. She followed, trying to quell her desire to ask him what he knew. Trying to ignore the strange sounds of lust coming from above them.

The woman's blood dripped into the middle of a star etched into the cavern's hard rock floor. While this blood glistened wetly, there were deeper, older patches that suggested similar sacrifices had been performed here.

Around the star was a protective circle of stones. These were a burnished black, just like the ones that ringed the town, but they were much smaller.

Nikki put out a hand. Energy crackled through the air—a buzz that got steadily angrier as her fingers drew closer to the unseen wall that protected the star. Flickers of blue cut through the air, lightning-like wisps that lashed out at her hand. It felt foul, some-how. Depraved.

She clenched her fingers and dropped her hand back to her side.

Michael looked up at the woman again. "I think we've found one source of Dunleavy's energy. But whether this sacrifice feeds his demented soul, his dark gods or the circle you say rings this town is any-one's guess."

She nodded, keeping her gaze on the stones rather than the happenings above them. "We can't leave her here."

"She won't live, even if we do manage to get her down."

"I don't care." Facing death was one thing. Doing so while forced to endure the ministrations of some-thing not even *remotely* human was another.

She walked past him, closer to the ring. The stones reacted, seeming to glow deep within their black hearts. Sparks crawled across her skin—an unpleasant sen-sation that made the tiny hairs over her body stand on end. Rubbing her arms, she swept her gaze around the circle, trying to remember everything Camille and Seline had told her.

There was always a key. Always one stone that could unlock or destroy the spell. All she had to do was find that stone. But it was not easy to do when they all looked the same.

Her gaze came to rest on the stone on the north edge of the circle. It was a little smaller, a little less obvious, than the rest.

She walked around to it. There could be no finesse about this. She didn't know enough about magic to negate the power of the stones, and brute force certainly couldn't dismantle a circle of this size any more than it could a circle the size of the one that ringed the town. But she'd bet *this* circle was set up to protect the star and its sacrifice against someone who knew something about the ways of magic, not someone armed with little more than a silver knife.

Yet silver was the one thing immune to magic. The only thing that could cut through a magic barrier such as this with the ease of a knife through butter.

She flicked the knife into her palm and knelt, studying the stone. Wisps of blue arced through the air, their foul energy scorching her forehead.

"Do you know what you're doing?" Michael asked from the other side of the circle.

She met his gaze. "You'd better hope so."

The thing above them let loose a strange sort of squeal. Nikki's gaze jerked upward. The slug had disengaged itself and was slithering around the woman's legs, heading for the ceiling. Nikki hefted her knife with half a mind to throw it, but at that moment the thing reached the roof and disappeared into a fissure.

"I'd take that as a sign," Michael commented blandly.

"Maybe it's had enough sex, and the retreat is its version of rolling over and going to sleep."

A smile tugged the corners of his mouth. "I still prefer that you don't do this."

"You know of any other way to get that woman down?"

He lifted a hand toward the circle. Energy buzzed, the sound a high-pitched scream of fury. Nikki raised her eyebrows. That reaction was far stronger than the one that had greeted her. Dunleavy *hadn't* expected Michael to get this far.

"No," he said. "I'm afraid I don't."

"Well, I'm not leaving her there," she said flatly.

"And I don't care what trap Dunleavy has set. I'm going to spring it."

"Wait—"

She didn't. She slashed the knife toward the stone, backing the blow with as much force as she could muster. The air screamed, and energy lit the darkness, blue flashes of light that crawled across the blade and up her hand, burning deep. She bit her lip, ignoring the sensation and keeping her eyes on the rock. An invisible force pushed at the blade, momentarily resisting her blow. Then the knife hit the stone, and the force of it reverberated up her arm, jarring her spine.

For a moment, nothing happened. Then there was a blinding flash, the boom of an explosion, and a wall of heated air threw her backward. She hit the ground with a grunt and flung her hands over her head, trying to protect her face. Shards of stone blew through the air, tearing at her clothes, her skin. Then Michael flung his body over hers, protecting her from the worst of the damage.

After a while, silence returned. Except the silence wasn't really silent, but filled with a dripping sound far stronger than before. Surely the woman couldn't have had *that* much blood left, Nikki thought, wanting to look, but at the same time not wanting to see. If the force of that explosion had blown *her* off her feet and back a good ten feet, what had it done to the poor woman hanging above?

"You don't want to know," Michael commented, his lips caressing her ear as he spoke. "Are you okay?"

She nodded, wondering if he even realized he'd read her thoughts. "What's that dripping?"

"Water." He lifted himself off her and touched her arm, gently assisting her into a sitting position.

Despite his warning, she couldn't help looking. What was left of the woman didn't really resemble anything human. Just a bloody, shapeless mass.

She briefly closed her eyes. *Damn it,* she'd been trying to *save* the woman, not kill her. Why couldn't something go right for a change? She swallowed the bitterness of bile and guilt and took a deep breath. "I guess I should be thankful her death would at least have been quick."

"Yes." His confirmation didn't ease her conscience any. His thumb brushed at the moisture on her cheek, a gesture as gentle and caring as the look in his eyes. "You gained a few cuts in the explosion."

"So did you." She carefully wiped away the smear of blood from his chin. "Are you hurt anywhere else?"

"My back." He shrugged. "Nothing major."

She gave him a deadpan look. "I saw your version of 'nothing major' with your shoulder. Turn around."

"I do not think this is the time or—"

"If you'd just stop arguing about everything and do as I ask, it would have been over hours ago."

"As usual, you exaggerate." Amusement gleamed in his dark eyes as he turned around.

His shirt was crisscrossed with tears, revealing bloody skin underneath. None of the cuts were deep, as he'd said, but some of them did bisect the runes on his back. Was that why he'd been able to read her thoughts? Was one of the damaged sections responsible for shutting down the link between them?

"You're right. There's nothing here that won't wait until later."

"Maybe next time you'll believe me."

"Not when you have a history of understating wounds."

She looked past him. The black rocks were no longer in an orderly circle. Of the eight that had been present, she could see only six. With any luck, the explosion had blown up the other two. And perhaps that meant that Dunleavy wouldn't be reusing this sacrifice site anytime soon.

She glanced at the roof, this time following the dripping water until she found the source. A fissure had opened up near the southern end of the circle, and the water was pouring steadily from that, washing across the star etched into the rock, bathing away the barely congealed blood—though she doubted it would ever erase the deeper, darker stains.

Little rivulets of moisture were beginning to work their way toward her. She pushed to her feet, glad of Michael's support as the cavern spun briefly around her.

"I don't think Dunleavy will be able to use this place again," she commented. "The water will make it too difficult."

Michael nodded. "But I dare say he has other places ready to go."

"Yeah." She dusted off her palms on her skirt. "And if they're anything like this, we'd better try to find them."

He raised an eyebrow. "And what of the two sacrifices you were told to halt?"

"I'm beginning to think they were merely a means to keep me occupied and off the trail."

"Believe me, Dunleavy *will* kill those people if he said he will."

"I know. But I think we're better off trying to find the source of his power—and destroying it—than running around trying to figure out who is next on his hit list." After all, they were probably all on his hit list. She was certainly under no illusion that he'd let her and Michael go.

"We could spend days searching through these tunnels," he said. "It's literally a maze down here."

And they didn't have days, only hours. Forty-seven of them, to be precise. They had to narrow the search area down. "Where is this cavern in relation to the town?"

He hesitated. "Somewhere near the eastern edge."

Meaning that they'd ended up heading away from the Standard Mine rather than toward it. "So, if the Standard Mine is west, and we know for certain there's a sacrifice circle there—"

"We haven't actually seen it, so you can't say that for sure."

"Yes, we can." Her gaze met his. "He's using compass points."

"If the magical barrier is as large as you say, he'd probably have to. I doubt whether he'd be able to feed it all from one central point."

She raised an eyebrow. "So you think there's a central point as well?"

"We've already found it. The roof of the whorehouse."

She closed her eyes and fought the rush of memories, although the man on the roof had died a cleaner death than the woman here. "Would they use it again? They surely must know we've discovered it." And hadn't that been the whole point in the first place?

"I think they'll have no choice. Dunleavy probably figures we have enough keeping us occupied to prevent us from keeping a close watch on that roof."

And in reality, he'd be right. "If this place is the maze you say it is, then it might be better if you search alone. Once you find something, you can come back for me."

"I don't fancy leaving you alone after what I discovered in Kinnard's hole."

She looked at him questioningly and mentally asked, *Why?*

Energy stirred the air, and his gaze narrowed in sudden concentration. *Fighting the spell,* Nikki thought. *Fighting the commands being placed on him.*

Because it seems Kinnard has taken quite a fancy to you. He answered her question through the link without even seeming to realize he'd done so. Nor did he seem to realize he'd basically recognized that *she* was the woman in the photos and not Christine.

And though she felt like dancing at the breakthrough, she controlled the urge. There was still a long way to go before he was totally free of the effect of the runes. And until he was, she had to play it carefully. While those photos certainly suggested Dunleavy knew who she really was under this disguise, there was still a small—albeit *minute*—chance that he didn't.

"I can protect myself. Dunleavy may think he holds all the aces, but I hold one or two little surprises up my sleeve."

"Yeah, both of them silver." His tone held a teasing edge. "But those little stickers aren't going to be of much use if Dunleavy decides to send his goons after you."

"He won't, because he needs me alive for the ceremony."

Michael raised an eyebrow. "Are you so sure of that, you're willing to bet your life on it?"

"Yes." If only because Seline had killed Weylin's twin. They'd captured him in the midst of the ceremony, tortured him, then consigned his soul to hell. Which meant that if Seline was right, then she—or at least someone representing her—*had* to be at Weylin's ceremony so that he could reverse the spell and bring his brother's spirit back to life. And she was not only Seline's doppelganger, but someone Michael loved. Double bang for his ceremonial buck, so to speak.

All they had to hope was that Seline was correct in her assumption that the past events were actually important.

"I'll escort you back to the entrance."

"No. I can go by myself. We need to find the other sacrifice sites before Dunleavy has a chance to protect them any further."

His concern whisked through the link, warming her soul. "I don't think—"

She placed a finger to his lips, stopping him. "Trust me. I *can* look after myself."

It was a phrase she'd repeated often enough, and something sparked in his eyes. Amusement or recall, it didn't much matter which, because he was getting closer and closer to breaking the chains around his memories.

"Okay."

He brushed a hand down her cheek, slid it around her neck and pulled her toward him. His kiss was both demanding and passionate. And despite the danger of doing it here, she couldn't help responding just as intensely.

And with their bodies crushed so close, she was fiercely aware of every part of him. From the rush of longing burning through the link, to the way her breasts crushed against his chest, right down to the restrained hardness pressing luscious heat against her abdomen. His body remembered her even if his mind was still chained.

He pulled away with a suddenness that made her gasp. Then she saw the fiery glint in his eyes. It was passion and something else. Something far deadlier.

"There was blood on your mouth, just a smear," he explained, his voice soft yet strained.

Yet his teeth weren't extending, even though his demon had risen to the surface. He was gaining control again, despite the spell on his back. She nodded. "I'll meet you back at the house later."

He stepped away, then stopped again, reaching out to brush a thumb across her mouth. "Be careful."

"I will."

He wrapped the shadows around his body, disappearing from normal sight, but not her enhanced sight. He was a whitish blur that ran quickly toward the tunnel and disappeared.

She bent to retrieve her knife. The blade was nicked, the end broken. Even so, it was a useful enough weapon against a vampire or shapeshifter. She shoved it back into its sheath, walked around the star and headed for the other tunnel.

And tried to ignore the weight of the earth pressing down on her as she made her way back to the entrance.

When the beams of sunlight began filtering through the darkness ahead, she gave a huge sigh of relief. She wiped the sweat from her eyes and tried to convince herself that her reaction was due to the oppressive atmosphere in the tunnels rather than fear itself.

She'd been in tunnels in San Francisco and she hadn't felt like this. Nor had she when she and Michael had traveled to Jackson Hole and confronted the dead and his past. But those tunnels hadn't really reminded her of the tunnel that had trapped her. This one did.

With a leap, she grabbed either side of the opening and hauled herself up, wriggling and cursing and wishing her butt were a little less heavy.

When she finally reached the surface, she collapsed in an ungainly, sweating heap, trying to catch her breath and wondering why her muscles were aching so much when she was supposedly so fit.

"That has to be the most inelegant exit I've ever seen," a voice said drily.

She bit back the urge to curse and looked around. Kinnard was sitting on the steps of the dead ranger's house, idly twirling a long reed of grass in his hand.

"What are you up to, Kinnard?" she snapped, hauling herself into a sitting position before dusting off her hands.

Kinnard's gaze slithered up her exposed legs. She snapped her skirt down and he grinned.

"Just waiting for you to come up for air, girlie."

"Were you down in that darkness, spying again?"

"Maybe I was. Maybe I wasn't." He flicked the blade of grass away and stood. "That vampire of yours won't be able to fight the creatures waiting at other sacrifice sites alone, you know."

She raised an eyebrow. "And just how do you know we found the sacrifice site?"

"Half the town heard the explosion. I'm surprised you and the vamp weren't more seriously hurt."

"We run fast."

"You must. Just be warned—the next time, it could be deadly."

She rose to her feet. "Or so you would like me to believe."

"Oh, I didn't mean deadly to *you,* girlie."

"Then what *did* you mean?"

His gaze slid to the town. She grabbed his arm, wrapping her fingers around his cold, almost slimy, flesh and called to the fire deep within. Flames responded, leaping from fingertip to fingertip, touching, but not really burning, his skin. Kinnard's eyes widened in surprise and, perhaps, a touch of fear.

"You hurt any more of those people down in that town," she said, keeping her voice flat, "and I'll hunt you down and burn you to cinders."

He jerked his arm free and stepped back. His flesh was white where she'd touched him, her fingerprints seemingly burned into his arms.

"You try that, and your vampire lover dies."

"I don't think your master is going to be too impressed if you kill one of the two vital elements he needs to bring his brother back to life."

Kinnard snarled at her, and it was her turn to grin. "Yeah, I figured it out. I may be blond, but I ain't dumb."

"Aren't you?" He snorted softly. "Then why are you here rather than finding the man who will die in an hour's time?"

She stared at him, her heart racing. No one else was supposed to be killed. Dunleavy had set that task only to keep her occupied—hadn't he?

Yet Seline had warned her that five would die. Surely, though, those would all be the sacrifices. Unless, of course, Emmett Dunleavy had killed more people than Seline was aware of. But if that were the case, how did Weylin know? He'd been nowhere near Hartwood when his brother had died.

Or had he?

Realizing that Kinnard was waiting for a reply, she said, "Dunleavy's changing the rules already? We must be closer than I thought."

Kinnard hawked and spat. She shifted her foot and the glob landed in the dust near her toes.

"It's Dunleavy's game you're playing," he said. "He can do what he wants."

"Not for much longer."

The old man merely grinned. "You wanna bet, girlie?"

"Not with a lecher like you."

"And not when you know the odds are on our side."

She stepped back. She wasn't about to get into a war of words with this man—not when she had a feeling that was exactly what he intended. "Remember what I said, Kinnard. You kill someone else, and you burn."

She turned and walked away, but his gaze followed her down the slope—piercing her spine and sending chills racing across her skin.

And yet when she looked over her shoulder, Kinnard was gone. His stare had been her imagination, nothing more.

Hadn't it?

Somehow, she suspected not. He was still watching her, even if she could no longer see him. The foul caress of his gaze still burned deep.

She turned a corner and, finally, the sense of him watching disappeared. She blew out a relieved breath and let her gaze roam across the old buildings crowding the main street. It was extremely quiet. Either everyone had finally passed out from all the booze they'd consumed over the last few days or Dunleavy had decided it was better to keep them docile and conserve his strength in the process.

Her gaze went to the two-story building at the end of the street. Though the day was still reasonably bright, the whorehouse's roof seemed oddly wreathed in mist. It was as if the clouds that raced the threat of rain toward the town had paused for breath over that particular building. Even from where she stood, she could feel the tremble of electricity in the air.

Another chill raced through her. Something was happening up there, something she really didn't want to discover.

But what choice did she have?

She scanned the remaining buildings, not sensing any life in any of them. Not that she really would. Her talent had never been sensing life, but rather *un*life. Even before Michael had turned her world inside out, she'd been able to sense other creatures—even if she hadn't been fully aware of it. The circle around this town had shut down that ability, but if she and Michael shut down at least one other sacrifice site, would the rest of her abilities start to seep back?

She suspected they might. She also suspected Dunleavy would try to ensure they didn't shut down any more of his sites. He had to know Camille and a dozen other circle operatives were waiting outside the barrier, waiting for the chance to get in and hunt him down.

So how did he plan to escape?

Another tunnel, perhaps?

Her gaze hit the whorehouse again, and after a moment's hesitation, she walked toward the old building. The buzz of electricity got stronger, crawling across her skin like biting ants. The closer she got, the more her skin burned. By the time she reached the stairs, it felt like she was being eaten alive.

Biting her bottom lip and resisting the strengthening desire to scratch at her skin, she hesitated on the bottom step and stared upward. The fog had closed in on the top few steps, making it impossible to see what was up there. But flashes of light bit through the gloom. Either this mist was accompanied by lightning or someone was performing magic on the roof.

She flicked a knife down into her palm and cautiously began to climb. The old stairs creaked under her weight, the noise snapping through the misty hush surrounding her.

The lightning stopped, and so did she. She tightened her grip around the knife, her knuckles almost white. Nothing moved on the fog-bound landing above her, and no sound beyond the soft rasp of her breathing broke the silence. Yet the air itself seemed to quiver in expectation.

Someone was waiting. Someone she couldn't see.

She took another step forward and slashed at the fog with her knife. It curled away from the blow, reminding her, oddly, of the way plastic disintegrated when touched by flame.

She climbed on, slashing at the mist with every step. But as she neared the top landing, the retreat of the mist slowed, then stopped. She paused, staring at the wall of white a few steps above her. Was it just her imagination, or did deeper shadows lurk in the heart of the mist? There was no sound, no creak of wood, no movement to stir the white wall and indicate life, yet every instinct screamed that she was no longer alone.

Lightning bit through the mist—blue flashes that smelled as foul as they felt. The ants eating at her skin became more frantic, telling her that whatever was happening on the roof was reaching a peak. She had to move or she'd be too late.

She took a step and sound rumbled toward her.

A growl she'd heard before.

The wolves were back. Yellow flashed through the white—canines, bared in warning. She raised the knife, the blade gleaming with silver fire in the fog. A wolf stepped out of the mist, teeth bared, hackles raised.

"This knife is silver," she warned, slashing the blade back and forth through the tendrils of mist swirling between them. "Silver is deadly to shifters."

The wolf didn't react. Maybe it *was* a real wolf and not a shifter.

She climbed one more step. The wolf crouched, its growl rumbling harshly through the night.

"Don't," she warned softly. "I *will* kill you if I have to."

The wolf's yellow gaze met hers. There was no humanity in those glowing depths. No understanding.

A real wolf, then.

She bit her lip, but she knew she had no choice. She had to stop whatever was happening on the roof, and the only way to do that was to go through this wolf.

She raised her foot to take the next step, and at that moment, the wolf leapt. She threw herself sideways, hitting the wall of the building with enough force to crack the wooden boards, and slashed at the wolf with the knife. The blade scoured the creature's side. It seemed to do little damage, but the animal landed awkwardly and tumbled down to the next landing. She hitched up her skirt and ran the last few steps to the top landing.

Only to discover that the wolf wasn't alone.

The smell of blood and approaching death stung the tunnel's dank air. Michael paused, breathing deep the smell, feeling the richness of it through every pore. The source wasn't far ahead.

The darkness in him stirred, then settled. For whatever reason his demon had risen, he was again regaining control. And as much as he enjoyed the taste of blood in the air, he had no intention of sampling the offering.

And that's what waited ahead.

An offering, not one of Dunleavy's sacrifice sites.

He moved forward more cautiously. The tunnel curved around to the right, then widened out, becoming a junction with two other tunnels. There, in the middle, lay a man.

In the infrared of his vision, the stranger's body was a mass of pulsing red—but the heat of his blood was dying, just as the man was dying. He was naked, his torso marked with purple patches that indicated he'd taken a beating sometime in the last few hours. His hands and feet were tied with what looked like fishing line, the silvery thread glowing as brightly as the blood congealing on the floor near the stranger's neck.

Michael stopped beside him. The man's eyes were wide and staring, and the stark look of terror seemed frozen on his face. Odd, given he wasn't yet dead.

On his neck were bite marks. Dunleavy had obviously fed off him before he'd slashed the man's neck. But he'd avoided the jugular, so the rush of blood was slower, as was the dying. As with the woman they'd discovered hanging from the ceiling, there was nothing he could do to help this man. He'd lost far too much blood, and most of his organs had already begun to shut down.

Michael squatted down and lightly touched the man's face. Narrowing his gaze, he reached out with his thoughts, trying to touch the stranger's mind. For a moment, it was like trying to push through treacle. Energy danced around him, burning up his back and across his shoulders. He frowned, ignoring it, concentrating on reaching the man's thoughts. The sensation fled, and suddenly he was reliving the horror inflicted on the stranger.

Dunleavy had beaten him, defiled him. Then he'd frozen the man's thoughts and actions and fed off him. The bastard might like the fear, the horror, inflicted while violating his victims sexually, but when it came to feeding, he preferred them unknowing and helpless.

Oddly enough, though the sense of violence was clear and fresh in the man's dying thoughts, there were no impressions of Dunleavy himself. Just sensations. Emotions. And memories of Kinnard dragging the man into this tunnel.

Michael closed the stranger's eyes and quickly snapped his neck, granting him a speedier death. Then he rose and went to look at the man's feet. Like the victim on the roof of the whorehouse, the stranger had the imprint of lips burned into his soles.

Something had fed while Dunleavy was defiling his victim.

Something he suspected might resemble a sluglike creature.

A creature whose energy was similar to Kinnard's.

Whether or not the two were one and the same, he couldn't really say, because there were *some* differences in the flow and resonance of body heat between the two. But that could very well come from the differences in form.

He'd never heard of, or met, a shifter who took the form of a large slug, but he'd hardly lived long enough to meet all the creatures on this earth. But he'd known vampires who fed on emotions rather than blood, and they could die just as easily as regular vampires.

What killed Dunleavy would kill his sick little minion.

He rubbed a hand across his jaw as he looked toward the nearest tunnel. The air there seemed fresher, indicating there might be some sort of opening close by. Maybe the same one Kinnard had used to drag the stranger here.

But he wasn't here to find an exit. He glanced at the other tunnel. The air there was thick and rich, full of the stench of earth, water and age. And, underneath all that, the slightest taint of blood. That was where he had to go.

Again, power burned across his skin, and for a moment, his thoughts became confused. He should go right, find the exit . . .

He shook his head, and the pressure on his mind became more intense. He swore, fighting it, fists clenched against the urge to follow the orders pressing into his mind. He'd faced telepathic assaults before, and this was very similar. But during those other assaults, his own telepathy had been strong enough not only to repel but to attack them. This was far stronger than anything he'd faced before, and it had its base in magic rather than mind-strength. There was no attacking, only surviving.

The witch was right, which meant she was probably right about other things—including the runes on his back and the magic surrounding this town. Including him knowing her more intimately than he believed.

Just thinking about her appeared to clear the force hammering through his brain. Her warm, cinnamon scent seemed to spin around him, through him, and sunshine flowed through his mind—a radiance that was at once passionate and familiar, and one that filled him with strength.

He didn't only know this woman. He loved her.

Yet he hadn't really loved anyone since he'd fallen for the woman who had turned him. He hadn't even truly loved Christine, despite the years they'd been together.

Or was that all another lie concocted by Dunleavy and his magic? He didn't know the truth from fiction anymore, and *that* was the most frustrating thing of all.

He swore, then spun around and stalked toward the dark tunnel. The air became foul and cold, the walls slick with moisture and slime. It was a good thing the witch wasn't with him. This place would remind her too much of the tunnels that had almost snatched her life . . .

Damn it, why couldn't he remember her name? And why did it feel like she was as vital to his life as blood itself? He *had* to get rid of these runes, *had* to remember.

He had to kill Dunleavy—not only as revenge for Christine, but for snatching away his memories of the amber-eyed witch.

Ahead, moisture dripped, and the metallic taint of blood became sharper. He slowed, tasting the air, listening to the distant beat of life.

Only there wasn't one heart pounding through the silence ahead, but four.

Three of them were strong, one weaker. One a sacrifice—three guards, then.

Michael smiled grimly. Dunleavy wasn't giving

him much credit if he had only three guards. Either that, or he was extremely confident about the abilities of his guards.

Or perhaps it was as the witch said—Dunleavy didn't intend to kill them. Not yet, anyway.

He walked forward more cautiously. There was no sound from up ahead, other than the steady beat of life. If those ahead breathed, he couldn't hear it.

The tunnel began to widen into another cavern. Ahead, the light of a campfire danced, spreading bright fingers across the slick black walls. Silhouetted against the flames was a wolf. The other two guards stood to the left and the right, lost to the darker shadows still haunting the edges of the cavern. Even with the benefit of infrared, he couldn't see them. They were obviously using the boulders that lay scattered across the floor from a past landslide as cover.

He stopped and cast away the shadows hiding his form. The wolves would know he was there by smell alone, so it didn't matter whether he was cloaked or not.

The wolf near the flames growled a low note of warning. Michael ignored it, his gaze moving to the figure hanging from the ceiling. Unlike the first sacrifice, this one was a man, and he was currently free from the attentions of the slug creature. He was unconscious, but the beat of his heart was strong, even if it was a little erratic, indicating that he hadn't been up there all that long. His torso bore the dark splash of bruises, and the stench of vomit entwined with the richness of blood. Dunleavy had obviously beaten him until he was sick, and only then had he sliced off the man's hands and feet. The question was, was this a ritual necessity, or merely another sick perversion on Dunleavy's part? Knowing Dunleavy, it was probably the latter.

He swept his gaze around the shadows beyond the flames, locating the other wolves by the beat of their hearts. Then he looked at the pack leader.

"If you attack me, you die."

The wolf's lips curled, revealing gleaming canines.

"I know you can understand me, shifter. I intend to free that man, and if you get in my way, you'll pay."

The wolf rose onto all fours, its low growl reverberating through the cavern. To the right and the left came the slow sound of claws clicking against stone. The other two were moving in, but they weren't yet ready to attack. Maybe they were waiting to see what their leader did.

Michael moved forward. Energy surged across his back, stinging with the sharpness of bees. He frowned, trying to shrug away the sensation, but met with little success.

The wolf crouched, then sprang. Michael blurred, avoiding the wolf's lunge, then ran for the fire. He didn't want to kill the shifter, but he knew he might have no other choice. He leapt over the flames and felt the fingers of heat playing down his legs. He hit the ground on the other side and saw the star and its accompanying circle of stone. He knew he wouldn't be able to get the man down until the circle had been broken.

The buzz of energy got stronger. He shook his head and felt the stir of air to his right. He swung, hitting the wolf square in the jaw, feeling teeth score his fist before the force of his blow knocked the creature sideways. The other wolves attacked, coming in from the left and the right. Michael dropped, allowing one of them to soar over his head before twisting and kicking the other in the gut. It made an almost human grunt of pain as it hit the ground and slid into the fire, scattering the wood. Sparks flew, firefly bright in the darkness, and flames leapt high. The wolf scrambled to its feet and leapt away from the fire, its coat singed but otherwise unharmed.

He rose, the bite of energy across his flesh so severe it felt like a thousand needles piercing his skin. It was hard to concentrate . . . hard to think . . .

Too late, he became aware of movement behind him. Teeth sank into his flesh, worrying and tearing at his skin, spilling warmth down the back of his leg. As pain flashed white hot through his body, he heard the scrape of nails. Another wolf was coming at him.

He swore and twisted around, smashing his fist against the snout of the wolf that tore at his thigh. Flesh and bone gave way under the force of the blow, but the wolf refused to release its hold. The frantic beat of the second wolf's heart warned that the creature was close. He dropped, dragging the first wolf down with him, his breath hissing from clenched teeth as the movement tore away more of his flesh.

The second wolf missed by inches. It landed several feet away, scrabbling to gain purchase against the slick stone and stop the impetus of its leap before it slid into the fire.

A yellow blur moved past it. Teeth gleamed. The third wolf launched—going not for extremities or torso, but straight for the neck, the jugular. Trying to kill, not maim.

The witch had been wrong. Or Dunleavy's game plan had changed.

He knocked the creature away, then reached around, unlocking the death grip the wolf had on his thigh. The wolf put up little fight—his blow had shattered the creature's nose, and the mere act of breathing had become a battle. One Michael ended by breaking the shifter's neck.

He grabbed the creature by the front legs and rose. Agony burned through every nerve ending, its epicenter his torn and bloodied flesh. His leg buckled, and for a moment he didn't think it would bear *his* weight, let alone that of the dead wolf. But forcing his knee to lock and hold, he swallowed nausea and blinked away the sudden sting of sweat. The air howled its warning as he swung the dead wolf around, using it to batter away its pack mates. He staggered sideways and felt the caress of flames across his skin. Then he caught his balance and blurred, running for the stone circle.

The scrabble of claws suggested the remaining two wolves weren't far behind. And they were gaining with every step, because he could barely run even at a human pace, let alone move with the inhuman speed of a vampire.

He felt rather than saw the impetus of their leap, noted the closeness of the stones and dropped flat. Electricity buzzed across his face, and warning flickers of blue fire cut across the night. The black stones were within arm's reach, which was exactly what he'd intended.

The wolves twisted in midair, trying to reach him as they flew over his prone form. Maybe they weren't aware of the danger of the black stones. Or maybe they simply didn't understand the magic involved.

Either way, they hit the invisible shield, and the magic reacted. Blue fire flared brightly, surrounding the two wolves in tendrils of flame, burning them, consuming them, with very little fanfare.

Once the two were little more than ash and scraps of bone, Michael pushed into a sitting position. Firming his grip on the dead wolf, he swung it as hard as he could at the nearest stone. Most circles like this were created to protect against intrusion from magic, the living, or the *un*dead. Very few were designed for protection against the *dead* dead, simply because, in most cases, there was no need.

The circle didn't react to the wolf's body when it hit the nearest stone and sent it ricocheting away. With a sound that was almost a sigh, the circle's energy faded away.

Michael blew out a relieved breath. Now to get the man down from the ceiling. His gaze followed the line of rope holding the stranger up, and he saw that it was attached to the large boulder lying at the northern edge of the circle. He pushed to his feet and hobbled over. Releasing the knot, he carefully lowered the stranger until he was far enough down to catch hold of him, and then he pulled him out of the pentagram before lowering him completely to the floor.

At that moment, pain hit him.

Not his pain.

Nikki's.

Eleven

THE MAN ATTACKED, giving Nikki no time to think, just react. She ducked his blow and slashed with the knife, cutting through the thick material of his shirt and slicing a thin line across his stomach.

The man's howl was one of fury more than pain, and he swung his fist. She fell back, but not fast enough, and the ring on his middle finger scraped across her jaw as the blow moved past. He followed that blow with another. Again she fell back, not really wanting to hurt this man, knowing by the glazed look in his brown eyes that he was attacking under Dunleavy's orders, not of his own volition.

Her retreat was stopped when her back hit the railing. She swore and tried to step sideways. Heard the rumbled warning close to her thigh and knew the wolf wasn't going to allow an escape that way.

Nowhere to run. No choice but to maim.

The stranger's fist bit through the air again. She dropped and spun, sweeping her leg behind his, knocking him off his feet. He landed with a crunch that shook the whole landing. She scrambled forward and tried to chop a blow across his windpipe to temporarily paralyze him, but he caught her hand in his pawlike fist and squeezed so hard that pain shot up her arm, and a scream forced its way up her throat.

As if they had a will of their own, her flames appeared, dancing eagerly from her fingertips to the stranger's hand. For a second, her pain was forgotten as she stared. It looked for all the world as if the flame imps had come to life.

The stranger howled and released his grip, shaking his hand in an attempt to rid himself of the slivers of flame that skittered across his skin.

She switched her knife to her bruised hand and completed the blow to the stranger's neck with her left. He made an odd gargling sound, his burning fingers forgotten in the greater need to breathe.

The flames died as she rose, but warmth kissed her fingertips, as if the energy of the flames was being drawn back into her body.

Which was impossible, surely. She certainly hadn't felt anything like that when Lenny had tried to kill her. But then, she'd intentionally wanted him to burn. Wanted him to hurt, to suffer.

She hadn't wanted to hurt *this* man, just distract him enough to immobilize him. So did that mean she had differing levels of control available? She hoped so. She really didn't want to burn every single person she was forced to defend herself against into a cinder.

She sheathed her knife and stepped past him and onto the roof, just in time to see a sluglike creature slither away from the naked form lying in the middle of the pentagram. It slid down through the cracks between the wooden roofing and disappeared. A shudder ran through her. Obviously, whatever that thing was, it wasn't overly choosy about whom it had sex with. Male, female, near dead, dead . . . it didn't really matter.

She blew out a breath and walked over to the body. It was a different man lying here, and while part of her wanted to know what had happened to the remains of the first victim, she very much suspected that it was better *not* to know.

He was lying in the middle of the star, his arms and legs outstretched, as if he were welcoming the death visited upon him. His expression backed this up—he was smiling, his blue eyes frozen in a look of warmth.

And like the first man they'd found on this roof, he had a small knife wound in his chest. Blood still trickled out, the flow sluggish as it crept down his side. There was a similar wound on his head, suggesting that, like the first victim, he no longer had his heart and brain.

She glanced down at the black star etched into the roof. There was no sense of power coming from it, no tingle of energy cutting through the air. While the slug had crossed those dark lines without harm, she wasn't about to test them. If Camille and Seline had taught her anything, it was a high respect for magic. Just because she couldn't feel any energy coming from the black pentagram didn't mean it was inactive.

Still, she had to do *something* about it. Dunleavy was using this place to feed either his strength or that of his dark gods. For that reason alone, it had to be destroyed, and the only means she had to do that was her fire.

That would mean destroying evidence—this man,

the bloody room downstairs, the woman's remains, her head . . .

She swallowed and tried to ignore the gruesome images that surged into her mind. Destroying evidence was a better option than leaving this pentagram here and allowing Dunleavy to use it to kill more people. And besides, given what she'd learned about the Circle in the last few months, she very much doubted whether the police would even be aware that something foul had happened here. This place would be cleaned of all evidence, the survivors would be given the best medical attention and counseling available, and their memories would be "rearranged." How the Circle would handle the dead, she didn't know—but if she'd learned anything about the organization, it was that they took care of those left behind. The families of the dead would be compensated in some way.

She reached down inside herself for the power of the flames. This time, she intended to burn, intended to destroy, and the flames that sprang to life across her fingertips echoed that intention. They were fierce and hungry, and they didn't resemble flame imps in the slightest.

The scrape of a nail made her jerk around. The wolf had stepped onto the roof, and the flames reflected in its yellow eyes, making them glow eerily.

It stepped forward, its snarl low, fierce and deadly. She stepped back, the fierce golden fire of her flames burning back the fog, allowing weak sunlight to filter in and lift some of the shadows. But sunlight only made the wolf's intentions more obvious. It would stop her any way it deemed necessary.

From behind the wolf a figure rose. The stranger staggered to the roof's entrance, his face white and his breathing still little more than a rasp.

"Get her," he said, in a low, dead voice that didn't match the man or his injuries and oddly reminded her of Kinnard. "Just remember to injure, not kill."

The wolf stalked forward. She retreated, her gaze on the stranger more than the wolf. His brown eyes were still glazed, unblinking. Did that mean Dunleavy was controlling his actions, but not actually seeing what this man saw? Why else would he not react to the flames burning across her fingers?

The wolf walked around the edges of the pentagram. With the stranger blocking the exit to the stairs, she had no other choice but to back toward the far wall. Once she hit that, her only options were to either fight or risk the two-story drop.

Her gaze went to the pentagram. She had to destroy it. It was one source of Dunleavy's power, and the more they destroyed his supply options, the better chance they had. And the better chance Camille and the rest of the Circle had of getting in here to save the day should she and Michael fail.

Not that they *would* fail, because she had every intention of marrying her vampire, and no psycho out for revenge was going to stop her.

Her gaze went to the stranger. She couldn't let him die, though, and she very much suspected that might happen if she flamed this roof. Dunleavy had control of his mind, and wherever Dunleavy was, it surely wasn't close enough to see the fire until it was too late.

The wolf had reached the top of the pentagram. A

few more steps and it would be within range. She stepped sideways, raised her burning hand and reached for more of the power surging through her veins.

"Burn this place to cinders," she said softly.

Fire exploded through her, around her, and the air was suddenly thick with heat. The wolf yelped, a sound full of surprise, but she wasted no time seeing what had happened to it. She'd left it an escape route—over the roof edge. Shifters were tough; it could take a two-story fall without breaking a nail.

She spun and ran for the stranger. When she was close enough, she launched herself at him, twisting in the air so that she'd hit him feet first. He didn't react, merely stood there dumbly, confirming her guess that Dunleavy wasn't using this man's eyes. She hit him hard and sent him flailing backward. He hit the landing's back railing, and with a crack that sounded like thunder, the wood splintered and gave way. With arms flailing, the stranger fell into the fog and disappeared.

She barely had the chance to swear before the impetus of her leap took her over the edge and down into that same fogginess.

"Oh, *shit*!" was all she managed to say before the free fall was over. She hit the ground with enough force to jar every bone in her body and send her teeth through her tongue.

She slumped face first into the dirt and lay there for several minutes, trying to remember how to breathe, trying to ignore the pain pouring through every nerve ending. She'd never fallen two stories before, and it certainly wasn't an experience she'd care to repeat. It *hurt.*

Concern flooded through her mind, and suddenly there were warm hands on her back, her neck, feeling for a pulse, checking that she was okay.

"I'm all right," she murmured, and forced herself to roll over. "Just winded."

Michael's face was dark with dust, and there were smears of blood near his temple, as if he'd dragged bloody fingers through his hair. "Are you sure?"

She wiggled her fingers and moved her feet. "I'm fine. Really."

The relief and love evident in his gaze made her heart do its usual happy dance.

"I was in the mines and felt your pain." He paused and frowned. "Odd, really."

She smiled and touched a hand to his cheek. "Not as odd as you might think. Did you find anything?"

"Another circle. I destroyed it, though the pentagram is still viable." He glanced up at the roof of the whorehouse. Orange flames were now visible through the rapidly retreating fog. "Looks like the one up there is in the process of being destroyed, though."

She nodded and grabbed his leg, using it to help her sit up. He winced, and as she pulled her hand away, she saw the blood. "What the hell . . . ?"

He shrugged. "Dunleavy wasn't about to let me take one of his sacrifices without a fight. He had three wolves protecting the stones. I used one of their bodies to displace the rocks."

"Since your jeans are soaked with blood, you definitely need that wound treated."

He gave her a gentle smile. "Blood is easy enough

for me to replace. The man I rescued needs treatment first." He paused, looking past her. "Who is that?"

She twisted around. The man she'd knocked off the roof was lying on his back not far away. "Dunleavy left him as a guard on the roof. Is he okay?"

"He breathes. His heart beats."

She glanced at Michael. "Can you touch his thoughts?"

He frowned. Energy buzzed around them, a sharper heat than that coming from the flames above them. "I should be able to, but it feels like I'm fighting my way through molasses."

The runes in action. "Where's the man you rescued?"

In answer, he rose and offered her a hand. She placed her fingers in his, her skin trembling at the sheer warmth of his touch. He pulled her to her feet but didn't move immediately, instead touching her bruised chin with his free hand.

"I know you," he said softly. "I love you."

Elation winged through her soul. The wall around his memories was breaking down—and though she wished it would happen a little faster, at least it was happening.

"And I you," she whispered, then added through the link, *but when you remember my name, do not utter it out loud.*

Why?

Again, despite the spell, he didn't seem to think it strange for them to be connecting this way—even though he'd tried to use telepathy moments ago and couldn't. But maybe that was because Dunleavy didn't actually know about the deeper connection between

them. He'd blocked Michael's memories and, therefore, his path to the link, but as the memories seeped
back, so did his access to the mind-link.

*Because I'm hoping against hope that Dunleavy
still thinks I am someone I'm not.*

Seline.

Yes.

I knew that name didn't suit you. He brushed a
kiss across her lips, and then he gently squeezed the
hand he held before stepping away. "We need to take
care of Dunleavy's victim. I think he's in shock."

As he would be, since he'd basically been left to
bleed to death. "We'd better move the other man
first. We wouldn't want the building falling on him."

"If you save him, you're just saving another weapon
Dunleavy can use against us."

"He's not helping Dunleavy willingly, and I'm not
leaving him here to die."

Michael didn't look too enthusiastic about the task,
but he hobbled over to the stranger and hauled him to
an old water trough, dumping him inside. "The concrete will protect him from the heat," he commented.
"That good enough?"

She nodded and glanced up as something exploded
on the roof. Sparks flew high—blue and black shards
that glittered like diamonds against the bright flames.
The candles, perhaps. Black smoke curled upward,
oddly reminding her of the slug creature as it worked
its way through the rapidly disappearing mist.

A chill ran through her. Was that thing still in the
building? While she damn well hoped so, she very
much suspected it wouldn't be so easy to kill.

She turned her back on the burning building and

wondered why no one was coming to douse the flames. Even Dunleavy couldn't want the outside interest such a fire might evoke.

"This place is very remote," Michael said, his gaze skating across the building before meeting hers again. "And there's no one inside, other than the already dead."

"No strange slug creature?"

"No, unfortunately." He turned and limped across to the next building. A naked man was sprawled near the front of the building, his body bruised and bloody, his breathing rapid but shallow. In shock for sure.

"We'd better get him inside and get him warm," she commented, silently cursing the monster who'd done this. "And we need to stop the bleeding and elevate the wounds."

Michael nodded and, with a grunt of effort, hauled the stranger up onto his shoulder. The surge of fresh blood down his thigh was worrying. The wound was worse than he'd led her to believe, though that was something she should be used to. Even with his memory short-circuited, he was still playing the same old games and not telling her everything. She couldn't help the smile that teased her lips as she followed him down the street. Obviously, that was something that was never going to change.

Once they'd reached the house, they cleaned up the injured man's wounds and made him as comfortable as possible in the second bedroom. She found extra blankets, shoving several under his legs to elevate them and throwing the other over him to keep him warm.

"We're going to have to restrain him," Michael commented, coming into the room with rope.

"We can't. He's injured."

"He's also a threat. Dunleavy could take his mind at any moment, and while you might believe the fiend has no intention of killing us before tomorrow, I'm not so sure."

Her gaze skated down to his blood-soaked thigh, and she knew he was right. They couldn't risk it. She took a rope, tying one of the stranger's arms to the bed while Michael tied the other.

"Now, your turn," she said, as she straightened.

Amusement flirted with his lips. "Woman, if you want your wicked way with me, all you have to do is ask. You don't need to tie me down."

She grinned. "Sometimes I wonder. Get into the bathroom and clean yourself up while I go find something to bind up that wound of yours."

"The wound will heal—"

"A lot faster if it's treated. So stop arguing and go."

"Is this tendency to nag a new trait, or something I know about and put up with?" he muttered as he turned away.

She grinned as she followed him out the door. "Oh, it's something you know about." And it was a two-way street. He could nag her just as much as she nagged him.

She headed into the main room. A search through the cupboards uncovered a small medical kit. Inside were bandages and salve. She took both and walked into the bathroom. Michael was standing naked in front of the basin, washing himself down with a cloth. She hesitated in the doorway, her gaze skating down the lean, familiar length of him. Even after all the months they'd been together, it seemed she could never get enough of simply looking at him. She loved watching the play of muscles under his pale skin as he moved. Loved running her hands all over him, feeling the restrained power beneath the gentleness of his caress . . .

Her gaze hit his thigh. The flesh was hanging in bloody chunks, and the wound bled freely, staining the back of his leg and pooling near his heel. With a wound like that, there'd be no baths. Not until the blood stopped flowing and it had begun to heal, anyway.

"Damn it, Michael, why didn't you bandage that wound right away?"

He raised an eyebrow as he looked over his shoulder. "Because I'm a vampire, and the wound will not kill me."

"But loss of blood can weaken you, and you're losing buckets of the stuff." She knelt behind him and raised a hand. "Give me that cloth."

He did. She washed down the wound, then liberally applied the salve and bandaged it the best she could. After washing away the blood staining the back of his leg, she dropped a kiss on his butt, and rose before she was tempted to do anything else.

"Wet this," she said, handing him the cloth. "I'll have a go at the runes again."

He obeyed her orders and stood patiently for several minutes as she scrubbed the runes, his skin twitching and energy stinging the air. Then, with a slight growl, he spun, took the cloth and tossed it back into the sink. "Enough."

Her gaze met his, and her heart crashed through her chest. Not at the hunger that burned in his eyes, but rather from the love and desire that burned even brighter.

Lord, she wanted him, but it was too much of a risk with the remains of the runes still on his back and the glint of hunger in his eyes. "You should go eat."

"Yes," he agreed softly, taking the cloth from her hand and dumping it in the sink behind him. "I should, shouldn't I?"

She placed a restraining hand on his chest, even though all she really wanted to do was draw him close. "This is neither the time nor the place."

He caught her hand and pressed her back against the wall. "This from the woman who insisted on making love on a San Francisco bench while the rest of the world woke around us."

A smile teased her lips. "So you remember that?"

"I'm remembering lots of things. Like how much I enjoy making love to you in the afternoon."

His hand slid under her shirt and around her waist, his fingers almost molten against her back as he pressed her closer to his warm, hard body. Then his lips came down on hers, and for the longest time, there was no more talk, simply enjoyment.

After a while, his touch moved down her spine. It was a caress that spread like a wave through every nerve ending, leaving her whole body tingling in anticipation. He undid her skirt's button and zipper, and it fell with a sigh, puddling at her feet.

He pulled back, his breath warm on her lips as his gaze burned into hers. "Let's make love. Here. Now."

His words were little more than a husky growl that

made her tremble with desire. But it was the desire burning bright in his dark eyes—a desire that was not only sexual, but blood need—that worried her. He *was* controlling the need to taste her blood, but only just.

"Michael—"

He gave her no time to finish, his mouth closing on hers again. Her protests died, quashed by the force of his kiss. By the passion behind it.

With a husky groan, he pulled back again and ripped open her shirt, the buttons pinging across the bathroom floor as he pushed the material off her shoulders. His fingers were a flame that skimmed her back as he dropped the shirt beside the skirt. Then, with a slowness that denied the urgency thrumming through the link, he skimmed his hand up her stomach and began circling one breast with a finger. His gaze held hers, leaving her drowning in the dark pool of his desire as his caress gradually worked inward, reaching, but not quite touching, the aching, sensitive center of her breast. Sweat slicked her skin. His whisper-soft stroking moved to her other breast, and by the time he'd finished circling to the center, she was close to screaming with frustration.

His mouth claimed hers again, urgently, passionately. His hands skimmed her waist, catching the sides of her panties, thrusting them down. Then he stroked her, teased her, until the shudders of pleasure became almost too much to bear. At that moment, he lifted her, claiming her in the most basic way possible.

She wrapped her arms around his neck, holding him close as he thrust and surged inside her. Her body quivered with the sensations tumbling through her, her thighs clenching him tight as the pressure built and built, until she felt so tightly strung that everything would surely break. Then everything did break, and she was unraveling, groaning, with the intensity of the orgasm flowing through her.

His kiss became as fierce as his body, then his mouth left hers, and his teeth grazed her neck. She jerked away before he could pierce her skin. He groaned, his need for her blood so fierce it burned down the link between them. She caught his face between her hands, pulling him away from her neck, kissing him. The sharpness of his canines grazed her tongue, warning her that the danger was not over yet. Yet it was a danger that oddly heightened her desire, revived her need for him. She knew it was as much the glamour of a vampire in need of blood as the desire that still surged between them.

No blood, she warned forcefully.

He groaned, his kiss becoming almost savage. She thrust the link wide open, and their minds joined with a fierceness that was far greater than anything they'd reached physically. It was mind, body *and* soul. For one glorious moment, they were one person, one entity. One heart. One soul. And nothing, not even bloodlust, stood a chance against that oneness.

Together, they fell screaming over the edge, plunging into a sea of bliss more powerful than anything she'd experienced before.

When she remembered how to breathe again, she rested her forehead against his, and said, "Wow."

"Indeed." He kissed her forehead and lowered her to the ground. Hunger seared through the link, and she looked up quickly. Heat still burned in his eyes, and his body trembled as he fought the urge to slake his hunger.

"You were right. I should have fed first." He brushed a hand across her cheek, stepped away and bent to pick up his clothes. "We were extremely lucky hunger and the magic didn't get the better of me."

"I think self-control had more to do with it than luck."

"Maybe. But I won't be so foolish next time."

Next time, hopefully, they'd be free of Dunleavy's magic, and there wouldn't be a need to be careful. "Watch yourself out there. Dunleavy's going to be a little pissed about us destroying another of his pentagrams."

He nodded and zipped up his pants. "I want you to walk around the house and make sure all the windows and doors are locked."

She raised an eyebrow. "Why? Dunleavy's a vampire. He can't come into a house uninvited."

"Maybe. But we don't yet know what, exactly, Kinnard is, and I'd rather he didn't know you're here alone."

"He's going to know that if he sees you outside."

"I'll blur, so he won't even see me."

She had a suspicion Kinnard knew exactly what they were up to, no matter what they were doing. She flicked a knife down into her palm, then flipped it, handing it to him hilt first. "Take this with you. It's silver, so no matter what Kinnard is, it'll affect him."

"I do not need a weapon to take care of a worm like Kinnard."

"That worm is too cagey to let you get anywhere

near him. At least you might be able to throw the knife and nick him."

He stared at her a second longer, then took the knife and put it through his belt at the back of his jeans. "I won't be long. You be careful."

"I always am."

"Yeah, right," he said drily and headed for the front door.

Nikki locked it after he left. Then she gathered her clothes and walked into the bedroom to get another shirt. After dressing, she checked all the windows, making sure they were locked and shuttered. Not that she thought it would help. She had a suspicion that if Kinnard wanted to get in here, he could. And it was a certainty that the slug thing would be able to enter.

Goose bumps ran across her skin, and she rubbed her arms. What *was* that thing? She didn't know, but she knew someone who would. Camille. She bit her lip, wondering if she dare risk calling the old witch. But what would it gain her, other than a bit more knowledge? If Kinnard or Dunleavy found out about it—and she suspected they somehow would—then someone in this town would pay the price. There'd been enough deaths here already. As much as she hated working blind, that was exactly what they had to keep doing.

She blew out a breath and headed into the main room. Michael wasn't the only one who needed to eat to keep up his strength. It was way past time she ate something too. And way, *way,* past time she got some caffeine into her system.

Because she had a feeling she was going to need

every ounce of energy she had access to over the next twenty-four hours.

Michael had almost finished taking his fill from a sweet brown mare when he realized he was no longer alone in the stables. He retracted his teeth, licking the last droplets of blood from the mare's neck to help heal the wound, then gave her a reassuring pat and stepped to the stall door.

Kinnard leaned against the opposite stall, a malicious gleam in his gray eyes. "Human blood is far sweeter, vampire. Have you not sampled your witch's blood yet?"

Energy stirred around him, and the need to taste her blood began to course through his system. But he'd resisted it while in the throes of passion, and its flame was nowhere near as strong now. The question was, why did Kinnard and his master want him to taste her so badly? Given the depth of the need they were trying to force into his mind, he'd surely kill her.

Was that what they wanted? For him to kill her?

It couldn't be, though—not if the witch was right and they needed her alive for the ceremony.

"Animal blood has certain advantages over human. Not that a worm like you would ever know the difference." He switched to his vampire vision and studied the haze of life coursing through Kinnard's gnarled body. He'd been right earlier—Kinnard and the slug had very similar energy patterns. He reached back for the knife in his belt, holding the hilt in his fist, the blade resting against his wrist and arm, concealed from Kinnard's prying gaze. "What are you doing here, Kinnard?"

"I came with a warning, vampire. If you or the witch destroy any more pentagrams, the remaining people in this town will die."

Michael eyed him skeptically. "If you kill those people, you take away your boss's source of power for the circle protecting this town."

Kinnard hawked and spat. "It doesn't much matter now, because the new moon is less than a day away. He has enough power to ensure the strength of the circle until then."

The truth? Or a lie Kinnard and his master were desperate for them to believe? "Where is Dunleavy?"

Kinnard's smile was mocking. "You've seen him more than a dozen times already, vampire."

"So the witch was right. He's a shapeshifter?"

"A shifter with several forms. He might even be the man you think you've tied so securely in that house of yours."

Energy caressed the air again as Kinnard spoke. Michael rolled his shoulders, trying to shake the sensation. The man tied to the bed wasn't a vampire. Wasn't Dunleavy, as much as Kinnard and the magic wanted him to believe otherwise.

"Does anything resembling truth ever come out of your mouth?" he asked.

Kinnard's mocking smile grew. "More often than you think, vampire."

"Right now, what I'm thinking is that we'd be better off with you dead."

Kinnard snorted. "As quick as you think you are, you're no match—"

Michael didn't give him the time to finish. He threw the knife as hard and as fast as he could. Kinnard squawked and blurred, moving with vampire speed. But even then, it wasn't quite fast enough, because the blade bit into Kinnard's shoulder rather than his heart. Almost instantly, blue fire began to lick from the wound, stealing across his skin as the sharp smell of burning flesh stung the air. Kinnard's scream was high and inhuman. Energy lashed the air, flaying Michael's skin, burning across his back and shoulders. He ignored it and launched at Kinnard, intending to finish what the knife had started. Kinnard's eyes widened, and he threw out a hand, as if that alone would stop the impetus of Michael's leap. White light flashed, temporarily blinding.

Then it was gone. And so was Kinnard.

Michael hit the ground and rolled to his feet, looking around. The bloody knife was sitting on the straw at his feet, but Kinnard himself seemed to have disappeared into thin air. Yet the smell of burned flesh and the scent of fresh blood still stung the air, indicating the old man was still close. He picked up the knife, then swept his gaze around the rafters and saw the faint haze of life in the far corner.

"You'll pay for that, vampire," Kinnard spat. His voice had changed, had become harsh, cold and somehow younger. Dunleavy speaking through his proxy. "Or your witch will. I shall feast on her body, and then I shall take her life, sending her soul to hell in exchange for my brother's."

"Over my dead body."

"Oh, that's part of the plan, never fear." Kinnard's voice was fading away, the haze of his life shifting, mutating. "Enjoy her while you can, vampire, because at midnight, she will be mine."

Kinnard's energy squeezed through the cracks in the stable's wooden roof. Michael ran for the door, but by the time he had it open and got outside, Kinnard was gone. And no amount of searching could find him.

Michael swore and punched the nearby wall. The old wood splintered, sending several slivers into his skin. His flesh immediately began to burn, and he cursed his own stupidity. After more than three hundred years of existence, he should know better than to hit wood . . . he stopped. *Three hundred?*

Energy danced across his skin, and the questions crowding his mind faded. But they didn't completely disappear, and he knew, without doubt, that the runes that appeared to be no more than scars on his back were at the center of his memory loss. It was time to get them removed—as much as that same magic might try to prevent it.

He tore out the splinters and shook his hand to free it of the burning. Another thing he was certain of was the fact that Kinnard was not getting hold of the witch. If Michael had to drag her out of this town kicking and screaming, then he damn well would.

And why did that thought seem oddly familiar?

He frowned, but he knew his memory wasn't going to get any clearer until he did something about the runes. And for that, he needed the witch's help.

He made his way back down the street. The old whorehouse had almost burned to the ground, but no one seemed worried about it. He scanned the nearby buildings, noting the stir of life in several of them.

The whores were still plying their trade with the few miners who were awake, yet the beat of life pounding through their veins spoke of stress rather than pleasure.

He reached out with his thoughts, trying to touch their minds. Again, it felt as if he were trying to reach past a thick wall of molasses. This time, though, he touched enough surface thoughts to realize he wasn't the only one being controlled. Those women weren't whores. Kinnard had snatched them from the street and brought them here to play that part.

And there wasn't a damn thing he could do to stop it. Not when his psi abilities were being so elusive. He cursed softly, turned away and walked back to the witch's house.

She was in the small kitchen area and glanced around as he entered, but her welcoming smile quickly faded. "What's wrong?"

He placed the bloody knife on the table and continued toward her. "Kinnard was waiting for me in the stables."

Her gaze skated down his body, then rose again. "You're okay?"

"Yes. He merely came to give me a warning." He stopped in front of her, cupping her cheek with a hand. "You have to leave."

She rolled her eyes. "Please, we've been through this a hundred times before."

"I don't give a damn if we have. Kinnard intends to come for you at midnight, and I'm not going to risk him getting past me." He brushed his thumb across her lips and gave her a crooked smile. "I may not be able to remember your name, but I know I could not live without you."

"Nor I you." She leaned forward and placed a gentle kiss on his lips. She tasted of honey and butter and all the good things in life he'd longed for since his turning, and he had finally found them.

"But I can't—"

"You can, and you will."

"Michael—"

"No. If what you say about the ceremony is true, then by simply leaving, you destroy Dunleavy's plans."

"That's *if* what I've been told is true. Trouble is, Dunleavy doesn't seem to be operating on the same premise we are," she said. "Besides, if I leave, he will begin killing off Circle members."

Dread clenched his gut, even though he wasn't entirely sure why. "What?"

She blew out a breath, puffing the blond-brown strands of fringe away from her forehead. "You and I are members of an organization known as The Damask Circle. Dunleavy has gotten hold of a list of our people. If I leave before the ceremony, he'll start killing the people at the top of that list and work his way down."

It was on the tip of his tongue to say he didn't give a damn about the list or the people on it, but he just couldn't force the words out. Because he did give a damn, even if he couldn't remember why.

"So he holds all the aces."

She shrugged. "He thinks he does. Me, I think we're in pretty damn good shape." She hesitated, her gaze dropping to his thigh. "Well, *I* am, anyway."

He smiled and wrapped a hand around her waist,

pulling her close. Her body was warm and familiar, the rapid beat of her pulse a siren's song that called to the man in him rather than the vampire. With her breasts pressed so snugly against his chest, he couldn't help being aware of her arousal, just as she was no doubt aware of his. He wished they were home—wherever home might be. Wished he had the time to give in to passion's flame and love her as thoroughly as she deserved.

But that wasn't an option right now. Not when there were a couple of madmen running around . . .

Or were there?

He remembered what she'd said earlier, remembered what Kinnard had just said, and frowned. "Have you seen Dunleavy at all?"

Her sigh was a sound of frustration. She stepped from his embrace and reached for the still-steaming cup on the kitchen bench. "Once," she said. "Just after he'd kidnapped you."

"But not since then?"

She shook her head and leaned her hip against the bench. The sunlight streaming in through the window behind her lent warm highlights to her hair, and in that moment he realized her natural color was brown rather than the blond he kept seeing.

"Why?" she asked.

He crossed his arms. "Because I think it's odd that we haven't seen him at all."

"I thought we'd decided that all this magic happening around us had him drained and basically immobilized."

"We did. But what if that's what we were supposed to believe?"

She sipped her coffee and said, "Even if that were true, how come we haven't seen him?"

"Maybe we have. Maybe we just haven't realized it."

"You're the one who said you'd be able to see Dunleavy if he was around. Are you telling me now that's not true?"

"No. I said if Dunleavy was here, I should be able to see him, because you cannot hide the basic energy readout of a vampire."

"And Dunleavy is definitely a vampire, so why haven't you spotted him?"

"Didn't you say Dunleavy was also a shifter?"

"And a sorcerer. So?"

"So what if he's a type of shifter we've never seen before? His energy pattern wouldn't be the same as most vampires', because most vampires come from human stock rather than nonhuman races, such as shifters."

"But even if that is the case, wouldn't you have noticed the difference? There's only us, those people down in the town and Kinnard here." She shuddered. "And whatever Kinnard is, he's definitely not human."

"No. He's that slug thing we saw taking advantage of the woman."

Blood drained from her face. She took a quick drink of her coffee, but it didn't bring the color back to her cheeks. "I knew he was a slime bucket, but I didn't suspect—" Another tremor ran through her. "Yuck."

"Indeed. But I'm beginning to suspect he's a whole lot more than just a nasty little creature."

"Meaning?"

"When I was talking to Kinnard in the stable,

Dunleavy threatened us—or, more specifically, you—through him. But it wasn't so much the threats, but what *else* he said that got me thinking."

She took another sip of her coffee, then said, "Like what?"

"He said we'd seen Dunleavy more than a dozen times already. He also said that Dunleavy was a shifter with several forms."

"I told you that yesterday."

"You told me he could be a shifter like his brother, able to take the shape of anyone he has consumed. What I'm saying is that I think Dunleavy is restricted to two other forms."

"Kinnard's obviously said something else to make you think that."

"It isn't so much what he said, but what he did."

"And that was?"

"I threw the knife at him and got him in the shoulder. Blue fire erupted across his body."

She nodded. "That's consistent with silver being used against a shifter."

"Yes, but when I attacked him, he used magic to escape."

She stared at him for a moment, and then her eyes widened as what he was implying hit her.

"Yes," he confirmed softly. "I think the man we know as Kinnard is actually Dunleavy himself."

Twelve

KINNARD AND DUNLEAVY one and the same? As much as Nikki didn't want to believe it, it *did* make sense. It would explain why Dunleavy was nowhere to be seen, and why Kinnard had been able to cross the pentagrams unaffected. It had been *his* magic rather than that of his so-called master's.

"I should have cindered the little maggot when I had hold of him earlier," she muttered. Instead, all she'd succeeded in doing was warning him that she had some abilities that weren't under the control of his magic. No doubt he'd now try to counter that. Michael caught her hand and pulled her back into his embrace. She closed her eyes and pressed her cheek against his chest, listening to the slow but steady beat of his heart. She wished her own would follow suit. In many ways, this was her first official assignment for the Circle—something she'd been wanting for months now. And yet here she was, so damn scared it felt like her heart was going to gallop out of her chest.

"That's natural," Michael said softly, "if only because it *is* your first mission."

She pulled back enough to look him in the eye. *That's not the reason I'm scared.*

No?

I'm afraid of losing you. Which was ironic, considering she'd joined the Circle to ensure she *didn't* lose him.

He kissed her forehead. *That won't ever happen.*

But it already had. For a few days, she'd had no idea where he was or what was happening to him. She didn't want to ever have that feeling repeat—yet she knew it would undoubtedly happen, because that was the nature of their work. As he'd tried to warn her before she'd joined the Circle.

You can't guarantee that, she countered. *No one can.*

No. But I guarantee nothing short of death will ever keep me from your side.

She smiled and rested her cheek against his chest again. The idea that his death would also mean hers had somehow lost its terror in their months together. What would be truly unbearable was living without him—and sharing his life force had at least guaranteed *that* would never happen. *So the dead man vows.*

The dead man doesn't make many vows, and he keeps the few he does make.

Have I ever mentioned how much I love you?

His smile swam through the link, filling her mind with sunshine. *Not in recent history, no.*

Then consider it mentioned.

I don't suppose you'd consider mentioning your name?

Amusement bubbled through her. *I would, but simply mentioning it brings on an attack from the runes on your back. I think you have to remember it in your own time.* Besides, it wasn't as if he'd totally forgotten her. The strength of the emotions tumbling down the link were evidence enough of that.

Speaking of runes, it might be wise to try washing them away again. I have a suspicion Dunleavy might make an attempt at getting to you through me.

She pulled back again. "Now?"

"The sooner the better. He might be working on a spell as we speak."

She nodded and led the way to the bathroom. While she filled the basin with hot water, he stripped off his shirt. When the basin was full, she grabbed the soap and water and began working away at the black marks all over his back.

"What are we going to do about Dunleavy?" she asked.

"We hunt him down and destroy him. At least now we know exactly what we're hunting."

Energy was beginning to touch the air again, and his back muscles twitched and jumped. Welts were flickering into existence across his skin, then just as quickly disappearing, as the power touching the air lashed his skin. But he didn't say anything, so she attacked the runes with greater vigor. How much time she had left very much depended on his resistance to the runes' force.

"What about destroying the other pentagrams?" she asked. "At least then, Camille and the others will be able to get in and help us."

"Kinnard warned that if we destroyed any more pentagrams, he'd kill everyone in this town."

"He's going to do that anyway," she bit back. "You really don't think he's simply going to walk away after all this, do you?"

"Neither Dunleavy brother has ever walked away without causing as much havoc and death as he could manage."

She hesitated, but curiosity got the better of her and she asked, "Did Christine get caught in one of Emmett Dunleavy's death-and-destruction binges?"

She caught his grimace in the mirror. "No. Christine paid the price for *my* stupidity."

"What happened?"

"We were living in Chicago at the time—"

"You and Christine?" she interrupted, surprised. "In the same house?"

"No, not in the same house." His gaze met hers in the mirror, dark eyes filled with a heat that made her toes curl. "I have only lived with two women in all my years as a vampire. And I have truly loved only one."

She sighed softly. If there was one thing she was sure of, it was the fact that she'd *never* tire of hearing him say things like that.

He smiled. "We lived in the same district and had been lovers for years. When her husband died, she used his legacy to open a small milliner's store. Over the years, her business, and her fame, grew."

She didn't bother commenting on the fact that he'd basically admitted he and Christine had been lovers while her husband was still alive. Given the utter loneliness she'd sensed in him when she first met him, she could hardly take him to task for grabbing happiness where he found it. Besides, it had all happened long ago, and the people involved were long dead. "So how did your Dunleavy—Emmett—get involved with her?"

"He didn't. I caught him trying to kidnap a woman and beat him up. My mistake was not killing him."

"Why on earth didn't you?"

He shrugged. "At the time, I thought I was doing the right thing. I didn't realize he was anything more than a bloodthirsty vampire intent on a kill."

"I thought you killed bloodthirsty vampires?"

"Nowadays, yes."

She raised her eyebrows. Did those words mean that Weylin Dunleavy's spell had faded to a point where Michael no longer thought he was living in the past?

"Back then," he continued, his words confirming her thoughts, "I had more of a 'live and let live' attitude. At least until Christine was killed."

So Christine had been the first step on his road to becoming a key member in the foundation of the Circle. Well, that and whatever had happened when he met Seline, here in this same town. "How did Emmett know you were involved with her?"

He grimaced. "Christine's success made her very welcome at many society gatherings. I was her regular escort. Neither of us was exactly hard to track down."

"How did she die?"

"Emmett shot her. She bled to death in my arms."

"I'm sorry." She brushed a kiss across his wet shoulders. "But at least being shot was a quicker death than what Emmett could have offered."

"That's the problem. He did do worse. He raised her from the dead and turned her against me."

And he'd been forced to kill her all over again. "Then he deserved the death you gave him."

"Yes, he did. But here we are, and once again, others are paying for something I did."

"If there's one thing I've learned in my time with you, it's that the mentality and actions of psychos are not the same as those of normal human beings. What's happening here is not your fault, just as what happened to Christine was not your fault."

"If I'd killed him—"

"You don't have clairvoyance. You can't see the future. Hindsight is wonderful, but at the time, you thought you were doing the right thing."

He smiled and turned around, drawing her into his arms and kissing her soundly. "Thank you," he said, pulling away from the kiss and gazing down at her.

She returned his smile. "For what?"

"For listening. For understanding. I have carried the guilt of Christine's death for a long time."

"Just as you carried the guilt of Patrick's death?"

The warmth in his face died a little. She saw the struggle in his eyes and felt, via the link, his instinctive need to shut her out battling with the desire to finally acknowledge, and therefore release, some of the pain of his past.

He pulled her close again, wrapping his arms tightly around her, as if drawing strength from her closeness. Which was ridiculous. If any man was an island, it was this vampire.

"It was my desire to be a crusader—to save the world from monsters—that cost Patrick his life."

"You went after Jasper and his brother," Nikki said, remembering what he had told her back when they had first met.

"Yes. I killed his brother, but Jasper escaped—and

took his revenge by taking *my* brother in turn." Michael's face twisted with grief. "It's one of the reasons I vowed never to care about anyone again, so they couldn't be used against me like that. And I never did—until you."

The quiet words made Nikki's heart sing despite the obvious pain he still felt at Patrick's loss. She stroked his cheek, saying, "Even if you'd never gone after Jasper, you don't know that Patrick wouldn't have met the same death. One thing I learned from my years on the streets was the fact that fate cannot often be sidestepped."

"I know that. Accepting it is a different matter, however."

"You do good work, Michael."

"And yet it still costs the ones I love deeply. It's why . . ." His brow furrowed as his voice trailed off.

Nikki knew what he was thinking, even if he did not consciously recall it himself. *It's why you never wanted me involved in your life like this. Involved with the Circle.* But she was not about to admit that to him, even now. Because she was a part of this, whether he wanted it or not.

He turned back around and she continued scrubbing his back. The black lines were fading, but the buzz of energy was just as strong, and the welts rippled across his skin in a red wave.

"So," she said, suspecting she'd better keep him talking, keep him distracted from the magic. "How are we going to kill Kinnard—or Weylin Dunleavy—when he can protect himself with magic?"

"I don't know. Magic is not my field of expertise." His gaze met hers in the mirror. "And as much as I want you to leave, this is one case where I think I need help."

"Well, you've got mine, whether you want it or not. Even if Dunleavy wasn't threatening to kill everyone here, I wouldn't leave you here to fight him alone."

His amusement ran through the link. *I seem to remember hearing words to that effect before.*

Once or twice, she replied with a grin. Aloud, she added, "Dunleavy warned us against destroying any more pentagrams. What if he just meant the ones he's using to feed the circle protecting this town? What if we destroyed the one he intends to use for the sacrifice?"

"Would it achieve anything?"

"Well, it might delay the ceremony a little." And even a few minutes could make a difference when it came to finding Dunleavy.

"He'll have it protected."

"Then we take the protection out, too."

Michael nodded. "And then we begin the hunt for Dunleavy himself."

It was a plan. Not much of a plan, but it was better than nothing.

He twisted around, grabbed the cloth from her hands and tossed it into the sink. "Let's get moving."

She didn't argue, just turned around and walked into the bedroom to grab her coat. The day was rapidly cooling, and it would probably be cold as a freezer tonight. She had no idea what it would be like in the mines, but she was bundling up, just in case. She checked on their hostage, happy to see he was breathing easier, then walked into the main room.

Michael was at the sink, washing the blood from her knife. He flipped it and handed it to her hilt first.

"The pentagram he'll be using in the ceremony will no doubt be protected by a larger circle of stones than the ones he has around his sacrificial pentagrams," she said, slipping the knife back into its sheath. "I doubt whether my knives will be strong enough to move any really large rocks."

He nodded and bent, searching through the cupboards underneath the sink. Whatever he was looking for, he obviously didn't find it. "You do realize he can perform the ceremony without the benefit of a pentagram. All it really does is protect him and his victim from unwanted attacks."

"But he's trying to raise his brother's spirit. Without the pentagram, he risks bringing something far worse into being."

"There *is* nothing worse than Emmett Dunleavy," Michael said grimly. "Are you ready?"

She wanted to say no, if only because she had no desire to scramble around mine shafts again. But she didn't have any choice, so she nodded and headed for the door.

The day had definitely gotten colder. The thick gray clouds crowding the sky were now accompanied by a fierce wind that held the bite of winter. She shivered and hastily buttoned her coat.

He pressed a hand into her back, guiding her toward the mine entrance near the other ranger's house, but they'd barely taken three steps when a scream ripped through the air.

Nikki stopped, her heart in her mouth and a chill racing across her skin as she stared toward the town.

It had been a sound of sheer terror, and one she'd heard before—yesterday, when the mutilated body had been discovered in the whorehouse.

She swallowed, though it didn't ease the sudden dryness in her throat, and glanced up at Michael. His expression was grim, but he didn't say anything, just grabbed her hand and pulled her into a run.

The screaming went on and on. But as they entered Main Street, it stopped. In many ways, the ensuing silence was far worse.

Michael glanced at her. "It's the Hollis Hotel."

It would be. That was where the women who'd been living in the whorehouse had been sent. They climbed the steps and walked through the double, half-glass doors. The interior of the hotel was small, dark and smoky. Men sat in the shadows, visible only through the sudden glow coming from the tips of their cigars. Others leaned against the small bar, nursing drinks that looked as unsavory as the men themselves. The air was thick with the scent of unwashed flesh, beer and urine. None of the men seemed inclined to investigate the screams, nor did they seem to think the sudden silence or Michael and Nikki's entrance worthy of notice.

Michael pulled her past the bar. Her gaze collided with the barman's as he dried a glass with a tea towel as grubby as the floor, and she noted the curious blankness in his eyes. On one level his mind was obviously working—he was cleaning the glass, pouring beers when they were needed—but she doubted he'd be capable of anything more than that. Dunleavy hadn't allowed it.

They climbed a rickety set of stairs. At the end of

the short hall sat a woman. She was hugging her knees close to her chest and resting her face on her knees, her dark hair spilling like a curtain around her exposed legs. Though she was no longer screaming, her whole body shook. Shock, or fear, or a combination of both.

"Get a blanket," Michael said, releasing her hand.

Nikki opened the nearest door, but the room wasn't empty. A man and a woman were on the bed, having sex. Nikki averted her gaze, grabbed one of the blankets that had been thrown onto the floor and hastily exited. If the squeak of the bedsprings was anything to go by, the man didn't even miss a beat.

Michael was kneeling beside the distressed woman. Nikki joined him and eased the blanket around the woman's trembling body. She didn't react. Didn't speak.

"Traumatized." He glanced up at Nikki, his expression neutral. Only his voice hinted at the fury she could feel inside him as he added, "She walked into the middle of it."

"It's amazing she's still alive."

"Not really." His fingers went to the woman's neck, catching the silver chain and pulling it around to the side, revealing a large silver cross. "Dunleavy had already been weakened by silver, so he probably wouldn't have wanted to risk getting so close to it just yet."

"Which reminds me." She dug into her pocket and pulled out the small chain and cross she'd given him long ago. "You'd better put this back on."

He opened his hand, and she placed the cross into his palm. His skin didn't react to it—he'd been wearing the cross for some time now and had developed a certain amount of immunity because of it. He put it on, then caught her hand and kissed her fingers. "I thought it had been lost when Dunleavy snatched me."

"You're remembering?"

"Bits and pieces." His gaze went back to the woman, and his eyes narrowed slightly. Energy caressed the link. Obviously, her latest attack on the runes had finally yielded some decent results.

"Dunleavy was in slug form when she walked in. There were two others in the room—one a man, unmoving and frozen, and the other a woman. Dunleavy was suckling the soles of the woman's feet while part of him used her sexually and the rest held her down, then tore her apart."

Nikki closed her eyes, but it didn't stop the horror that crawled through her mind. Her stomach churned, and bile rose. She swallowed, thrusting away the violent images and fighting to remain calm.

Even so, her hands were shaking as she knelt beside him. The woman didn't even react when Michael's fingers moved from her neck to her forehead. "Dunleavy made her stand there and watch as he finished his bloody task," he said softly. "Then he made her watch as he shifted to his true form and drank every drop of life from the man."

"Why do that, then let her go?"

"Dunleavy feeds on emotion as much as blood. Forcing her to watch him tear apart the woman, then drain the man, gave him a triple hit of fear."

"So why let her go?"

"He was probably too bloated to kill her. Besides, as I said, there was the silver."

She very much suspected Dunleavy had left this woman alive because he had other plans for her. "Can you help her? Or at least block her memories?"

He blew out a breath. "I don't know. Dunleavy's control runs deep, and my telepathy is just coming back."

He raised his other hand. Touching the fingers of both hands to either side of the woman's temples, he closed his eyes. Silence fell, broken only by the woman's rapid, gasping breath. But the link was far from quiet. It burned with power. Burned with the force of his words as he battled to gain mastery over the woman's mind.

After a while, he dropped his hands. "I've done what I can. I cannot erase the lock Dunleavy's magic has on her self-perception, so she will continue to see herself as a whore for the moment. But I've erased her immediate memories."

"What did you replace them with?"

As if in answer, the woman looked up. Her face was tear-streaked, eyes huge and fear-filled. But her body no longer shook with such intensity, and the sense of deep shock was already retreating from the blue of her eyes.

"Did you get that goddamn snake?"

"Yes," Michael said softly. "We did. But I'm afraid you won't be able to use the room again for a while. We created a bit of a mess."

She shuddered. "Don't you be worrying about that—I ain't ever going back into that room. That thing was a monster, and there might be more living in the walls."

In the walls, in the ceiling and in the floor, Nikki

thought, sharing a glance with Michael. Dunleavy had access to them all, thanks to his slug shape. How the hell were they ever going to track him down?

Michael rose, caught the woman's hand and helped her rise. "You should go downstairs and get yourself a drink." He pressed some cash into her hand, and power caressed the link again. "Take the night off, and take a long bath. I think you deserve some pampering."

"You know," she said, her fingers clenching around the cash, "I think you're right."

She pushed past them and walked unsteadily down the hall. Michael's gaze met Nikki's. "She's from Arizona. A preacher's daughter."

"Shit."

"I can think of several stronger words that would be more appropriate," he muttered, and something dark and dangerous glittered in his eyes. "But it's really no surprise. Emmett always had a penchant for corrupting the virtuous. Looks like his brother is much the same."

Her gaze went past him, settling on the door. "Do we need to go in there?"

"No. Dunleavy is long gone, and we've already seen the destruction his feeding frenzy produces."

She let out a relieved breath. A smile tugged his lips and he caught her arm, pulling her into his embrace. For a moment he did nothing more than hold her, and she was more than glad to simply stand there, allowing the warmth and strength of his touch chase the chills from her flesh.

After a short while, he kissed her forehead. Then he

slid his hand down her back and guided her down the hall.

The stairs creaked with each step, a sound eerily loud in the strange hush that filled the bar. The barkeep still polished his glass, and the woman they'd met upstairs was leaning over the bar, grabbing the key tagged "bathroom."

But everyone else was gone.

Nikki stopped on the bottom step and said, "This can't be good."

"No." His hands touched her shoulders, gently propelling her to one side. He walked past her to the bar. "Where did everyone go?"

The barkeep shrugged disinterestedly.

"When did they leave?"

Again a disinterested shrug. Energy caressed the air, and Michael glanced at her. "They left the minute we'd disappeared up the stairs."

"Meaning Dunleavy was somewhere close?"

"If he was, I couldn't see him."

"But if he was underground, you wouldn't, would you?"

"No." He pushed away from the bar and walked across to the doors, carefully looking right, then left. "No sign of anyone in the immediate vicinity."

"There had to be at least ten men in this room," she said, walking across the room and stopping beside him. The street was empty, except for the odd tumbleweed being blown along by the wind. "Ten men can't walk out of this place and then completely disappear."

"In this town, they might be able to. Remember, the ground is probably riddled with mine shafts."

"Yeah, but not all of them would be usable. And surely the rangers would have closed all the ones around the town. This place is a tourist attraction, remember, and they wouldn't want to risk lawsuits by having someone fall down an unused shaft."

"I doubt even the rangers would know the location of all the shafts. Hartwood had hundreds of operable mines in its heyday, and many of them were one-man operations that didn't consider themselves accountable to anyone when it came to permits and plans."

"So where does that leave us?"

"Well, there's one thing in our favor—ten men are going to throw off a mass of body heat that I can track. We'll check the town, and if they aren't here, they have to be in the mines. Wait here."

He opened the door and walked out, his gaze scanning the area before he looked over his shoulder. "It's safe."

She joined him as he walked down the steps. "You think Dunleavy plans to sacrifice them all? One big bang before the ceremony that brings his brother back to life?"

His expression was grim when it met hers. "No, I think he's planning an attack. He wants to kill me and capture you."

That was just what she needed to hear. "Dunleavy would surely know that ten humans wouldn't be much of a match for the two of us. I mean, those men aren't going to fight like they really mean it."

"We can't say that for sure. And he has at least one more shifter at his beck and call."

When they reached the cross street he hesitated, looking right and left, then tugged her left, heading down Green Street toward Fuller. "It does mean, however, that if we want to try to destroy that pentagram, we'd better do it before he realizes what we're up to."

"But that's only giving him time to plot his attack. Shouldn't we be trying to find those men and somehow short-circuit his hold on them?"

"Unless my psi abilities kick into full gear, I don't have the strength to counter his magic. As for tracking down the men, that could be exactly what he wants us to do."

"I very much suspect we'll be playing into his hands no matter what we do," she muttered, looking up as a bell chimed. Ahead, an old wooden church stood on the street corner. Though much of the redwood had faded with age, the building itself was in remarkable condition, especially considering the rundown condition of the surrounding buildings. The bell chimed again and she glanced up. The wind was hitting the bell tower with some force, and the old bell was swaying back and forth as if it were being rung by some invisible hand. "That church almost looks as if it could still be in use."

He shrugged. "Maybe the rangers have someone come in to do services."

She chewed on her lip for a moment, studying the old building and wondering if the bell ringing was just a coincidence, Dunleavy playing tricks, or a hint from forces beyond the grave. Forces she'd never actually believed in until Michael came along and altered her perception about what was and wasn't real. "Have you been inside?"

"I had no reason to be. Why?"

"Well, if it's being used, there might be something useful inside. Like a cross or holy water."

"The only cross that would be of any use would be one made of silver, and I doubt they'd risk possessing such a valuable item."

"But we might find holy water. And if we sprinkled the water around the outside of the pentagram, wouldn't it stop Dunleavy from entering the circle?"

"It'll probably have the same effect as silver—burn him, but not stop him."

"But that's better than nothing, isn't it?"

"I suppose it is."

He tugged her toward the old church. They climbed the steps and discovered the entrance had thick wire mesh padlocked across it.

"It looks like the place is not in use after all," Nikki said, disappointed.

"Except that I have a feeling we were brought here for a reason. Stand back," Michael ordered.

Nikki obeyed. He gripped one side of the mesh, yanking back on it hard. His muscles rippled under his jacket as the locks gave way and the wire pulled free from the wall. He pushed the wire out of the way, opened the door and went inside.

Sunlight glittered through the stained-glass windows, sending sprays of red and gold across the harsh white walls and washing warm rays of sunshine through the gloom. Dust motes danced in the light, but she wasn't sure if it was an indication that someone had recently walked through here or merely an aftereffect of the wind whistling past her ankles. The faded polish on the floorboards wasn't dusty enough to hold footprints and offered her no clues.

She stepped inside. Pews were stacked up against the walls, and down at the far end stood a raised dais and table. To one side of that was a door. The air was cold—colder than it was outside—but the faint smell of lavender teased her nostrils. She walked toward the dais, her footsteps echoing loudly. She half expected a priest to come running out, telling her to hush. The church had that sort of feel—like it was occupied and waiting. Yet the thickness of the dust suggested the opposite was true.

"Nikki . . ."

The edge in his voice made her glance over her shoulder. "What?"

He'd taken only a few steps into the church, though she knew the old legend about vampires being unable to cross holy ground was untrue. "There's something here."

She stopped, her heart leaping to the vicinity of her throat. "What?"

"I don't know. It just feels . . . wrong."

Usually, *she* was the one getting those feelings. "How wrong?"

"Evil."

"Odd that you're feeling it rather than me." Though it *did* still feel like something was waiting.

She rubbed her arms and studied the small door to the right of the dais. Whatever the sensation was— whether it was good, evil or something else entirely— it was coming from that direction. "There's no one in that room?" she asked, nodding toward the door.

He shook his head and fully entered the church, his steps echoing as harshly as hers. The air seemed to become colder. Tenser.

"But *something* is near."

He caught her hand and she held on tight, drawing strength from his warmth, his calm. Together, they moved forward.

"It's the door," she said as they drew close. "It's coming from the door."

He nodded. "We've faced something like this before."

"We have?" She stared at the knob and saw the slight shimmer. Then she remembered. "Not a devil spawn?"

"I'm afraid so."

"Why would he risk calling forth a wraith as dangerous as that to protect a door in an old church?"

"I suspect we'll have the answer to that once we get the door open." He released her hand and squatted in front of the door, studying the knob. "The magic binding the spawn isn't recent. It's been here for quite a while."

"How can you tell something like that?"

Amusement played around his lips as he glanced up. "I've been hanging around old witches for more years than I care to remember. You pick up on these things." He rose and headed for the stack of pews sitting in the corner. "I'm afraid there's only one way to spring the trap."

"Is there only one devil spawn bound to that door?"

"Probably."

"So where's the other one?" Devil spawn always came in pairs.

"Who knows? It could be in the room beyond this door. It could be protecting Dunleavy, or it could be anywhere." He grabbed the top pew and hauled it down.

"That's a cheery thought," she muttered, stepping away from the door.

With a grunt of effort, Michael hefted the big wooden pew and tossed it at the door. It hit with a crash that was almost deafening. The door buckled and splintered under the force of the impact. As the pew fell, the wood hit the handle. For a second, nothing happened. Then a scream bit across the silence—a wail so high-pitched it was almost inaudible. Goose bumps fled across her flesh and she rubbed her arms, stepping back again. She knew what was coming, and she didn't want to be anywhere near the pew when it arrived.

Steam began to pour from the metal, steam that glittered like diamonds in the thin strands of sunlight streaming in from the nearby window. It boiled, convulsed and somehow found form. It became a ghostly creature with rows of wickedly sharp teeth and soulless eyes.

Her mouth went dry. She'd gotten too close to one of these things in Jackson Hole and still bore the scars on her calf.

The creature screamed again. There was a sharp retort, a bright flash, and then the devil spawn—and the pew—were gone. Dunleavy had obviously ordered the creature to destroy whatever touched the handle—which was exceedingly lucky for them. Water was the only thing that could stop or deter the spawn, and there wasn't much of that to be found in the church.

"One down, one to go," she muttered. "Do you think the spell will reset itself?"

"Spawn are usually only set the one task. They aren't the brightest of creatures." He looked at her. "You can't sense anything else in the room beyond this door?"

She shook her head. "But that doesn't mean anything. I didn't sense the first spawn until we got closer to it, either."

"True."

He pressed his fingers against the remains of the door and pushed it open. She watched, her heart in mouth. Nothing happened. The small room beyond was empty except for dust.

He stepped inside and she followed, crowding close to his back and peering over his shoulder. "Nothing's here."

"Something *is* here," he countered.

"What?"

"I don't know." His voice held an edge of frustration. "The runes on my back are interfering."

She grunted and moved past him. Under normal circumstances, she'd be the one feeling the evil. But the circle around this town had snatched that ability away, along with her kinetic skills. While some of those skills somehow seemed to have leached to Michael, surely she'd feel it too if she got close enough to whatever was hiding in this room. After all, she'd sensed who—or what—was with her in the Circle's test room. And according to Camille, that shouldn't have been possible.

She reached out, skimming her fingers in front of her, scanning, but not actually touching, the walls. On the third wall, energy caressed her fingers.

"Here," she said, leaning closer. "There's something here."

The wall was badly plastered, the paint cracked and peeling and covered in dust. It looked solid. Only the slight shimmer in the air—a shimmer that was similar to and yet different from the sort of energy that the devil spawn gave off—revealed the fact that something other than dust was present.

Michael's shoulder brushed hers as he leaned in. "I can't see anything."

"Maybe that's because the magic is telling you not to."

"Possibly." He straightened. "I'll fetch another pew and we'll see what happens."

She stepped back. "I doubt it's another spawn. It doesn't feel the same."

"It could be some other type of wraith. Or demon. Dunleavy's a sorcerer, so he has a supermarket of evil to choose from."

"Now there's a comforting thought."

He came back in carrying a two-seat pew. "Stand back."

She did. He lifted the pew and tossed it end first at the wall. There was a mighty *crack* that sounded like half the wall had shattered under the impact. The shimmer in the air grew brighter, and the pew kept on going, disappearing right through the wall.

"What the hell . . . ?" She scooted over. The wall looked solid, unmarked. So where did the pew go? "What happened?"

"Either the magic consumed it or the magic is hiding something. Like another door. Try one of your knives."

She flicked the damaged blade down into her palm and cautiously eased it into the shimmer. Wisps of lightning crawled away from the knife, revealing what lay underneath. Another door—or the pieces of one. The pew had split the old door in half, and both sections were flopping limply toward the deeper darkness haunting the space beyond.

She met Michael's gaze. "Why would Dunleavy be hiding this door?"

"I suspect we'll find the answer by investigating what lies beyond." He raised a hand, tentatively touching the shimmery air. Flickers of light crawled away from his flesh. "It's a concealing spell, nothing more."

"The front door was padlocked, and no one's been in here for ages." She hesitated, remembering the dust dancing through the sunlight.

"Dunleavy could easily have gotten the key," Michael replied, obviously following her thoughts. "He has control of the rangers, remember. And since he had a devil spawn protecting the door to *this* room, there has to be something worth guarding down there."

"So we're going in?"

"We are. But me first."

She grinned. "I must be psychic. I just *knew* you were going to say that."

He chuckled softly, brushed a kiss across her lips, then stepped through the shimmery air. "There are steps," he said after a moment. "Only two or three of them, by the look of it."

She stepped through the shimmer. Energy crawled across her skin, stinging like ants before fading away. The darkness enveloping the room beyond gave way as her vampire-like night sight kicked in. There were shapes in the darkness below them, but she couldn't quite make out what they were. "Looks as if there's a bit of a drop to the ground."

"Maybe." He shifted, putting one foot on the first step, testing it before he put his full weight on it. He did the same with the second one. "They seem fairly secure."

He stepped onto the next one, but it was one step too many. With a splintering crack, the old wooden step gave way, and he dropped like a stone into the darkness.

Thirteen

MICHAEL HIT THE ground with enough force to jar just about every bone in his body. For a moment, he lay on his back and listened to the silence.

Other than the odd scuttling beetle, there didn't seem to be anything down here with him.

"Michael?" Nikki appeared above him, her body backlit by the sunlight in the room behind her, making her blond hair appear a more natural brown.

He blinked. *Nikki?*

Emotion flooded the link, wrapping him so tightly in joy and love that for a moment he couldn't even breathe. Not that he actually needed to.

You remembered!

Finally. He grimaced. *I'm sorry it took me so long.*

Better late than never. Are you hurt?

No. But I'm getting rather tired of falling through floors. Even if it *was* more than likely the reason he'd finally remembered. He pushed to his feet and looked around. The room was small and square, the walls bare rock. Old wooden shelves lined the wall near what remained of the stairs. They were filled with an assortment of old cans, bottles and other whatnots.

On the opposite side of the room, what looked like

another storage area had been carved into the rock itself, and this contained a long wooden box. Unlike the shelving, the box looked new.

He glanced up at Nikki. *It's not much of a jump. You want to come down or not?*

How will I get back up?

I'll boost you.

Then I'll come down.

She knelt on the second step and climbed over the edge, hanging by her fingertips for several seconds before she let go. He steadied her as she hit the ground, keeping her upright. She threw her arms around his neck and kissed him soundly. It was a kiss he was more than ready to return.

Welcome back, she thought when they finally parted.

He smiled. *I'm not sure all my memories have returned, but at least now I can call you something more than "woman" or "witch."*

Thank God. Though . . . don't say my name aloud, she reminded him. It might not matter, but she didn't want to take the chance. She turned around, scanning the room in the same careful manner he had. *What's that?* She pointed toward the box. Flames leapt across her fingers as she did so, throwing warm light across the darkness.

I don't know yet. It seems to be lined inside, because I can't see past the wood.

He walked over to the alcove. The box was about six feet long, made of rough-hewn planks, and was hinged and locked at the top.

You know, she said, a touch of uncertainty running through her mind-voice, *that looks an awful lot like a coffin.*

The graveyard is on the outskirts of town. They wouldn't be burying the dead in the church cellar. Yet he had to agree with her—it did look like a coffin.

He hovered his fingers over the old padlock and felt energy run across his fingertips. Some kind of magic protected whatever was inside the box. Likely the second devil spawn.

Stand back, he warned. *Just in case.*

He grabbed a bottle from a nearby shelf—empty, from the sound of it—and smashed it across the padlock, but nothing happened. Maybe the spell was on the coffin rather than the lock itself.

"It's too easy a trap to spring if you know where it is," said Nikki. "Weylin must be using it differently."

She was likely right. "Then be on your guard," Michael counseled. Devil spawn or not, there was still magic on that casket. He tightened his grip and pulled back as hard as he could, wrenching the lock away from the box.

No magic, she said, relief evident. In the heat of her flames, her eyes appeared to glow a rich, warm gold.

There's still magic inside. He undid the clasp and carefully lifted the lid. He wasn't sure what he expected to find, but it really wasn't a body.

Ohmigod, she said, peering past him. *It's Weylin.*

Emmett, not Weylin, he said grimly, recognizing the small differences. The fatter cheeks, the scar near the eye, not to mention the fact that his extremities weren't actually connected to his body. The sour, almost petulant, look to the mouth was exactly the same, however.

Her eyes widened. *But Emmett's been dead for*

close to a hundred years! He can't possibly be this well preserved.

He can, and is, with the aid of magic. He skimmed his hand across the top of the box. Power crawled across his skin, stinging like bees.

But— She hesitated, the horror in her amber eyes stronger. *Why?*

The soul needs a proper house. In this case, its original body.

She swallowed convulsively. *How could Weylin have maintained the spell for all these years?*

It would have taken regular sacrifices. He glanced at the floor. In the light of the fire dancing across her fingers, it appeared to be nothing more than dirt, but when he switched to vampire vision, the stains of old blood leapt to life.

There was no sign of a pentagram, but then, it would be easy enough to draw one in the dirt. And maybe he didn't need one. The old legends about vampires not being able to enter holy ground had some basis in truth—because some evil *couldn't* enter. The devil spawn was here only because it had been summoned by someone within the confines of the church. For the most part, evil tended to avoid churches.

Are you sure Weylin intends to use the sacrificial site in the Standard Mine to perform his ceremony later tonight?

She hesitated. *That's where Emmett died. Seline therefore believes that's where he must be brought back to life, but honestly? I'm not so sure. She did say she'd have to be in Hartwood to be certain, and she couldn't risk that.* Her gaze rested on his. *Why?*

Because he's been doing sacrifices here for many

years. I was just wondering if he'd risk moving his brother's bod—

He cut the words off as an odd sort of hissing filled the silence. His gut clenched, and he knew without looking what that hissing would be. Grabbing Nikki's arm, he ignored the flame that jumped from her flesh to his; it didn't burn. Instead, he yanked her behind him as he slowly turned around.

Yellow-tinged smoke billowed into existence in the corner of the small room, curling through the darkness with unnatural heaviness.

The second devil spawn, as she'd predicted.

He pressed his hand against Nikki's stomach, keeping her behind him but forcing her backward.

What do we do?

Her fear crowded his mind, becoming his own. Though in his case, it was fear more for her than himself. *Get out.*

It'll come after us the minute we make any sudden movement, and we don't have anything to protect ourselves here.

Nothing stops a spawn. Not until it finds something to consume.

Water can repel it, and water can also contain it.

Her voice was so matter-of-fact he glanced over his shoulder at her. *How do you know?*

She grimaced. *Um . . . I didn't tell you about my encounter with the second spawn in Jackson Hole, did I?*

No. Though it does explain the burn scars on your calf. The ones you kept waving away as not being important.

Hey, I obviously lived, so it didn't matter. There

was a slight thud as her back hit the shelf, and tin rattled. *Is there anything big enough on these shelves to satisfy the hunger of the spawn?*

The spawn was finding shape, gathering substance. They didn't have much time left to decide what to do. *On the shelves, no. But the pew I threw at the door is lying to our right. That might do the trick.*

That thing is going to attack the minute you move.

It certainly was. Right now, it was simply hanging there, a twisting, boiling mass of smoky evil waiting for something to happen. *I don't suppose there's any water on that shelf?*

There are bottles. Could be booze, though.

In a church?

Hey, they do use wine in ceremonies, don't they? Just check.

The shelf rattled, and the spawn's mass became agitated.

You might want to go a little faster.

If I go any faster that thing will attack.

Her tension and fear simmered through the link, sharper than before. Glass clinked, and the spawn zipped sideways, as if trying to see where the sound was coming from. In the warm light still leaping from Nikki's hands, its eyes gleamed like soulless diamonds.

Got something. She hesitated, then sniffed and added, *It's water. I think.*

Okay, the minute I move, you spray that water across the room. Hopefully, it'll deter the spawn long enough for me to grab the pew. He paused. *Ready?*

No. Her spirit reached out to his, wrapping him in heat and love. *Now I'm ready. Let's do it.*

Okay. He took a deep breath, then said, *Go!*

He dove for the pew. The spawn screamed and zipped toward him, its vaporous tendrils reaching out, ready to smother and consume him.

Michael hit the ground, sliding through the dirt as he grabbed the pew. The spawn screamed again, teeth gleaming as it tried to wrap vaporous arms around him. Water slewed through the air, glittering brightly in Nikki's flames. The droplets lashed across the spawn's mass, and it hissed, backing away. Michael lifted the pew and threw it toward the coffin. The spawn howled in fury and lurched forward, touching the pew. There was a retort, a bright flash, then the pew and the spawn were gone. Michael blew out a relieved breath and climbed to his feet.

Why did you throw the pew at the coffin rather than the spawn? Nikki twined her fingers through his and squeezed lightly.

Because I figured the spawn might have been programmed to protect the coffin from any real damage, whereas the first spawn had been set to attack anyone who touched the handle.

Anyone but Dunleavy.

He nodded. *By throwing a heavy pew at the coffin, I made the spawn attack the pew rather than us.*

But why would Dunleavy have a spawn here when he's protecting the coffin with magic?

Extra insurance. He squeezed her fingers, then released her. *We'd better get out of here.*

She raised an eyebrow. *We're not going to try to destroy the coffin?*

I doubt that we can. I don't know enough about magic, and I'm sure the magic protecting Emmett is pretty powerful.

He cupped his hands, and she stepped into them. He boosted her up, ensuring she'd climbed safely onto the second step before following her.

"Where next?" she asked, dusting her hands on her skirt. "The Standard Mine?"

"Yeah. I don't think we have any other choice." It was either that or sit back and wait for Weylin to come to them, and he'd never been one to do that.

"Neither have I," she said, responding to his thought. A smile teased her lips. "Which is why I'm always so surprised at your reaction when I act rather than wait as ordered."

"That's because you tend to rush in where angels dare not tread." He caught her arm and pulled her into his embrace, kissing her quickly. "Or vampires, as the case may be."

He slid his grip down to her hand and again twined his fingers through hers. "Let's go."

They walked into the church's main room. He scanned the outside of the building as they headed for the door, using his vampire vision so that he could detect blood heat. No one waited for them. However, tension crawled through his limbs, and he had a peculiar feeling that the men from the bar would soon be making an unwelcome appearance.

"It's odd, you know," Nikki commented as he released her hand to put the wire mesh back in place.

"What's odd?" He couldn't do much about the lock, as he'd broken it when he'd snapped it free. But he hooked it onto the latch. From a distance it would look as if the mesh and the lock had been undisturbed.

"These feelings you're getting. It's almost as if you're somehow siphoning my abilities."

He glanced at her. "Could be. After all, you're siphoning mine."

She gave him a skeptical look. "Am not."

"Then how do you explain the fact you've developed perfect night sight?"

"But—" She hesitated. "I don't see blood rushing through bodies or anything like that."

"No. But from what you said, your vision is somewhat similar." He led the way down the steps and into the main street. It was eerily quiet. *Too* quiet. Even the blustery wind made little sound as it blew around the old buildings.

"So how is something like that possible?"

"I'm told it's because of the bond we share." He hesitated and decided to finish the sentence through the link, simply because he couldn't shake the sensation that they were being watched. *Seline thinks that because I shared my life force out of love rather than need, the bonding between us became far deeper than normal. It made us one.*

Her frown deepened. *But you have talents I'm not developing. And vice versa.*

True. But we haven't been together all that long. It could take years for the assimilation to be fully complete.

And years before we know which talents we can share, and which we can't?

He nodded. Right now, he was wishing that they could share *all* their talents. He had a feeling it would come in handy when they were finally battling Dunleavy.

They turned the corner and headed up the hill toward the old mine. The wind was colder here, fiercer. Yet, through it, he could hear a heartbeat. Many heartbeats, in fact.

The men were waiting up ahead.

He scanned the horizon, but he couldn't see anything, which meant they were probably underground. Maybe they were waiting near the pentagram. Maybe Dunleavy did expect them to do precisely what they were doing.

He stopped. "I think we should try getting to the Standard Mine pentagram through the shaft near the ranger's house."

Her gaze searched his. "You sense something?"

"Those men are waiting up ahead."

Her gaze jumped to the top of the hill, then back to his. "Where?"

"I don't know. I can hear the beat of their hearts, but I can't see them with vampire sight. If we're in that smaller shaft, we're at least coming from a direction they might not be expecting. Plus, there's less room for them to come at us."

She nodded, and he changed direction, heading back down the street and across to the house. The wind had blown off a lot of the dirt covering the mine shaft's hatch, making it hard to tell whether the shaft had been used recently or not.

He flung back the door and peered inside. No sound. Nothing to indicate anyone or anything waited inside the dank blackness. He met Nikki's gaze.

"When I give you the all clear, come down."

She nodded and crossed her arms, her determined stance at odds with the fear lurking in her eyes. That determination was part of the reason he'd fallen in love with her. Part of the reason he would always love her.

She'd become part of the Circle simply because she was determined to share his life—determined to share everything, good *and* bad.

And for the briefest of moments, he wished he could simply give it all up, just walk away and enjoy an eternity of being with her, loving her. But he couldn't. He'd vowed, after first killing Emmett, that he would hunt and kill the evil that preyed on good. That vow was the reason he'd made Seline's half-formed desire for a paranormal army to battle evil into a reality.

A reality he'd almost abandoned when the newly formed Circle had sent him against Jasper and his brother, and had cost him Patrick in turn. He had managed to kill only Jasper's brother that day, and Jasper had taken his revenge in the most hurtful way, depriving him of his own brother, with whom he had only recently been reunited. Yet he was glad now that he hadn't abandoned those vows. There had been casualties, true . . . but he had done a lot of good over the years. And, besides, the Circle had brought him to Nikki. How could he possibly regret that?

Yes, evil would always be around. But if he had any say in the matter, the Circle would always be there to battle it. It was the reason why he was still financing the Circle to this day.

And though he now had more to lose than ever, he finally had something more than a vow to fight for. To live for.

He leaned forward, briefly, fiercely kissed the love of his life, and then dropped into the hole.

Nikki shifted her position so she could see him a little more clearly. Power surged through the link, and after a moment or two, Michael looked up. His eyes were as forbidding as the black shadows crowding the edges of the puddle of afternoon sunlight in which he stood.

"Come down."

She bit her lip, but she eased over the edge and into the tunnel. He helped her down, then twined his fingers through hers and led the way forward. The darkness leapt into focus as her eyes adjusted, but she felt no easier now than she had before. It still felt like there was a ton of earth above her, just waiting for the chance to bury her again.

She shivered and pushed the memories away. That wasn't going to happen here, simply because this time, the madman they were chasing needed her alive.

They reached the cross-tunnel again. Water flowed past their feet, trickling down the right-hand tunnel for several feet before sweeping sideways.

"Obviously there's another tunnel down there," she commented.

He nodded, his expression remote as he listened to the silence.

"You hear anything?"

"Yes." He glanced at her. "The heartbeats are stronger. They're moving toward us."

"Dunleavy must know we're trying to destroy that pentagram."

"Maybe." He lightly squeezed her fingers. "I'll try to find a way around them."

While she hoped that was possible, she suspected they'd have no choice but to confront the oncoming henchmen. Dunleavy had planned his revenge well, and it was doubtful they'd be able to slip past his net this late in the game.

Which meant the final confrontation would occur during the ceremony tonight.

Goose bumps trembled across her skin. She could only hope that Seline had been right in her assumption that the ceremony couldn't be completed simply because she *wasn't* Seline. Because if she and Michael failed, that was the only thing stopping Emmett's evil from being unleashed on the world yet again.

We won't fail, Michael commented, his mind-voice calm and almost soothing. *I have every intention of getting you to that altar and officially making you mine.*

And here I was thinking you'd forgotten that little detail.

Amusement bubbled through the link, wrapping warmth around her heart. *Forget our wedding? Never! Though maybe you're having second thoughts about marrying such an old man . . .*

As long as that old man keeps loving me as well as he did today, I'll have no complaints.

Then I shall endeavor to—

His words cut off suddenly, and he stopped. She followed suit, listening to silence, hearing nothing but the steady gurgle of water. The air was thick and cold and moved easily past her cheek, indicating there was an outside entrance somewhere up ahead.

What? she asked eventually.

The heartbeats have ceased.

Her stomach began to churn. *Oh God . . . He's killed them?*

I don't know. I certainly can't smell blood, and if he's killed them, I would.

Could they have moved back up top? The air is moving, and it wasn't before.

Maybe. He tugged her forward again. *I've a feeling we'd better get to that pentagram while we can. Dunleavy is weaving his net around us.*

It's been around us the whole time.

Yes, but now it's growing tighter.

They hurried through the darkness. Though Michael made little noise, her steps echoed, the sound slapping off the wet walls loudly enough to make her wince. One thing the Circle hadn't taught her was how to run without noise. Maybe she'd suggest that lesson when—or if—they got out of here.

They reached another junction. Michael barely hesitated before pulling her right. She had no idea where they were in relation to the mine or the town, having lost all sense of direction about twenty steps in.

They'd barely gone three steps when noise scuffed across the silence. She glanced over her shoulder. *Michael . . .*

I know.

But—

I know. His mind-voice was terse. *They've been there for a few minutes now.*

So why didn't you mention it?

I didn't want to worry you.

I thought you were going to stop doing that.

I said I'd try. I didn't say I'd stop completely.

Now, that was definitely the vampire she knew and loved. *So when were you going to tell me we were being tailed? A heartbeat before they attacked?*

Give me a little more credit than that.

Okay. Two heartbeats, then.

Amusement shimmered down the link. *That's more like it.*

She shook her head. *So, is there anything else I should know?*

Have I mentioned there's something ahead?

No. Her thoughts were more acerbic than annoyed. *What?*

There's one heartbeat. I think it's the last shifter.

Can we go around him?

I'm trying, but he's shadowing us. Remember, they know these tunnels. I'm only following instinct.

He tugged her to the right again. The walls began to close in, and the rough-hewn support planking gave way to natural rock. The air became danker, thick with the scent of age and disuse. Ghostly tendrils of slime appeared, sprouting from the ceiling like a living thing and slapping wetly across her face. It felt like the fingers of the dead grasping for her.

A chill ran across her skin, and she edged a little closer to Michael's back. This tunnel was way too similar to the one that had almost claimed her life.

Stone rattled behind them, the noise echoing harshly. The men were closer than before, and fear scooted through her. While she really *did* believe ten men weren't a match for her and Michael, the situation they were in now was far from normal, and she was without the benefit of her basic abilities. Sure, she had her fire, but she didn't particularly want to kill any of those who followed them, and that would hamper her actions and perhaps make it more difficult to protect herself.

The tunnel twisted and turned, leading them deeper into the darkness. The walls closed in, brushing her shoulders and tearing at her shirt. She bit her lip and hoped like hell they weren't being herded into a dead end.

After a few minutes, the walls began to ease back, but she felt no sense of relief. Though she could hear little beyond the harsh note of her own breathing, she couldn't shake the sensation that the men were close enough to almost touch.

The link sprang to life, wrapping around her fear, gently easing it away. *They're not yet within reach.*

How far, then?

A few minutes.

And the shifter?

Paralleling us.

What about the pentagram? How far away are we from that? Though she asked the question, she very much doubted whether they'd get that far. This all reeked of a well-laid plan.

If my sense of direction isn't leading us astray, we shouldn't be that far from it.

Good.

The tendrils of slime began to recede as warmth touched the air. Not that it was actually *that* much warmer. She shivered again, this time more from the cold than fear.

The tunnel began to open up, eventually leading into another cavern. Her footsteps seemed to echo forever, lending the darkness a feeling of enormity. Michael paused, and the sensation of wrongness hit her so strongly it felt like a punch to the gut.

There's something here, she gasped.

Magic. His mind-voice was grim. *We'll have to watch where we step.*

It's on the floor?

To our right. I'm not sure what it is, beyond the fact that its source is evil. He squeezed her hand gently. *This ability I'm siphoning is far too new for me to properly assimilate. You can't sense anything more?*

Nothing beyond evil. But Dunleavy's spells have nulled my psi skills.

Then, by rights, they should have stopped my using them as well.

Not if he didn't know we could share. And considering *they* were only beginning to discover what was possible, it was hardly likely that Dunleavy could know. Even if he had read Michael's mind when he'd had him under full control, it wouldn't have mattered. Of course, that was presuming Dunleavy thought she was Seline. And there was a ton of evidence suggesting he didn't.

He tugged her forward again. The floor around them was littered with rocks and deeper, darker spaces that suggested holes.

Old mine shafts, Michael said. *It looks like the miners decided to dig deeper for treasure here.*

Right through the rock?

Rock wouldn't have stopped them if they were following a vein of gold.

It would have stopped *her.* But then, she'd never

have been a gold-digger in the first place. Riches of *any* kind had never called to her—except when it came to the richness of emotion. Something she'd been afraid to reach toward for more years than she'd cared to remember.

They were barely halfway across the cavern when he stopped. She was just about to ask what the problem was when she saw it. Or, rather, him.

The shifter who had been shadowing them stepped from the tunnel on the far side. In his hand was a wooden stake.

Fear leapt into her throat, and for a moment she couldn't even breathe. Then she raised her hand and called to the fire. It leapt to life, spewing from her fingers in a flaming ball that shot light across the cavern as it arced toward the shifter. He stumbled backward, eyes wide with fear that she could almost taste. But her flames were not meant for him. They hit the stake and wrapped around it quickly. With a squawk that was barely human, the shifter dropped it. It was little more than ash by the time it hit the ground.

She tugged Michael's hand. *We need to go.*

It's too late for that.

A scraping sound made her spin, and she realized what he'd meant. The ten men who'd been following them now crowded into the old tunnel opening. They were trapped, with no option but to fight.

Michael spun and kissed her briefly. *Take care of the shifter. I'll take the men.*

He was gone before she could argue, so she ran at the shifter. He smirked, and in that moment, she recognized him. He was the driver of the van.

His form shimmered, then re-formed, becoming that of a wolf that snarled and leapt for her. She flicked the knife into her palm and slashed at him as she dodged his leap. The blade scoured his side, and blue fire flickered. The wolf yelped as he hit the ground, then he twisted, leaping for her again.

She sidestepped him, slashing again with the knife. The sharp point tore past his coat and into flesh, deeper than before. He howled and twisted in midair, his sharp teeth slashing. His canines tore across the back of her hand, skidding up her arm. She cursed and backed away. His form shimmered as he hit the ground, becoming human once again.

"For this," he said, pointing to his bloody side, his voice gruff with anger and pain, "you die."

"I don't think Dunleavy will approve of that plan." And what the hell was it with shifters thinking she'd be easy meat?

"I don't give a fuck what Dunleavy wants. No bitch is going to wound me and live to tell about it."

The words were barely out of his mouth when he rushed for her. She dove out of his way, hitting the stone with a grunt and rolling back to her feet.

Air stirred. Too late, she saw the shifter's leg sweeping toward her. The force of the blow against the back of her legs sent her flying. Her butt hit the ground with enough force to jar her spine, and her breath was punched from her lungs, leaving her wheezing. The air stirred again, warning her. She rolled to one side and barely avoided the foot aimed at her head. She twisted around, lashing out with her legs and striking his legs, sweeping them out from beneath him in much the same manner as he had hers. She scrambled upright as he crashed to the ground, but the shifting haze crawled across his body again and, in wolf form, he launched at her.

She dodged and pivoted, smashing her booted heel into his side and kicking him into the rock walls. He hit with enough force to make him grunt. She gave him no time to recover, throwing the knife as hard and as fast as she could. This time, she didn't miss.

The shifter was dead before his body hit the floor.

One less murderous kidnapper for the world to deal with, she thought, retrieving her knife and ruthlessly battering away the remorse that ran through her. She hadn't meant to kill him, but he'd nevertheless deserved it. He wasn't one of the townspeople Dunleavy controlled, but a willing participant in his games. A clean death was probably more than he deserved.

She spun and ran to help Michael. There were only five of the original ten men left, but they were forcing him backward, away from the tunnel and toward the deeper darkness that stank of evil. And then she saw how five men were managing to do this. Three of them were armed with stakes.

"Hey you!"

One man turned at her yell. She launched herself at him, hitting him feet first in the gut and sending him flying backward. He hit the wall with a crack loud enough to suggest broken bones and slid to the ground. She scrambled upright, but he didn't move. Hoping she hadn't hurt him too badly, she spun and tackled the next nearest man.

This one was waiting, and his blow cracked across

her face, sending her sprawling backward. She half yelped in pain, and through the blur of tears, she saw him coming at her. She dropped and hooked his feet, making him stumble. Then she jumped upright, and before he could catch his balance, pushed him in the back. He hit the ground, sprawling on his stomach and sliding along the slick rock for several feet. She slipped her broken knife into her palm, flipped it so she was holding the blade, then stepped close to his sprawled form and hit him with the hilt as hard as she could. He didn't move. She checked his pulse, then spun and ran back to help Michael with the remaining three men.

There was blood on Michael's arms and a cut on his cheek. They'd pushed him so far back that the magic they'd both sensed now pulsed around his body, spinning purple shards of light across the darkness. Fear for him rose, but she pushed it away and reached for the fire again. She aimed it at the stake the man closest to her was holding, then launched herself after her flaming arrow, intending to knock him down and away from Michael.

Only he twisted at the wrong moment, and she pushed him sideways rather than away. He cannoned into the other two men, pushing them forward— straight into Michael, thrusting him backward into the pulsing curtain.

"No!"

She lunged forward, trying to grab him, to stop his fall. The light closed around her hand, sucking her forward, her feet skidding across the stone even though she fought the pull.

Then evil leapt into focus and someone grabbed

her, yanking her backward. She spun, knife raised. Saw Kinnard's mocking expression and a bright flash of light.

Then there was nothing.

Nothing but darkness.

Fourteen

MICHAEL GRABBED A fistful of the nearest man's shirt, attempting to remain upright as the air howled around them.

The stranger instinctively stepped back, and for a moment, they both teetered over the edge of the whirlpool of magic that sought to suck them to God knew where.

Michael reached out with his thoughts, trying to touch his anchor's mind, trying to break the control Dunleavy had over him in order to save them both. But at that moment, the man raised the stake he held in his hand and stepped forward. The whirlpool grabbed them, dragging them into its depths.

And suddenly he was free falling, tumbling down and down and down.

Even a vampire couldn't escape a hole as deep as hell itself. And he wasn't about to get trapped in hell.

Though disoriented, he flung out his arms, trying to get some idea of what was around him. He hit flesh first and grabbed the man, knowing he had to save him if he could.

His free hand brushed walls, but they were too

smooth to provide any real purchase. Then he hit wood, but it slithered past too fast for him to grab.

More smooth rock. Another piece of wood.

This one he managed to hook his arm around. The abrupt halt tore at his muscles, and the sudden deadweight of the stranger damn near popped his left shoulder out of its socket.

He hissed, fighting pain, fighting to keep his grip on the wooden beam and the stranger against the pull of the magic and gravity. He blinked the beads of sweat from his eyes and looked around.

They were in one of the vertical shafts. It wasn't all that wide, and aging beams lined the drop, with supporting beams spanning the gap north to south. If he'd hit any of them in those first few moments of free falling, he probably would have broken his back. But luck had been with him and he'd fallen right through the middle.

He couldn't see the top of the shaft, and he had no idea just how far he'd fallen. He glanced down. The beams continued on for a while, and then the wood gave way to unnaturally smooth rock. Dunleavy's doing, he suspected. The bastard was probably trying to ensure the hole was deep enough to cage a vampire. If he'd fallen much farther, he would have been caught in that cage.

Material tore, and the stranger dropped a little. Pain ripped up Michael's arm, burning through the rest of his body. He swore softly. The man's weight must have torn ligaments when they'd come to that sudden halt. And it wasn't as if he could shift his grip and make both of them more comfortable.

He needed help.

Needed to know if Nikki was okay.

He reached out to her, but the link between them was little more than a black wasteland. He swore again. Dunleavy had her. He knew that without doubt.

He tried instead to use his kinetic skills, but they were still locked in glue. Nikki was right. The circle around this town was blocking basic psychic abilities. So why could she use her flames? And how could he siphon her ability to sense evil when that, too, was a psychic skill? Was the fact that they *shared* that skill somehow an issue?

Right now, that was a question he didn't have the time to ponder.

He glanced down again and lightly toed the stranger in the face. "Wake up." Though he knew it probably wouldn't succeed, he tried to reinforce the words telepathically. The man's mind was a mental minefield he didn't have time to traverse. He had to get to Nikki. Had to get moving.

He toed the stranger again, less carefully this time. The man jerked and cursed, and Michael hissed in pain as the fool's action sent them both into a gentle swing.

"Keep still," he snapped.

The man's gaze jerked to his. There was no awareness of the situation, no life in the blue of his gaze, only a curious blankness. He was still under Dunleavy's control.

And Dunleavy wanted Michael suffering, then dead.

The stranger swung the stake he'd somehow clung to, rapping Michael across the shins. Michael cursed and shook the idiot, trying to make him lose his grip on the stake, but it didn't do any good. The wood hit him again, and the nails that had been rammed along its length tore past his jeans and into flesh.

There was only one thing to do, and he did it.

The stranger didn't even scream as he fell. After a few moments, water splashed. With any luck, Dunleavy had left the stranger with enough common sense to tread water—though whether he'd be able to stay afloat long enough for Michael to get him help was anyone's guess.

And right now, he had more important things to worry about. Dunleavy's threat rose to haunt him. He pushed it away savagely and hooked his other hand around the beam. Pain slapped through him, and his breath hissed through clenched teeth. His shoulder had definitely been damaged, but at least he could still move it. Could still hold on with it, though it hurt like hell, and his grip was a lot weaker than it should be.

He took a breath and swung his body, hooking his feet around the beam before carefully climbing onto it. Once secure, he took another breather, wiping the sweat from his eyes as he glanced up. The next beam was about eight feet away. Not much of a leap if he stood.

He edged his way along the beam until he reached the wall. Using it to steady himself, he rose slowly to his feet. For a minute, the tunnel swam around him. He blinked the sensation away and looked upward, judging the distance. Then he lunged.

He caught the beam, holding on tightly as his body swung like a pendulum and pain burned white hot up his left arm. Ignoring it, he swung his legs, hooking them around the beam and clambering on top of it.

He repeated the process over and over.

By the time he neared the top he was drenched in sweat, and the burning in his shoulder had spread to the rest of his body. He was shaking with exhaustion, and his vision was so blurred he could barely see.

He needed blood. Needed to replenish what he had lost.

And he didn't have the time to do it, because Nikki was running out of time. The longer Dunleavy had her, the more he could do to her. The images he'd seen in the woman's mind rose to haunt him again, and he swore savagely.

Nikki wasn't being abused yet. He'd know it, feel it, if she were.

But that didn't mean she wouldn't be if he didn't get there soon.

He looked up. The top of the shaft was about ten feet away. As wretched as he felt, it might as well have been a hundred. He scanned the rim, looking for something he could grab if he missed the edge. Three of the side supports were rotten near the edge, thanks to the water dribbling down the side of the shaft. If he grabbed those, they were likely to splinter and give way. The fourth was the only one out of the water's path, and it looked secure. That was the side he had to aim for.

He shifted his position so that he was more in line with the edge. Then he flexed his fingers and jumped. Exhaustion had sapped his strength, and his leap wasn't as high as it should have been. He cannoned into the side of the shaft rather than the top of the hole, and scrabbled wildly for the edge even as he began to slide back down into the shaft. His fingers slid across the stone, and at the last possible moment, hit a crevice. He wedged them deep, halting his fall, his arms shaking with the effort of holding on. After another shuddering breath, he hauled himself up enough so that he could place his foot on the top of the nearby support beam.

Then he launched himself out of the shaft. He hit the slick rock surface of the cavern and slid along for several feet before crashing into another rock.

He didn't do anything—*couldn't* do anything—other than lie there for more minutes than he cared to count. His breath was a harsh rasp that echoed through the silent cavern, and every nerve ending shook—ached—with pain. And though the air was thick and damp, the smell of blood was sharp. His blood, coming from the wounds on his thigh and arm. He'd have to tend to them before he moved, or he'd be in trouble long before he got to Nikki.

He pushed into a sitting position and tore off a shirtsleeve. After wrapping it around his leg and securing it, he looked at the wound on his arm. It was deep enough to see bone. Luckily, it had been caused by the nails in the wood rather than the wood itself, and it would heal cleanly—unlike the slice he could feel burning on his cheek. But the cut on his arm was bleeding profusely, and he couldn't afford to lose any more blood.

He grimaced. Blood was blood, and though he couldn't survive on another vampire's blood, sucking down his own would at least help counter lightheadedness, while licking the wound would quicken the healing process.

He stood. The cavern spun around him, then lurched to a sickening stop. He wiped the sweat from his eyes and raised his arm, suckling his wounded flesh as he stumbled forward.

There was no sound beyond the trickle of water in the darkness ahead or behind him. No heartbeat. No sense of magic.

Trepidation rushed through him, and he broke into a run. The tunnel widened, became a bigger shaft. He followed it, reaching for the memories to guide his steps. He slid right into one side shaft, then right again into another. The past loomed before him, and as he slid into a third shaft, he came to a sudden halt.

A body hung from the ceiling, dripping blood into the center of the pentagram. A pentagram protected by a small circle of black stones, and nothing else.

Dunleavy was using the Standard Mine pentagram all right, but it was for one of his regular sacrifices, not the ceremony that would bring Emmett back to life.

Seline was wrong, just as Nikki had suspected.

Weylin was going to perform the ceremony where his brother's body lay—under the church.

It was the cold that woke Nikki. For several seconds she lay still, keeping her eyes closed as she tried to determine where she was and what was going on.

To her right, someone was murmuring. The harsh tones suggested it was Kinnard—or rather Dunleavy, in his Kinnard guise.

Beyond the sound of Dunleavy's voice, there was little other noise. The wind was a distant howl, but the air around her was thick and still and icy. She was lying on dirt rather than stone, which was odd, because it felt sandy rather than clayish.

She cracked open her eyes. A flashlight sat on old, wooden shelving, its bright light spilling across the ceiling and down the walls. She was in the church, not the mine. Michael had been right.

The murmuring had moved and was now coming from behind her head. She cautiously tried to shift her foot and discovered that both legs were tied, along with her hands.

And she realized something else. She was naked. Images of what had been done to the women in the whorehouse and the hotel filled her mind, and fear swelled. But fear was what Dunleavy wanted, what he fed on, and she ruthlessly pushed it away. The little worm wasn't going to get the better of her—and he certainly wasn't going to get *her* without a damn good fight.

She opened her eyes and tilted her head back. "You praying to those gods of yours to save your soul? If not, you'd better be, because I'm going to make sure you're sent back to the hell that spawned you."

Dunleavy's gaze met hers, the ghostlike depths filled with amusement and scorn. "Girlie, you're in no position to be threatening me."

"If you think that, you're a fool."

"And if you think your vampire is going to come to your rescue, *you're* a fool. He's either fallen to his death by now or he's trapped in a hole deep enough to swallow the Empire State Building. Either way, there'll be no last-minute reprieve."

"I don't need a vampire to rescue me." And Michael wasn't dead or trapped. He was hurt, granted, but he was free and coming for her. His anger and determination burned through the link—a force so great she couldn't reach past it, couldn't tell him she was alive and unhurt. But he'd know, the same way she'd known about him.

"No?" Dunleavy's tone was scathing. "Let's take stock of your situation, then. You're naked. You're tied up. You're in a pentagram that will allow no one but myself and those I serve to enter."

Meaning she could get out if she somehow managed to get free? That was what his words implied, and she hoped it was true. She began working on the ropes binding her arms, twisting and tugging as imperceptibly as she could while he continued talking.

"And if you're thinking you can raise your fire, think again. I've changed your particular muting spell to cover that little psychic talent."

Her flames weren't a psychic talent—not according to Seline, anyway. But she wasn't about to disabuse Dunleavy of the notion—not when it could be the one thing that saved her.

"I warned you when I first met you that you didn't know as much about me as you thought. You still don't, and that lack of knowledge will kill you."

He snorted. "I'll have to give you top points for courage. Ain't many women who'd be feeling so smart-mouthed when lying in that position."

"Ah, but you see, I'm not just a woman. I'm a witch.

And over the years I've faced, and defeated, evil far worse than you."

"You're no witch, girlie. I've known who you are since you stepped into Hartwood. Why do you think I decapitated that particular woman?" He snorted and shook his head. "You, my dear, are no more dangerous than any of them other whores now that your powers are fully muted."

She gave him a cold, hard smile. "Which doesn't negate the fact that I *will* kill you, and then ensure your bastard brother rots in the fires of hell like he deserves."

He hissed at her and stepped forward, his fingers clenching around the ceremonial silver knife shoved carelessly through the belt at his waist.

"And won't your dark gods be pleased if you kill their sacrifice before the appointed time?" She arched an eyebrow, feigning an indifference she didn't feel. "You think they'll still grant your brother his freedom?"

He hissed again and spun away, and she heaved a silent sigh of relief as she continued tugging and working at the bonds on her wrists. The left one was definitely looser, but freedom from the ropes was nowhere near close enough.

Life sparked through the link, and the relief she felt belied her earlier tough words. *Where are you?*

In town, approaching the church. He hesitated. *You okay?*

He hasn't touched me yet.

His relief was a tidal wave that all but drowned her. *I had visions . . .*

So did I. But I don't think he's completed the full

ritual yet, and I don't think he'll try anything until then.

I hope you're right.

So did she. *I'll try and keep him off balance until you arrive. Maybe he won't notice your arrival until it's too late.*

It was a slim hope, but better than nothing. She turned her attention to Dunleavy. He was back to mumbling.

"Hey, slug boy."

He looked up, eyes glimmering with anger. "You will feel my flesh on yours, you know. You will feel me in you as I tear your limbs apart, and my gods take your heart and then your mind."

"Like hell." Yet even as she said the words, fear trembled through her.

Dunleavy sucked deep and smiled. "Ah, there's nothing that tastes quite so good."

Damn it, she *couldn't* let him get to her. He wasn't going to get fat on her fear, not if she could do anything to stop it.

"Why the gnome face, Dunleavy?" she bit back. "You're a shapeshifter like your brother, so why haven't you taken on the forms of your victims? It would have confused the situation more, and kept us guessing."

"This is the face I was born with, and the one I am most comfortable with."

"And the slug?"

"We may come from a family of shifters, but I am not able to take on multiple human forms. I can only share my brother's because I am his twin."

"So the ugly boy got the ugly form?"

Hate glittered in his eyes. Hate and old anger. Yep, this was definitely one of his hot buttons.

"That form is more versatile than most would think."

"But I bet you weren't exactly welcome amongst the shifter fraternity." Especially considering what he liked doing while in that form . . .

He snorted. "They're all—" He stopped and swung around. "So, your lover is free."

"You never can keep a good vampire down," she commented, twisting and tugging on her bonds less cautiously. Now that Dunleavy knew Michael was free, her window of escape had shrunk.

"It won't matter, you know. I'm not foolish enough to leave the church unguarded."

Even as he spoke, the sounds of fighting began to drift down into their hole.

"And here I thought you didn't have too many conscripts left in town."

Dunleavy flashed her a cold, cruel smile. "There are the women and the barkeep. And since your vampire considers himself a protector of women, I doubt whether he'll use full force on them. It'll delay him, and you will die."

He began to murmur again. She knew she couldn't let him complete whatever spell it was he was working on, so she tilted her head back, her gaze locking on the coffin. Reaching deep, she called forth her flames, putting as much force into them as she could, willing them to burn wood and flesh and bone until there was nothing left, not even dust.

Power burned through her body and leapt from her fingers in a huge ball of fire. Dunleavy made a strangled sound in his throat and flung out a hand. White light darted across the room, clashing with the flames. For an instant, they stopped, as white light and red rolled and boiled around each other in midair. Then another wave of power surged through her, though this time the call was not her doing. It was almost as if the flames themselves were calling for more energy. The fireball burned brighter, then broke away from the white light and leapt across the coffin.

Dunleavy's furious howl wasn't even remotely human. Nikki tugged harder on the ropes and wished she could reach for some ghosts. With all the people Weylin had killed in this place, they'd surely be eager for retribution. But that took time and energy, and she didn't have enough of either. One arm came free. She twisted, grabbing the rope binding her right wrist and pulling on it as hard as she could.

Air screamed above her. She looked up and saw the hilt of the knife aimed at her head. She threw herself away from it, the rope burning into her wrist as it brought her to an abrupt halt. The knife hilt smashed across the side of her face, and everything seemed to go red. Skin tore, bone cracked. And, despite her vow, she screamed.

There was an answering bellow from above, and fury burned through her mind, through her soul. *That was the answer,* she thought dazedly. That would free them. Save them.

"Move and she dies," Dunleavy yelled. "Your choice, vampire."

"If you don't move, your brother burns." Michael's voice was cold, harsh.

And weary. Nikki blinked back tears and fought

the pain that threatened to sweep her into unconsciousness. Dunleavy stood above her, his arm raised, the silver knife glittering in the harsh light of the flames behind them.

"My magic protects my brother. The flames only consume wood."

She closed her eyes and reached for the link. *You can use the flames to attack Dunleavy. He won't be expecting that.*

You sure?

Yes. Why she was so sure, she couldn't say. But she'd always trusted her instincts, and she wasn't about to stop now. *Do you remember that moment of oneness when we last made love?*

I'm not likely to forget something as beautiful as that.

Sunshine ran briefly through her mind. Despite the precariousness of their situation, she smiled. *If we repeat that, I think we might be able to use our psi skills. Dunleavy's spells nullify the particular talents of a particular person. By binding our minds, we bypass his spell.*

"Show yourself," Kinnard continued. "Come down here. But cautiously, mind you, or the girlie pays the price."

"I'm coming down."

Through the blur of tears, she saw his silhouette appear briefly above them. Then he crouched and leapt down. She tried to look at him, but Dunleavy's boot hit her cheek. Pain flashed white hot through her face, and bile rose to her throat. She swallowed heavily and remained still.

If I had the strength and the time, I'd rip the bastard apart limb by limb for what he's done to you.

I'm okay. It was a lie, and he undoubtedly knew it. *We need to link.*

Done. He thrust the link wide open, and suddenly, she was with him, in him, part of him. Their souls twined, merged, and every fiber of their beings rejoiced in a joining that was sensual, powerful and very definitely otherworldly.

Power surged through them, and flame flickered to life across Michael's fingers. He raised them.

Dunleavy's eyes widened. "That's not possible."

"I warned you, Dunleavy," Michael said. "You didn't know enough about either of us."

Dunleavy made a gargling sound, and the knife plunged toward her. Michael made a flicking motion with one hand, and the knife was torn from Dunleavy's fingers. Then that energy was battering Dunleavy, and he flew across the room, smashing through the shelving before sliding to the ground.

Michael's gaze met hers. Suddenly, the power that flowed through them both was concentrating on her, sweeping down her limbs, across her fingers and around her ankles. The ropes binding her fell away.

Get Dunleavy. Was it her thought or his? She wasn't sure, and in the end, it didn't matter. Not as long as Dunleavy was taken care of.

She rolled onto her hands and feet and crawled out of the unfinished pentagram. Pain was a distant echo, held at bay by the oneness, but they'd both pay for it later. She knew that without a doubt.

Michael hadn't moved. He raised another hand, and suddenly Dunleavy was there, right in front of them, squirming like the worm he was as he dangled several feet off the ground.

"You know, if I had the time, I'd ensure your death was as painful as I could possibly make it."

Michael's voice was flat, devoid of any sort of emotion. Yet she could feel his anger, his weariness and—most of all—his desire to just get it over with so they could get back to their lives.

"But as much as you deserve to die the way your brother died—the way you made your victims die—I can't be bothered wasting the time. I have wedding plans to finalize."

With that, the power surged. Dunleavy screamed—a high, unearthly sound that vibrated off the walls and sent chills racing down Nikki's spine. Dunleavy's silver knife rose from the ground and slashed with unearthly force across his neck. The screaming stopped, and the power died. Dunleavy hit the ground, his body flopping at odd angles, his head rolling away into the darkness. Michael dropped beside her and carefully dragged her into his arms. She wrapped her arms around his neck and pressed the good side of her face against his chest, listening to the wild beat of his heart, knowing her own strained just as badly.

"So," she said, her voice cracked with exhaustion. "What now?"

"Now, we sit here and watch the bonfire while we wait for the cavalry to come and pick up the pieces."

And that's exactly what they did.

Fifteen

NIKKI GLANCED AT the clock as she leaned a shoulder against the windowsill. It was hard to believe that in ten minutes she'd become Mrs. Michael Kelly. Even though she'd been rushing around all week finalizing the details, part of her kept insisting it was nothing more than a giddy dream.

Now the day was here, and it wasn't a dream. She'd been grinning like an idiot all morning. Even the weather gods had decided to bless them. Despite the fact that it had rained for most of the week, yesterday and today had dawned fine and clear, giving the soggy ground a chance to dry out.

Not that there was much grass *or* soil to be seen in the immediate area. It had all disappeared under the sea of buttercups that had been specially planted for the day. The pretty flowers—her favorites—also sur-rounded the path that ran from the house to the rose-covered gazebo. In the warm morning sun, orange, yellow and red roses were glowing so brightly the building looked like it was aflame.

She'd wanted a simple wedding—just her and Mi-chael and a few close friends, here in the backyard of their home. But Michael had taken control of the ceremony, and the stunning vista before her was the result.

"I wasn't about to let my one and only marriage begin as a quiet affair," he said as he stepped into the room. "Not when the woman I'm marrying deserves a whole lot more than that."

She grinned, hitched up her dress and ran across the room. She flung her arms around his neck, kissing him soundly, then said, "You do realize, of course, that you've set the tone for the rest of our marriage."

He raised an eyebrow, his dark eyes glittering with love and amusement. "So now I have to sit back and watch you fritter away my millions?"

"Why else does a girl marry a very old millionaire?" Still grinning, she stepped back and studied him. He looked absolutely divine in the old-fashioned morning suit. "You scrub up rather well." Even the scar across his cheek had faded to a thin white line.

"And you, my love, look good enough to eat." He tugged her into his arms again. "I hope all those pearl buttons down the back of this dress aren't as hard to undo as they look."

"No. They're harder."

"Hey," Jake said behind them. "The groom is not supposed to be manhandling the bride until *after* the ceremony."

Michael kissed her quickly, then pulled back, a smile playing across his lips. "Who invited the spoilsport?"

Nikki's gaze met Jake's, her grin widening when she saw his expression—that of a proud father. Like Michael, he was wearing a morning suit, and with his longish blond hair swept back, he cut a rather rakish figure.

"I'm afraid the spoilsport and I come as a package deal."

"I draw the line at taking him on the honeymoon."

Jake's face twisted briefly—clearly remembering his own wedding day—and then his smile returned. "Like I've got nothing better to do than watch you two lust after each other the next two weeks." He shook his head in mock disgust. "Besides, I've seen Paris, and I very much doubt that you two will actually see much of it."

"That's very possible," Nikki said, smiling as she momentarily lost herself in the warm, dark depths of Michael's eyes.

Jake cleared his throat. "Enough already. Michael, you're wanted downstairs."

Michael caught Nikki's hand, raised it to his lips and kissed it. *In eight minutes, you're officially mine.*

I was yours the day after we met. I just didn't realize it at the time.

But you did realize it, and you didn't let go, and for that, I shall be forever grateful. He released her hand and left.

Jake stepped into the doorway. "You look smashing."

"You think?" She twirled, allowing the deep gold material to float around her. She'd never wanted a white wedding dress, simply because white didn't suit her, nor had she wanted anything remotely modern. It hardly seemed suitable when she was marrying a man over three hundred years old. When she'd seen this beautiful old gown in a Renaissance shop, she'd allen in love. And it had fit her perfectly, meaning it was meant to be.

"I think Mary would have been proud of you," he said softly, tears in his eyes. She blinked away her own tears, then leaned forward and kissed his cheek. "She'll always be with us, you know."

"I know." He reached down and twined his fingers through hers. "You ready?"

"You bet," she said, and headed outside to marry her vampire.

If you loved the Nikki and Michael series,
be sure not to miss the adventures of
some of the other intrepid Damask Circle
operatives in the first book
of the explosive Damask Circle series!

CIRCLE OF FIRE

by

Keri Arthur

And stay tuned for the next two books
in the Damask Circle series—
Circle of Death and *Circle of Desire*—
which will follow at one-month intervals.

Here's a special preview:

MADELINE SMITH DIDN'T believe in ghosts—not
until the night Jon Barnett walked into her life, anyway. Maddie drew her legs up to her chest and held
them close. Maybe *walked* was the wrong word to use;
his method of movement seemed more like floating.

Outside her bedroom, the branches of an old elm
scraped back and forth across the tin roofing. The
wind howled through the night—an eerie cry that
matched her mood of anticipation and fear. Snow
scurried past the windows, silvery drops that glittered briefly in the light.

It felt oddly fitting to be sitting on her bed, waiting
for the arrival of a ghost while an early winter storm
raged outside.

Only *he* insisted he wasn't a ghost at all.

She tugged the blankets over her knees and wondered if she should stoke the fire with a little more wood. Maybe the heat would keep him away. Or maybe he'd gotten tired of his game and simply forgotten about her. She believed that the desperation in his eyes was real enough; she just didn't believe that *he* was real.

Perhaps he was just a figment of her imagination—a last, desperate escape from the loneliness of her life.

The clock on the mantel began to chime quietly, and she turned to look at the time. One thirty. Maybe he *had* forgotten about her . . .

"Madeline."

She closed her eyes, uncertain whether fear or the unexpected pleasure of hearing the low velvet voice one more time had caused the sudden leap of her heart.

"Madeline," he repeated. This time a hint of urgency touched the warmth of his voice.

He stood in the shadows to the left of her window. Despite the storm that raged outside, he wore only a short-sleeved black shirt and dark jeans—the same clothes he'd worn when he had first appeared last night.

Tonight there *was* something different about him, though.

Tonight he looked afraid.

But he wasn't *real*, damn it! How could a ghost feel fear?

"Madeline, you *must* help me."

She closed her heart to the desperate plea in his voice. What he was asking her to do was impossible.

"I can't." She avoided his gaze and fiddled with the fraying edge of the blanket. "I don't know you. I don't even believe that you exist. How can you expect me to leave everything I have on the word of a ghost?"

"You must!" The sudden sharpness of his voice made her look up. "All I'm asking is for you to travel across the state, not to another country. Why are you so afraid to leave your retreat?"

Maddie stared at him. He seemed to understand altogether too much about her. No one else had seen her fear—not even her sister, who was as close to her as Maddie ever allowed anyone to get these days.

"There's nothing wrong with being cautious," she said after a moment.

He studied her, amusement flickering briefly in the diamond-bright depths of his blue eyes. "I never said there was. But life has to be lived. You cannot hide forever."

She ignored the sliver of alarm in her heart, ignored the whispers that demanded she ask how he knew so much about her, and raised an eyebrow. "And what does a ghost know about such things?"

He sighed, running a hand through his overly long hair. In the light of the fire, slivers of gold seemed to flow through his fingers. "I'm no ghost, Madeline. But I will be if you don't help me soon."

Alarm danced through her heart. "What do you mean?"

He walked across to the fire and held out his hands, as if to capture the warmth of the flames. Hair dusted his arms, golden strands that gleamed in the firelight. His fingers were long and smooth and tanned. Lord, he seemed real—and yet, if she looked closely enough, she could see the glow of the fire through his body.

"I mean that I'm stuck down this damn well, and I can't get out. I *will* die, Madeline, unless you help me."

Maddie closed her eyes and tried to stifle the rising spiral of fear. Not for her safety, because she sensed this was one ghost who would cause her no harm. It was just fear of . . . what? She didn't *know,* but there was something about this apparition that made her wary.

Perhaps she should play along with him. Surely he'd eventually tire of his game and leave her alone. Or perhaps she was just going mad, as most of her so-called friends had insisted she would.

Yet those same friends had never understood what she was, or what she was capable of doing. Nor had they ever tried to help her.

"Why can't someone else rescue you? You must have friends. Why don't you go haunt them?"

"Believe me, I would if I could."

His tone was dry and left no doubt that he would rather be anywhere else than with her. *Bad news when even a damn ghost doesn't want your company.* "So why can't you?"

He frowned. "I don't know. Some force keeps driving me toward you. I have no choice in the matter, Madeline. You're all I have."

And you refuse to help me. The unspoken rebuke was in his eyes when he glanced at her. Maddie bit her lip and looked away, watching the snow continue its dance past her window. Maybe she *was* going mad. She was beginning to feel sorry for a ghost.

"Why would you be able to reach a complete stranger and not anyone of real use to you?"

"I don't know."

He hesitated, so she quickly said, "If you want my help, you at least owe me the truth."

"Fair enough." He turned his back to the fire, but kept his hands behind him, as if still trying to warm them. "Whatever this force is, it brings with it a sense of danger. And it's connected with you somehow."

He seemed to say an awful lot without actually saying *anything,* Maddie noted. Maybe her ghost had been a politician in a former life.

"That made everything so much clearer," she said drily.

He shot her a look that was half amusement, half frustration. "Someone close to you is in danger and, somehow, they're drawing me to you."

Besides her sister Jayne, the only other person who qualified was Jayne's son, Evan. And if he *did* have that sort of power, it would be a recent development, meaning it was highly unlikely he'd have the sort of control Jon was suggesting. No, she thought grimly, there was only one uncontrolled misfit left in their small family unit.

"So how did you end up in the well?"

"Someone shot me when I was out exploring." He shrugged. "I must have fallen in."

Maddie raised an eyebrow. From what she could see of him, there was remarkably little evidence of a bullet wound. "Then you *are* dead."

He sighed and closed his eyes. "I was hit in the arm. The fall could have killed me, but I was . . . lucky."

The arm closest to her was a suntanned brown, well muscled and remarkably free of wounds. His hands were still firmly clasped together, which surely wouldn't be possible if the other arm had a bullet wound in it. Maybe it was her ghost who was mad, not she.

"Why can't I see any sort of wound, then?"

"Because I'm here astrally."

"That doesn't really explain why you're standing there with no wound." Or why she could see him. From the little she knew of astral travel, she shouldn't have even been able to do that, let alone interact with him.

"You're not seeing the wound because I don't want you to."

Which was probably a good thing given that she *did* want to get some sleep tonight. "Why don't you just shout for help?"

"As I explained before, I can't take the risk. Someone is out to get me. If they think I'm still alive, they'll just find me and finish the job."

A chill ran through her. "It could have been an accident."

"No."

She closed her eyes at the soft certainty in his voice. "Then if I come to help you, my life could be in danger."

"How would they know you're there to help me? You'd just be another tourist passing by."

The sudden weariness in his voice made her look at him. His form had faded slightly, merging with the night. Something was wrong, something more than the fact that he'd been shot. And she sensed he wouldn't tell her what. "Who do you mean by 'they'?"

"I'm not exactly sure. But someone in this town knew why I was here, and they moved pretty swiftly to get rid of me."

"Then tell me again what town you're in, and why you're there." If he was going to continue haunting her, she should at least try to understand a little more about him. And last night she'd been too busy trying to convince herself he was nothing more than a vivid dream to really listen to anything he said.

He stared at her, then shook his head. "How many times do I have to repeat myself before you believe me?"

His voice held an edge of desperation that made her wince. "You mentioned some town—Sherbrook, wasn't it?"

He closed his eyes for a moment, as if battling to remain calm. "Sherbrook is the name of the inn. The place is Taurin Bay."

An odd sense of foreboding ran through her. Evan had attended a school camp in Taurin Bay not so long ago. Jayne had gone along as cook and chief pot-washer. "That force you said was driving you to me—was it male or female?"

"Male." He paused, eyes narrowing. "Why?"

Evan—something told her it was Evan. Maddie licked her lips and wondered if she should call her sister—or was she just worrying over nothing again?

"Maddie, what's wrong?"

She stared at him blankly for a moment. "My sister has a thirteen-year-old son named Evan. Both of them were in Taurin Bay last month."

"Damn!" Jon ran a hand through his hair, then abruptly walked forward, stopping only when his knees touched the side of her bed.

He was close, so close. She could see the rise and fall of his chest, feel the whisper of his breath wash across her skin. Could smell him—a faint scent of cologne mixed with hints of earth and sweat. But he wasn't *real,* damn it!

"Over the last two years, sixteen teenagers have been taken from their homes and haven't been seen alive again. In each case, no locks or windows were disturbed. And each time, the teenager was taken on the next full moon *after* the family returned from Taurin Bay."

Her heart leapt. She raised a hand to her throat and tried to remain calm. "Evan is safe at home. This is ridiculous."

"Someone is drawing me here, Madeline. Someone who knows he's in danger. You're the connection between us. Tonight is a full moon. Go call your sister."

She scrambled off the bed and ran to the bedroom door. Then she hesitated, looking back at Jon. He hadn't moved, but his body had faded, losing its shape to the darkness. Only his blue eyes were still bright.

"Go call her," he said. "Then come to me. Save me."

Maddie turned away from his plea, though she knew he wouldn't be there when she returned. She ran down the hall to the phone in the kitchen, turning on lights as she went. Somehow, the darkness seemed too intense to face alone.

Fingers trembling, she picked up the phone and

dialed Jayne's number. It seemed to ring forever. Maddie bit her lip, hoping nothing had happened, hoping that Evan was in bed and safe.

"Hello?" a croaky, half-asleep voice said eventually.

"Jayne, it's me," she said without preamble. "Is Evan there? Is he all right?"

There was a slight pause, and Maddie could hear the rustle of blankets as her sister shifted around in her bed. "Of course he is. Why?"

Because I'm a fool. Because a ghost told me he may be in danger. "Humor your little sister and just go check, will you?"

Jayne sighed. "Maddie, have you been drinking again?"

Maddie closed her eyes. Whenever Jayne thought she had a problem, she always asked the same question—even though it had been six years and ten days since Maddie had last had a drink. Not since the fire that had taken her husband's life. The experts had never found an explanation for that fire, though they had theories aplenty. Maddie knew the truth, but she wasn't about to tell anyone—not even her sister.

She cleared her throat. "No. I had a dream, and I want to reassure myself that he's all right."

"For God's sake, it's after two." Annoyance ran through Jayne's voice, but at least she was still listening. She hadn't slammed the phone down yet.

"I'm well aware of the time. It will only take a minute to check on Evan. Please."

"I guess I better," her sister muttered, "or you'll be calling all night again."

Maddie heard Steve, Jayne's husband, murmur

something disparaging, then the squeak of springs as Jayne got out of bed. Maddie grimaced, hoping she *was* overreacting. Hoping Jon wasn't right. She stared out the kitchen window as she waited, watching the snow flurries dance across her yard. Then she heard the sound of returning footsteps and felt her stomach knot. *Please let Evan be safe.*

"Evan's sound asleep in bed, Maddie." Jayne's voice was a mix of exasperation and annoyance. "And so should you be."

This time Jayne did hang up on her, but Maddie didn't mind. Jon had been wrong. Evan was okay. She replaced the receiver, then thrust a shaking hand through her hair as she sagged back against the wall in relief. Maybe Jayne was right. Maybe all she needed was a good night's sleep—something that had eluded her ever since her world had disappeared into flames.

She closed her eyes, fighting the memories, fighting the sudden need to wash the pain into oblivion with a drink. *That* chapter of her life was over. She would not return, even through memories. And if Jon did come back, she'd tell him to go find someone else to haunt. She wasn't interested—not if the cost was to make her sister think she was stranger than ever.

His only chance of survival was a woman afraid of life. Jon shook his head at the irony of it and leaned wearily against the cold stone wall of the well. He'd seen the fear in the amber flame of her eyes, in the tremor in her hands as she ran her fingers through her chestnut-colored hair. She was afraid to move from the safety of her home.

And he would die if she didn't.

He smiled grimly and stared up at the pale stars twinkling in the dark bracket of sky far above him.

How he wished he could fly, simply wing his way up out of the well to freedom. But he couldn't even climb with his arm like this. He glanced down, noting that his flesh had swollen around the handkerchief he'd tied across his forearm.

Someone *had* shot him, but not with a gun, as Madeline had presumed. Someone in Taurin Bay knew what he was. They'd used arrows made of white ash, a wood that was deadly to those with magic in their souls when embedded in their flesh.

He'd broken off most of the shaft, but a section remained, and while it was probably the only reason he hadn't bled to death, it was also slowly but surely killing him.

Oddly enough, he felt no pain. Not now, anyway. Maybe it was the cold. Maybe it was the numbness beginning to infuse his body. Or maybe he was as thick-skinned as many of his friends believed.

He grimaced and closed his eyes. He'd thought about dying many times in his life, but he never thought it would come like this, lying helpless and alone in the cold, cold night.

And yet, in some ways, it was oddly fitting. He'd spent most of his adult life alone, so why not die the same way?

He wouldn't have cared much, either, if he'd had the chance to see his family one more time and ex-

plain why he'd avoided them so much over the last
ten years.

An owl hooted softly in the distance. He listened
carefully, then heard the soft snap of wings, the small
cry of a field mouse. If the owls were out looking
for a meal, it meant there was no one about to dis-
turb their hunting. And therefore, no one hunting
him. Trapped down this damn well, he'd be easy
pickings. A day had passed since he'd been shot. By
all rights, he should be safe, but he'd learned over the
years never to relax his guard.

He toed the water lapping the edges of the small
ledge. The water had been his salvation in more ways
than one. It had broken his fall and, no doubt, saved
his life. And it was drinkable, which meant he wasn't
in any danger of dehydration. But it might yet kill
him, too. His abilities gave him some protection
against the cold, but he knew he was starting to push
his limits. His plunge into the water had soaked every
bit of his clothing, and now he was so cold it hurt to
move.

If Madeline did find the courage to come to his
rescue, she might discover nothing more than a five-
foot-ten-inch icicle.

Madeline—what was he going to do about her?
How could he convince her that she was sane and
that he really needed her help? What had happened in
her life that made her so afraid?

A wave of dizziness hit him, and there was nothing
he could do except ride out the feeling. He probably
had enough strength left to contact her one more
time. If he couldn't convince her to help him, he'd just

have to hope that someone in the Circle realized he
was in trouble and came to his rescue.

Because if someone didn't, more kids would die.

The snow had turned to rain, which fell in a soaking
mist. Rivers of water were beginning to run past the
house, scouring tiny trenches along the freshly graded
driveway. The tops of the cedars, claret ashes and silver birches that crowded the fence line were lost to
the mist, and though dawn should have come and
gone, night still seemed to hold court.

Maddie raised the coffee mug she held between
both hands and took a sip. The wind was bitter, but
the wide old veranda protected her from the worst of
the storm, and her threadbare coat kept her warm
enough. She couldn't face going indoors just yet. As
much as she'd tried to go back to sleep, she couldn't.
The old house was too big, too full of ghosts . . .

Except for one.

She sighed and leaned back against a veranda post.
She couldn't shake Jon from her thoughts. Couldn't
shake the desperation she'd glimpsed in his eyes.

What if he really *was* in need of her help?

She sipped her coffee and stared out across the
snow-flung wilderness of her yard. In a last-ditch effort to salvage her life, she'd moved to Oregon to be a
little closer to her sister and nephew, and had bought
this house and its untamed three acres six years ago.
It had become her haven, the one place she felt truly
safe. She had no real wish to be anywhere else. The
flowers she raised in the barn she'd converted to a
greenhouse made small luxuries possible, and she

had enough money invested to see her through the hard times. Even Jayne had given up her efforts to get Maddie back into what she called "mainstream" life.

Maddie chewed on her lip. The question she had to face was simple: Could she simply stand by and let Jon die?

If she believed him, the answer was no. But that was the crux of the matter. Part of her was afraid to believe, and part of her was afraid not to. She took another sip of coffee and shivered as the wind ran icy fingers across the back of her neck.

Then she stiffened. Something told her she was no longer alone. Slowly, she turned.

Jon stood several feet away, his face as pale as the snow behind him, blue eyes still bright despite the shadows beneath them. He looked like death, and the thought chilled her soul.

"What can I do to make you believe me?" he asked softly.

There was a hoarseness to his voice that had not been evident a few hours before, an edge of weariness and pain that tore at her need to stay safe.

"Maybe it's not a case of me believing you. Maybe it's just a case of knowing I *can't* help you."

He ran a hand through his hair and looked away, appearing to study the silvery drops dripping steadily from a hole in the gutter. "Then you have killed me as surely as those who shot me," he whispered after a moment.

"No!" She closed her eyes. How could she ever survive the weight of another death, whether or not it was her fault? "Isn't there someone I could contact, maybe a friend in a better position to help?"

"My companions live in Washington, D.C., and my time is running out." He looked at her. "You're my only chance, Madeline. Please."

Something in his eyes made her want to reach out and touch him. She clenched her fingers around her coffee cup and turned away, knowing she had to react with her mind—not with her emotions, and definitely not with her heart. They had only led her to tragedy in the past.

"Why won't they suspect me?"

"You are . . . ordinary."

Ordinary. She almost laughed at the bitter irony of it. How often had she heard that in the past? No one suspected the truth, not even her sister.

"Madeline, I don't mean—"

"It doesn't matter," she said, turning to face him. "I can't change what I am. Nor can I deny that I'm afraid. But I just can't run off wildly without some proof."

He sighed. "I'm in no position to prove anything."

Mist drifted around him, darkening his hair where it touched. She wanted to reach out and touch him, to feel the heat of his body, to hold him close and caress away the lines of pain from his face. *Maybe I am insane. I want to touch this ghost in ways I never touched my husband.* Shaking her head, she stepped away from him.

Something flickered in his blue eyes, and a slight grimace twisted his generous mouth. It was almost as if he'd sensed the reason for her fear. *But that's ridiculous. He's a ghost—an astral traveler—not a mind reader.* The sharp ring of the telephone interrupted the heavy silence. Maddie glanced at her watch and frowned. It was barely seven. Who would be calling at this hour? She headed inside to answer it, then hesitated, meeting Jon's steady gaze.

"We won't meet again," he murmured. He reached out as if to touch her cheek, then let his hand fall. "For that I'm sorry. Stay safe, Madeline."

"No . . ." Maddie watched him fade until there was nothing left but the warmth of his voice in her thoughts.

She closed her eyes and fought the rise of tears. Damn it, why should she cry for a ghost when she hadn't even cried for her husband? She bit her lip and watched the mist swirl around the spot where he'd stood. Maybe because Jon had shown her more warmth in the few hours she'd known him than Brian had ever shown in the six years they were married?

The insistent ringing broke through her thoughts. She took a deep breath, then ran down the length of the veranda to the back door, fleeing her thoughts as much as running for the phone.

Slamming the back door open, she snatched the receiver from the hook and struggled to get her boots off. "Hello?"

"Maddie?"

She froze. It was Jayne . . . *Oh Lord, let Evan be safe*. Yet the note in her sister's voice told her something was terribly wrong. "What is it?"

"It's Evan," Jayne sobbed. "He's disappeared, Maddie. Just gone . . . without a trace."